CANDLELIGHT REGENCY SPECIAL

CANDLELIGHT REGENCIES

594 LADY INCOGNITA, *Nina Pykare*
595 A BOND OF HONOUR, *Joan Vincent*
596 GINNY, *Jennie Tremaine*
597 THE MARRIAGE AGREEMENT, *Margaret MacWilliams*
602 A COMPANION IN JOY, *Dorothy Mack*
603 MIDNIGHT SURRENDER, *Margaret Major Cleaves*
604 A SCHEME FOR LOVE, *Joan Vincent*
605 THE DANGER IN LOVING, *Helen Nuelle*
610 LOVE'S FOLLY, *Nina Pykare*
611 A WORTHY CHARADE, *Vivian Harris*
612 THE DUKE'S WARD, *Samantha Lester*
613 MANSION FOR A LADY, *Cilla Whitmore*
618 THE TWICE BOUGHT BRIDE, *Elinor Larkin*
619 THE MAGNIFICENT DUCHESS, *Sarah Stamford*
620 SARATOGA SEASON, *Margaret MacWilliams*
621 AN INTRIGUING INNOCENT, *Rebecca Ashley*
625 THE AVENGING MAID, *Janis Susan May*
626 THE HEART OF THE MATTER, *Diana Burke*
627 THE PAISLEY BUTTERFLY, *Phyllis Taylor Pianka*
631 MAKESHIFT MISTRESS, *Amanda Mack*
632 RESCUED BY LOVE, *Joan Vincent*
633 A MARRIAGEABLE ASSET, *Ruth Gerber*
637 THE BRASH AMERICAN, *Samantha Lester*
638 A SEASON OF SURPRISES, *Rebecca Ashley*
639 THE ENTERPRISING MINX, *Marian Lorraine*
643 A HARMLESS RUSE, *Alexandra Lord*
644 THE GYPSY HEIRESS, *Laura London*
645 THE INNOCENT HEART, *Nina Pykare*
649 LORD SATAN'S BRIDE, *Anne Stuart*
650 THE CURIOUS ROGUE, *Joan Vincent*
651 THE RELUCTANT DUKE, *Philippa Castle*
655 LOVE'S TEMPEST, *Elinor Larkin*
656 MISS HUNGERFORD'S HANDSOME HERO, *Nöel Vreeland Carter*
657 REBEL IN LOVE, *Veronica Howard*
660 TILLY, *Jennie Tremaine*
661 COMPROMISED LOVE, *Anne Hillary*
662 BRIDE OF VENGEANCE, *Rose Marie Abbott*
665 LADY THIEF, *Kay Hooper*
666 THE BELLE OF BATH, *Dorothy Mack*
667 THE FAINT HEARTED FELON, *Paulin*

THE VISCOUNT'S WITCH

Edith de Paul

A CANDLELIGHT REGENCY SPECIAL

Published by
Dell Publishing Co., Inc.
1 Dag Hammarskjold Plaza
New York, New York 10017

Copyright © 1981 by Edith Delatush

All rights reserved. No part of this book may be
reproduced or transmitted in any form or by any
means, electronic or mechanical, including photocopying,
recording or by any information storage and
retrieval system, without the written permission
of the Publisher, except where permitted by law.

Dell ® TM 681510, Dell Publishing Co., Inc.

ISBN: 0-440-19321-4

Printed in the United States of America
First printing—August 1981

CHAPTER ONE

"Vanessa!" The call from the doorway was crisp.

"Yes, Mary?" The tall, slender girl stopped, instantly wary as she rested the bundle in her hand on the gate. For weeks the woman had been ignoring her, joining most of the others in the village. Why was she stopping her now? Her son and husband must not be around, Vanessa wryly assumed.

Then she guessed. Mary wanted to be the first to obtain the latest gossip from the manor house.

"Vanessa," the heavy woman called again, shrugging against the unease which those remarkable green eyes always produced. "It's good to see you back. Is Mistress Martin's baby doing well?"

Vanessa gave a slight smile. "Yes, he is much improved. His breathing is easier," she answered politely in her husky voice.

"I don't know how you do it, child. You truly have the healing hands. I don't know what we'll do when we lose you."

Vanessa's green eyes widened in surprise. Why would they lose her?

Mary smoothed her apron with an irritated gesture. She had been foolish to plant the idea in the girl's mind so soon. First she needed her help.

"Come in, my dear," Mary said. "You look tired. I have some fresh bread and a cool cup of milk for you."

Vanessa hid her surprise at the invitation. Evidently

Mary's men were not around. Vanessa was tired and preferred to go home. These nursing chores depleted her so.

Mary saw her indecision and took her by the arm, ushering her into the house before she could devise an escape. The woman's heartiness did not fool Vanessa. Mary wanted something in return for such an invitation.

"Now isn't this better?" her hostess asked, sitting across from her with false brightness as she watched her eat. "You've been away from home for this past se'ennight, and you can be sure that lazy brother of yours has cleaned out the cupboards."

A sly look came to her face, and Vanessa felt the first twinge of apprehension. What had her halfbrother done now?

She would find out soon enough, she decided. Meanwhile, realizing she was hungry, she ate the food. It was five miles from Squire Martin's home, and walking in the hot sun had been tiring.

With the baby safely on the mend, the mistress had said the squire wished to take her home, but Vanessa had refused the offer, saying she preferred the walk after having been confined to the house so long while tending their child. There had been no objections. They both had been aware of the gleam in the squire's eyes. In compensation a gold coin had been pressed gratefully into her hand.

Surprisingly, Mary did not begin the expected prying questions. As soon as Vanessa was finished eating, the woman placed her leg on the chair and pulled down her stocking. She wished to get this done before her menfolk returned.

Vanessa eyed the pudgy woman accusingly. "You have not been doing what I suggested!" she cried, looking with dismay at the swollen foot and red leg with its forming ulcer. "You have not lost weight to make it easier for your legs. I cannot help you further if you do not assist yourself."

The woman thrust out her lower lip resentfully. "But I starve myself, and it does no good," she whined. "Not everyone is blessed with your slender form. Do try once more. You gave me much relief the last time."

So that was the reason for this generosity. Not only butter had been offered for the bread slices, but a currant jam as well. Vanessa gave a slight sigh. She was tired from her walk and the weary hours spent by the crib. Still, it was best to get it done now while the son was not about. And the husband? Did Mary suspect the extent of his sly pursuit?

She gently massaged the swollen leg, then placed her hands on each side of the broken skin. Her green eyes took on a faraway expression, as if she were listening to something beyond the woman's ken.

Mary shuddered, her face tightening with primitive fear. There was something supernatural about the silent performance which sent shivers down her spine.

"Witch," she muttered silently, and surreptitiously crossed herself before touching the amulet hanging around her neck.

Then she relaxed as the hot fullness, which was a constant ache, slowly left her leg.

"There, is that better?" Vanessa murmured, sitting back in the chair.

The woman nodded her thanks while carefully pulling up the coarse stocking. For the first time she noticed the lines of weariness on the girl's face.

Really, what did the men see in this slip of a girl? For the past three years, ever since Vanessa had turned sixteen, the women in the village had noticed how their men's eyes followed her whenever she was about. Was she really as innocent as she appeared, or was that part of her appeal?

She was tall for a girl and painfully thin with no shape to speak of. There could be no allure there. But her coloring was striking with blue-black hair against milky white skin.

But those eyes! They were pure green. Cat's eyes. Witch's eyes.

Again Mary's hand touched her amulet. Was Vanessa perhaps a daughter of a seventh daughter? Her mother had not been one to socialize. The women would have resented her reclusiveness if it hadn't been for her gentle nature. Her daughter looked much the way she had, although only she inspired a special awareness among the men.

In spite of the rising resentment and jealousy among the women, many still went to Vanessa when a back would not straighten. She was especially good with young children suffering from croup. Her fame had even spread to the manor house, and she had been called there to help the Martins' sickly son when doctors' nostrums had failed to work.

Because she felt cheerful from her relief, Mary's antagonism towards the girl abated. Ashamed of her previous feelings, she offered the rest of the loaf of bread to Vanessa in payment.

"Just so you have something to eat tonight," she said, and on impulse sliced a piece of cheese also.

Vanessa thanked her and placed it in the square of material she carried. It contained a change of dress and a nightdress she had taken when she had been summoned to the manor house.

Dusk was settling when she topped the low hill and looked down at the few buildings nestled by the small river. Martinham was a hamlet, seemingly forgotten or unknown by everyone except those who lived there.

Despite her weariness, Vanessa's restlessness stirred as her eye followed the thread of road out of town. The feeling was becoming stronger all the time. What was beyond the hill where the road disappeared?

One of these days she would decide she had taken enough from her half brother and would follow that road. Nothing could be worse than this constant need to be on guard. Her half brother was a year younger than she, but he was already a square brute of a man, much as his father had been.

She sank down on a fallen log by the road to rest for a moment. Poor Mother. She had never complained, but Vanessa had seen the flash of relief in her eyes when she had been informed that her husband had been found frozen dead that morning two years ago. He had taken that usual one too many in the Boar's Head and must have collapsed in a drunken sleep on the way home. The sub-zero weather had done the rest.

Unfortunately Vanessa's mother had lived only one year to enjoy her relative freedom. The following winter a chest cold developed quickly into a lung inflammation, and she was dead within a week.

Vanessa closed her eyes in pain as she recalled that last night by her mother's side. She had tossed in delirium most of the day, her breath coming in hungry gasps. Then suddenly she was lucid and held her daughter's hand in a painful grasp, her face straining with the intensity of her need to communicate.

"Listen . . . don't speak," she implored, her breath coming in loud rasps. "Leave . . . as soon as you can. You are not beholden to John. . . . He is not your true brother."

Vanessa had been leaning over her mother to hear the

faint whispers, and she drew back, startled by the confession. John not her brother?

"Your father titled . . . in love . . . we were eloping to Gretna Green. . . . His parents stopped us . . . made me take money and go away. . . . Samuel . . . gardener . . . heard everything . . . Married me for money . . . Needed a father for you . . ."

Her mother's faded blue eyes begged her to understand, and Vanessa laid a tender hand on her shoulder, although she had been shocked by the revelation.

"Be careful . . . John."

A paroxysm of coughing had racked the thin body, depleting the remaining strength. The eyes dimmed as she fell unconscious. An hour later she was dead.

Vanessa was overcome by her grief, and her mother's confession was placed in the back of her mind. She examined it later, letting the knowledge warm her.

She had felt no love for her father. As she had grown up, she had known it was her mother's constant watchfulness that protected her from his leering inspection when he was drunk.

To think her real father was titled! Her heart soared with excitement, and she hungered for further knowledge of him. If only her mother had told her sooner!

She imagined fanciful dreams of the two lovers torn from each other by irate parents, forcing them to return from the attempted elopement. She could vividly see the bewildered young girl being denounced while the son was no doubt sent to Europe on a grand tour. Had he known his sweetheart was with child?

She could not believe he had. He would never have deserted her. In her dreams he was tall and handsome and chivalrous, the man she herself dreamed would someday capture her heart.

In spite of her romantic inventions, the disturbing question would arise: Why had he allowed his parents to separate them? She sighed. She would never know.

In his more benevolent moods her stepfather had said she looked just like her mother when he had first known her, except for her eyes.

He tended to get angry when she stared wide-eyed at him, and she learned early to keep her lashes lowered when he was nearby.

"Why does Papa hate my eyes?" she had once asked her mother after one such occasion. "Why do people always say something about them? I hate my green eyes. Why couldn't I have your pretty blue ones since I look so much like you?"

Her mother had hugged her, answering with great sadness, "Don't ever say that. You inherited them from someone I dearly loved. Looking into your eyes, I can remember the great happiness once mine."

A rabbit hopped near Vanessa, bringing her back from her musings with a start. She had better hurry now before the sun set.

She skirted the hamlet, taking the path to the tiny hut nestled in a clump of trees. She was still tired and wanted to avoid the prying questions of the women in the village. They were always avid for gossip about the manor.

"Vanessa!"

She sighed. She had been seen by one of Sophie's many children, who had then alerted his mother, Sophie. They lived in the next house to hers.

"I'm glad I saw you before you got home. I mean . . ." Sophie paused, embarrassed, and Vanessa again felt the stab of apprehension she had experienced at Mary's house.

"Of course, it isn't your house anymore since Squire Martin had it padlocked."

Vanessa stared at her, certain she had heard incorrectly. "Whatever are you talking about?" she gasped.

"You mean your brother didn't get a message to you? He and the oldest Gable boy took off to go to sea right after you went to the manor. The squire was heard to say in the Boar's Head that he would rent your place to the Parson boy after he married next week. You know how desperately in need of houses we are. He couldn't rightly let you, a single girl, keep it now, could he? However could you raise the rent?" she ended, ever practical. "His man put the padlock on the next day."

Vanessa blinked, stunned. So it had finally happened. She had feared this would occur after her mother died last year, but John had taken a job at the squire's stables, and she knew they had a roof over their heads for as long as he kept it.

But he was now gone without a word to her. As usual, her brother had proved uncaring about everyone but himself. She was without a home. Her eyes widened with fear. Now she knew what the squire had meant when he had cornered her in his son's room.

A maid had fortunately arrived with hot water for the croup tent that day, and his pale blue eyes had laughed at her evident relief.

"Remember when you have no other place to go, I'm offering the job as nanny," he had said. "Things will be different then."

She had shivered at the hidden taunt. The devil! He had known even then that she had no house to return to.

"What am I to do?" she whispered in a ragged voice.

"I can't help, you know," Sophie said sharply. She would never had stopped this girl with the disturbing green eyes if her husband had been home. "Our place is no larger than yours, and the brats already sleep on the floor."

Vanessa said nothing. The last thing she would do was enter that house. The two rooms were always in a shambles, but she had excused the careworn girl only a year older than she. Four children in fewer than four years would wear out anybody.

At the sound of horses' hooves coming up the lane, they turned to see who was approaching. They both recognized the carriage. Only the squire could afford one so elegant.

What was he doing here? Vanessa wondered. Her heart gave a sickening lurch. She knew. He was coming magnanimously to offer her the position of nanny, using Sophie as a witness. If she refused, the town would soon know and consider her addled for turning down such a position. The word not to help her would go out. No one could afford to antagonize the squire. He owned everything: the town; the land they worked; the houses they lived in.

Panic filled her. Once she was in the manor, he would pursue her until she could fight no longer. Revulsion swept over her, and without further thought she ran into the woods behind the row of houses.

Her one thought was to flee before he saw her, before she could be forced to enter that carriage, before common sense warned how well she was trapped.

She ran recklessly, unmindful of how the branches tore at her clothes. Her primary need was to place distance between them.

Not until she reached the wide stream did she stop, gasping for breath. She could not have gone farther. A painful stitch was piercing her side, and she collapsed on the bed of moss.

She listened intently for sounds of pursuit but heard only the wind touching nervous fingers to the leaves.

Reason reasserted itself. Of course, he would not come after her. She suppressed a hysterical giggle, imagining the heavy, pompous man chasing her through the woods.

The full extent of her position now hit her. She was without a home, without food, without hope of help from anyone she knew. Her flight had been useless, might have even antagonized the squire to retaliate and withdraw the position offered.

Her chin firmed with determination. She would rather die than return to him under the conditions she knew would prevail.

Then she remembered the bundle still clutched in her hand. The bread and cheese! Mary would never know how prophetic her words had been, saying she would need it!

She untied the brown square of cloth, which doubled as a shawl, and examined her small hoard. How long did it have to last? With prudent care she took her small knife and cut a minute ration. She would eat only enough to satisfy her present hunger. When it was gone, she would have to ferret for more.

Fortunately it was summer, and she could gather wild berries and mushrooms in the woods. Surely, after a night's sleep, a plan would come to her.

She curled up on the soft moss, placed the bundle under her head as a pillow, and, in spite of her precarious future, was soon sound asleep.

CHAPTER TWO

The noisy chattering of a squirrel caused Vanessa to awaken.

She gazed around in bewilderment, then sat up, immediately alert. This was the beginning of a new life; her past was no more. Somehow she had to cope with her precarious future, and she wisely checked her resources.

She unwrapped the bundle again to examine its contents. One dress badly wrinkled. It was a lovely dress which her mother had redone from a discard from the manor. When the servant had come with the message that she was wanted, Vanessa had taken it along, not knowing if she would be eating with the servants or with the family. She had done neither. A tray had been sent to her so she had never left the sickly child's side.

One nightdress. When would she again sleep in a bed? A wooden comb, two ribands for her hair, and, most important, the partial loaf of bread and bit of cheese.

There was also the gold coin Mistress Martin had given her. But that was to be used only if she became desperate.

These were her total possessions. These and the dress she wore. She gazed down at it and gasped in dismay. In her reckless flight through the woods the branches had torn long rents in the material. It was hardly decent in its present state.

This was the final straw. Tears rolled down her face, and her body was racked with sobs. Was any girl ever in a more intolerable position? It would have been difficult enough for a lad, but for a girl it was impossible.

She was well aware that the squire was not the only man who desired her, although she could not understand why she was so attractive to men. She certainly never encouraged them and rejected the thought that she had any exceptional beauty. Lately even her companions were avoiding her. Since her mother's death she had often thought how lonely her position was.

Why couldn't she have been born a boy? This all could then become an adventure, similar to those she read about in the wonderful books she had borrowed from the squire's library.

She washed her face in the stream. One thing was certain: Tears would not help, and staying here would solve nothing.

Yesterday she had thought that someday she would be forced to follow that highway out of the village. The day had come. But she dare not travel on the road. Someone might see her and notify the squire. It would be best to follow the stream a little farther.

Should she travel north or south? North, she decided. From the bits of information her mother had let slip upon occasion, she had gleaned that she had been born near the Scottish border. She might never get there, but Scotland would be her destination.

The stream curved towards the little cottage which had been her home, and she slipped carefully along its shore, ever alert. Ahead was the small private pool where she bathed and did her laundry. Everyone in the hamlet used a section farther downstream. It was the meeting place for the exchange of gossip as well as for scrubbing, and that was one reason she avoided it. She preferred this little hidden pool.

Bathing was an uncommon practice that her mother had encouraged and that she enjoyed. She especially liked rubbing a handful of sweet-smelling herbs over her body when it was dry.

Dare she stop for one last bath? Her body itched from the scratches received during her mad dash through the woods. Yes, it would be her last time to enjoy it.

She entered the little glen with eager anticipation. She had been keenly aware of its serene perfection, when she had first found it, and had avoided mentioning it since then to prevent its discovery.

She stopped short in apprehension upon seeing clothes draped on the bushes. Someone else was here! She turned to flee, then gave a nervous giggle. These were John's clothes, which she had scrubbed and spread to dry and then forgotten!

When the message had come to go immediately to the manor, she had gathered only her few belongings and hurried to the waiting carriage. These had been here since then.

How John must have cursed her when he couldn't find his best set of clothes! A suspicion came to mind over his precipitous departure. Had the squire also manipulated that? John had always loudly proclaimed his desire to go to sea. The squire could well have heard of it and urged him to go, leaving her defenseless.

After slipping out of the tattered dress, she submerged into the water with a sigh of pleasure. Knowing that she should not linger long, she scooped up a handful of fine silt and rubbed her body. Long ago she had found that it did wonderful things to her skin, giving it a glowing, smooth perfection.

The air was already hot, and she picked a handful of

wild rosemary and rubbed her body. When would she be able to repeat this luxury?

She stared in disgust at her torn dress. Suddenly she had an idea. Hadn't she thought a boy better equipped to face what was ahead? If she traveled as a girl, her future would be fraught with peril. She would be powerless when the first man saw her, alone and in rags.

John's white singlet hung loosely on her, denying the sex of her slim figure. She put on the rest of his clothes—dark brown corduroy trousers, tan shirt, black sleeveless vest. While John had been heavier, she was inches taller than he. His clothes were sizes too large and hung on her, giving her a wistful appearance.

Only then did she think of her hair. Dear Lord, how was she to hide it? It flowed in a lovely blue-black river to her waist, thick and luxurious. While she disliked her green eyes, she was femininely proud of her hair.

There was no way to hide it, and she knew she had to complete the masquerade. Tears hung on her thick black lashes as she withdrew her small knife. Her lips trembled at the first cut, then firmed, and she sawed away until she was left with a close, shaggy crop. As it dried, curls formed. The long, heavy tresses had hidden their existence.

It was impossible to look in the reflecting pool; she would burst into tears. Instead, she stoically cut a slice of bread and cheese, then bundled everything in the square shawl and started on her way, her face set with determination. She should have discarded the dress, but she did not have enough resolution. Perhaps in the night, when no one would see her, she could sometimes try it on and pretend that this horrible situation had never occurred. Besides, it was the last dress her mother had made. She could not cast it aside.

Vanessa trudged wearily along, trying to ignore her hunger pains. She had stretched the bread to last two days. Last night she had eaten the last crumb. It was too early in the season for ripened berries, and the dry spell had prevented the growth of moisture-loving mushrooms.

She still followed the stream and, when passing a few farmhouses, had been sorely tempted to ask for food. But something warned her not to show herself.

Soon she would have to travel on the road. At an inn or a tavern there might be work she could exchange for food, whether washing dishes or mucking stables. She could not expect the relatively easier job of chambermaid, not if she presented herself as a boy.

The stream had widened into a river. Small creeks had fed into it, giving it strength and breadth. Rounding a bend, she noted that the road had also curved, coming closer. Then she saw why. A heavy rope spanned the stream, and a wide raft was tied to the shore, sturdy enough to carry passengers and carriages across. It was a ferry stop.

This was what she had been hoping for. Several carriages stood before the inn. The owner must derive a good profit from so fortunate a position.

She approached warily. It was one thing to be dressed as a boy, another to be so accepted. This was an ideal time to test her masquerade. From the number of carriages present the people must be quite busy in the inn and were no doubt shorthanded. She might succeed with her pretense.

She paused by the stable. Should she present herself at the stables or the kitchen? She loved animals, but the kitchen was where the food was. She might even be able to save some scraps to take with her when she moved on.

"Boy, take my horse!" a deep voice commanded imperiously.

Vanessa turned to the horseman, startled by his unexpected appearance. Fretting over her problem, she had not heard him.

The sun was full on him as she gazed up. She had never seen such a resplendent figure. The forest green riding jacket fitted with such perfection that one could see strong muscles with each movement of the wide shoulders. Nothing like him had ever been seen in her hamlet.

"Don't stand there like a dolt!" he continued with irritation. "Be careful he doesn't bite. He hurt his leg, and it will not improve his temperament."

He was speaking to her! She reached instinctively for the horse, still dazzled by the vision he made, tall and arrogant, looming high above her.

The horse rolled back his lips and snorted, and her gaze was pulled to him. Her eyes widened upon seeing his beauty. This was a horse that even the squire could only dream of possessing. What a fitting creature to carry such a man! Both were proud and vain, both from a world she had read about but never glimpsed until this instant.

"Hold his head!" he commanded more sharply as he swung off the horse. "I want to examine his leg and don't want to be bitten for my effort."

The horse rolled his eyes and skittered sideways.

Vanessa acted instinctively. She had been called by farmers many times to help with a lame animal.

"Whoa, pretty baby," she murmured, rubbing the horse's neck. "We'll soon get you better, you black beauty. Take it easy, lovely one, and you will have your oats and some sweet grass."

She continued her soft crooning as she wondered if so high-strung an animal would react in the same manner as a plodding farm animal. She felt a fine tremor run through the powerful beast and recognized it as the first response to her voice.

It was always so. First that tremor before the gradual relaxation under her crooning voice. Then the slight pressure as the animal leaned into her caressing hands, as if desiring continuous contact. It was then completely docile, as if hypnotized, and she could complete her examination without fear.

"Do you think it a break or a strain?" she asked anxiously. "It would be horrible to have to kill so lovely a beast."

"Don't even talk about a break," he snapped. "Diablo is too fine a horse to lose. You are too light to steady him. Get some men to hold his head so I can examine the extent of the damage."

"It is not necessary, sir. He will let you touch it," Vanessa assured him.

He stared at her in amazement, then at the horse. His astonishment grew.

His fiery mount was gently nuzzling the lad, his eyes half closed as if he were understanding the soft voice. The lad was rubbing the sweeping arch of the powerful neck as if he were patting a lapdog. Only he and his head groom ever dared do that. True, the beast was much improved since it had been bought last month, but this?

He realized with a start that he had shown an emotion, and he pulled himself upright, resuming the pose of haughty boredom he adopted in public. Why he thought he had to do so before a mere stableboy he did not know. There was something disturbing about those green eyes.

Vanessa watched in fascination as the long, strong fingers palpated the injured ankle. On one finger was a large gold signet ring of a beautiful, intricate design. She had never seen such lovely hands even on the women in town. All were calloused; many, begrimed.

"Damnation," he swore, feeling the slight swelling. "He hit a stone and stumbled. I had to walk him gently for the last mile. With luck it is only a pull. Get your stableman to place hot fomentations on that leg immediately. I will see about getting something to wash this dust out of my throat, then check how he is improving."

He strode to the entrance, tall and erect, assuming that Vanessa would instantly comply with his orders. He irritably slapped his riding crop against his handsome Hessian boots.

The elegant cut of his clothes could now be fully admired. Only a master tailor could have fitted the material to his wide shoulders so perfectly. The buckskin trousers moved like a second skin over his narrow hips and long, muscular thighs. Even the shadow of dust could not hide the exceptional gleam of the highly polished riding boots.

Who was this princely man with golden blond hair and angry blue eyes?

The horse nudged Vanessa, bringing her back from her thoughts. She drew the reins over a hitching post and went to the stable.

The place was in an uproar. The exceptional number of carriages was placing a strain on the stablehands. Evening was near, and the stalls were filling as weary travelers decided that it was more prudent to pause here for the night than continue.

The stableman was yelling orders to his scurrying helpers, and the general noise made even the tired animals nervous. This was no place to take Diablo, who was already skittish.

She led him to the river. She would take care of the

animal herself, and perhaps that golden man would give her a coin for her labors.

A waft of appetizing odors came from the kitchen, precipitating an agonizing pain in her stomach. She must see about getting some food, and soon.

The horse cropped the grass by the riverside while she rubbed him down with clumps of dry grass, slowly working her way to the tender leg. Her crooning monologue kept him content.

Gently she massaged the slightly swollen area. Then, placing her hands around the affected part, she let the magic come to her.

She had been twelve when first aware of the special gift she possessed. She had been playing with a friend when the little girl had slipped and fallen on her hand. Immediately the wrist began to swell. Both children were frightened. The girl's screams brought tears of sympathy to Vanessa's eyes as well as apprehension to her face.

Her arm went around her friend in childish reassurance, but the girl's sobs became louder as they looked with horror at the spreading purple bruise.

Instinctively Vanessa had cupped the injured member, wishing fervently that it would disappear so that she would escape a scolding. It had been upon her urging that the girl had climbed the fence in the first place.

A strange sensation enveloped her. She was still with her friend, yet oddly she felt as if she were standing a distance away, like an observer, while her hands moved gently over the bruise.

A pain shot into her own wrist. It was as if she had absorbed the injury into herself. The girl's crying had quieted to an occasional loud sniff.

"It feels better, Van." Her friend hiccupped. "The swelling is going down, too."

They both examined the arm in surprise. The hand was still discolored, but it had returned to its normal size.

Vanessa sat on the grass, the event having made her curiously tired. The pain had left her as soon as contact ceased, but now a lethargy possessed her. Seeing that she was no longer in the mood for play, the friend had gone away.

"Mamma, it was so odd," she later explained to her mother, with wide eyes. "It was as if I, too, had hurt my wrist."

Her mother had looked at her strangely, then pulled her close in a tight hug, as if needing to protect her.

"I suspected, but oh, how I prayed I was wrong!" she cried. "When your hands soothed my headaches, I was afraid you had the same gift possessed by my grandmother. Oh, my darling, what can I say to help you?"

"I—I don't understand," she said in astonishment, seeing the tears coursing down her mother's cheeks.

"The healing hands. You are gifted with healing hands," she explained inadequately. "Thank goodness people are more enlightened in these times and no longer believe in witchcraft!"

She held her daughter close, explaining what the special gift entailed in words that a twelve-year-old could understand. "Use it judiciously, my child. You can do much good with it, as you saw today."

The villagers had soon heard the story. A worried farmer's wife approached Vanessa to heal her husband's aching back so that he could finish the harvest. Once she had accomplished a second cure, her fame was assured.

She was much feted when further successes followed. People were proud to have a personal healer in their hamlet, and Vanessa was much petted and favored.

But as she neared her sixteenth birthday, the long-legged, awkward child suddenly became arrestingly attractive, with hair like a raven's wing, skin as white as milk, and strange green eyes which seemed to promise much. Suddenly people's attitudes towards her changed.

The men felt excited when near her, and the women were quick to realize it. Doors did not open so readily to her, and erstwhile female companions jealously guarded their beaux.

Vanessa was still asked to help when a child fell ill or when an animal was hurt. But now the men found their women close by when she was present.

It was a lonely time for Vanessa, who was at first bewildered by the villagers' growing coolness. Her solace became the books her mother brought from the manor house when she went to do the Martins' sewing. The girl became an avid reader, absorbing everything her mother sneaked home. No one at the manor seemed interested in the extensive library that the squire's father had accumulated during his lifetime, and the borrowing of books went unnoticed. Under her mother's tutelage and guidance she gathered a versatile education, which added to the distance growing between her and the village maidens.

Now Vanessa sighed as she patted Diablo. The swelling was gone, and he moved to the water to drink. He had no limp, but she decided it would be prudent to begin the rest of the treatment.

She pulled off her shoes and rolled up her pant legs before leading the horse deeper into the river. The cool water moved in a gentle massage. The horse stood quietly as she leaned her head on his neck while whispering sweet words into his ears.

She hoped that Diablo's princely owner would return soon. She felt fair faint from lack of food.

CHAPTER THREE

His lordship, the Viscount of Kingsley, the Honorable Sir Wainwright Radcliffe Larimor, Wayne to his friends, walked into the inn and was happy to see that it appeared better than most. Perhaps the food would prove edible.

He called imperiously to the harried innkeeper, who was reduced to quivering servility by this high-ranking nobleman. A private dining room was hastily prepared for the viscount. He was soon sitting before the fireplace with a goblet of surprisingly good wine, served by the innkeeper himself.

Wayne stared morosely into space. What a deucedly miserable thing to have happened! He had planned to be five miles from here with a comfortable bed and Roberts attending to his wants.

He shifted angrily in his chair. Since being called from London, he seemed to have lost control of his destiny, and he was vastly irritated. This injury to his prize horse seemed part of some confounded plot against him.

Dammit. He did not appreciate being coerced into doing something that went against his will. He frowned as he reviewed the past week's events, which had brought him to this sorry state.

His father, the earl, had made all arrangements before sending the message which brought him to his residence in Northumberland. There was no way to invent excuses without being insulting.

"An heir!" his father had thundered when he had

arrived upon being summoned from London. "It is time you thought about setting up a nursery. I will give you six months to find an acceptable woman and do what is expected of you. You are approaching thirty and have spent enough time on youthful pursuits. I am getting on in years and want you to begin taking on some of the tasks associated with running these estates.

"I had assumed that London would give you ample opportunity to chuse from a large selection of young chits, but so far you have not done so.

"I was lucky to be able to marry the woman I loved," his father continued, "and I promised your mother on her deathbed to give you the same choice." The deep voice rumbled a little softer. Theirs had been a great love, and the loss of his wife was still keenly felt.

"Surely you must have become enamored of someone during these past years!"

His lordship recalled various pairs of soft, clinging white arms, the beguiling loveliness held in close embrace.

"Yes, several," he said boldly with a glint in his eye. "But not among the vapid, simpering debutantes."

The two men stared at each other from similar deep blue eyes. Both stood equally tall and proud. The golden blond hair of the elder was dulled only slightly by encroaching silver.

"*Har-umph,*" the earl said, clearing his throat. "Then it's up to your aunt and me to expedite matters. I have been in contact with several of my close and dear friends who have daughters of marriageable age. You should find one among them who is acceptable." He closely observed his son's reaction.

"I will give you seven days to prepare yourself. Then you will visit them in monthly succession to assess the merits of each. In six months I want a decision, or your aunt and I shall chuse a wife for you. Is that understood?"

"Yes, my lord," he had replied stiffly. His first reaction was of resentment over the prospect before him. Then he admitted with resignation that his father was right. An heir was necessary. He was the last in direct line to carry on the title and control the vast holdings. If only the call hadn't come at this time. He had been in pursuit of the latest delectable newcomer met at a rout. He was certain he had edged out the competition, and it was frustrating to think that he must now forfeit his advantage.

He swallowed his irritation. Dammit, another month and it would not have mattered. The baroness Audrey would have been a feather in his cap. The pack was in full cry after her.

It was not unusual, as in the baroness's case, to find a titled woman bored with her marital life. She had married a man far too old and now enjoyed discreet *affaires*. Wayne preferred these liaisons. The women knew the rules of the game. When passion was spent, a gift of a diamond bracelet or jeweled earrings signaled the end.

The earl tugged the bellpull. The butler appeared immediately.

"Please ask the countess if she would be so kind as to join us," he ordered. "And bring tea. She will be expecting it."

The viscount's raised eyebrow was mocking. "So Aunt Dorothea is here. I have no doubt everything is then well planned!"

The earl ignored his son's sarcasm. "The season is almost over. You will miss little if you leave now," he replied drily. "If you find the first girl unpalatable in se'ennight, you may return and help with the estates until the next month's visit. But be assured of one fact: A wife must be chosen in six-month time!"

The butler opened the door, and the countess Dorothea entered. The young man hid a quick smile. Her entrance always reminded him of a full-rigged schooner with all sails billowing. One would never guess she was sister to his ethereal mother, who had passed away five years ago. He was really quite fond of the dear girl, and he took long strides to her side.

"How are you, my dear aunt?" he asked after placing a kiss on each cheek. "I am usually pleased to see you, but I have my reservations after hearing how you and Father have arranged my future."

She tried to look severe but ended by giving him an indulgent smile. "Someone had to do it. Your father has been warning you for the last few years that the time was fast approaching for you to settle down and accept your responsibilities."

He gazed at her reproachfully. "Are you intimating my time is spent only in gaming and wenching? Certainly you must be acquainted with how I have increased both yours and Father's holdings. The investments I have made for the estate have all been profitable."

"Yes, yes, we have been impressed," she admitted, tapping his shoulder with her fan. "You have proven to have a good business head. We hold no reproach. But a handsome man like you should now be thinking of a family. The name is an old one, and its future rests with you.

"We're cognizant of your reputation as a rake. Life doesn't end with marriage, you know," she added drily. "Who knows, you may be one of the lucky ones, like your father and my dear sister, and find that marriage is indeed made in heaven."

He lowered his gaze. Such a marriage had been his

secret desire. Unfortunately his married acquaintances proved wedded bliss to be a rare condition. Most liaisons had been family matches, and after the required child was produced, both went their own ways. It was not what he wanted in his marriage, but he was already resigned to the inevitable.

The se'ennight passed in preparation for his trip, and his trunks were finally tied high on the baggage wagon. The heavy vehicle started off first, since it must of necessity proceed more slowly. Roberts, his valet, and the new boy he was training as a page traveled with it. The lad appeared overly excited, his face abnormally pale with bright red cheeks. It was his first trip away from home, and he was evidently feeling apprehensive.

It had been Roberts's idea to train a page. He had informed his lordship that was how he had obtained his first lessons, which had helped him become so superlative a valet. Wayne had agreed to the training, especially when told that a page's first duty was to do his fetching.

"Too bad the custom to keep a page has faded, my lord," Roberts added. "A page lends a dignified elegance to a lord's presence. The new valets one sees nowadays simply do not have the proper background." He gave a disdainful sniff which relegated them to a lower level of competency.

Wayne had found his father in his study and said his good-byes. Boris, the butler, had approached him as he came down the stairs.

"Your lordship," he murmured, "this letter just arrived." He offered a silver salver with a pale blue envelope placed in the exact center.

The viscount recognized it at once, and his pulse quickened. He had received several like it. The heavy odor of tuberoses, which the baroness Audrey preferred, clung to the letter.

"Is an answer expected?" he asked, tapping the missive on his thumb.

"The footman is pausing to rest his horse before returning," he answered.

"Offer him some refreshment while I see if there is a return message," he ordered.

He repaired to the library, his mind spinning off possibilities. He knew what the letter held. Dare he take a quick side trip back to London? One day to get there, a night with the dazzling baroness, and the next day to catch up with his carriages. He could send word to Baron Wesley, the first on his father's list, that he was unavoidably detained. A broken wheel could be used as an excuse.

He broke the seal, and his eyes glistened as he read. This was better than he had anticipated.

The baroness was on her way to visit a cousin, she wrote. She was pausing at an inn only two towns away and had suddenly realized how close he was and thought longingly of him. She might tarry an extra day. Perhaps his lordship could find time to come and see her, even if for a short visit? She would await his reply.

He gave a triumphant laugh. This side trip would cause but a slight delay after all. No excuse need be invented. Travel was uncertain enough so that a precise time of arrival at Baron Wesley's need not be given.

"Tell the man there is no message," he ordered the butler, "and have Diablo saddled immediately." He then hurried out the door where his carriage awaited. It was a new acquisition, and he gazed at it proudly. It was designed for speed and stood magnificent in the sunlight with its new yellow paint and the Kingsley coat of arms discreetly displayed on the door.

His driver and two footmen sat erect, resplendent in their uniforms in his personal colors of deep blue and yellow. The four handsomely matched chestnuts were nervous to be off, and he gave his order.

"Go ahead with the wagon and wait at the inn where we planned to stop," he said. "Tell Roberts to wait there until I arrive. Something has come up which I must attend to, and I will be delayed."

With a "Very good, m'lord," they took off, eager to catch up with and pass the heavier wagon. It was a point of pride to arrive first at a destination, even if the baggage cart had had a head start.

Fentworth, the viscount's head stableman, brought round Diablo, his latest purchase. His eyes lit with deep satisfaction. Never had he seen such a beautiful beast. The price had been astronomical, but the animal was well worth it.

Wayne mounted the powerful beast, presenting an elegant figure. He was the despair of his friends. Nothing they owned could compare with this glistening black stallion. Everyone had stared with admiring jealousy when he had promenaded on Rotten Row.

Wayne did not know how well matched he and his beast appeared. The proud, haughty mien of the horse was a complementary duplicate of the handsome rider.

"I'm glad you are taking him after all, m'lord," Fentworth said, handing him the reins. "He needs a long ride to use up some of his energies."

Wayne merely nodded, his mind already tasting what was waiting for him two towns away. So open an invitation could mean only one thing. The game was nearing fruition. The fluttering lashes, the pretended coyness had been read correctly.

He wondered briefly what she had done with the old

baron, who suffered so loudly from the gout. He did not blame her for seeking enjoyment elsewhere. She was still young and much too beautiful to devote her life as a nursemaid to so ancient a man.

Wayne came out of his musings as the landlord entered with a laden tray, then refilled his goblet. He fell to and was pleasantly surprised at the flavor of the sauces.

He frowned as he recalled the events of the previous day. The baroness had been obliging and delectable, as anticipated. Yet why, when she begged him to stay the night, had he refused? He had left her bed, where they had repaired after lunch, aware of that niggling sense of something incomplete. She had been better than most, so why this feeling, which was becoming more annoying each time?

He shrugged his shoulders in irritation. Could it be that at this still relatively young age he was becoming less enamored of the game? That, seemingly, was the crux of the problem.

Once again he had found the quest more exciting than the final capitulation. He shook his head in disgust. Maybe if he abstained for a while, his first youthful eagerness would return.

Somehow he doubted it. He was more mature now and suspected he craved more from these relationships than momentary pleasure. His father was right. He needed a wife, and he prayed fervently he would be as lucky as his aunt had opined and would find someone to share his love.

He grimaced, remembering the parade of vapid, giggling creatures he had politely danced with at their coming-out balls. If one of these daughters he was being forced to visit proved to have half a brain in her head, he would propose to her, no matter what her beauty. All he asked was that she be passable in appearance. After all, only he had to look at her, and if she wasn't a beauty, he wouldn't have to be concerned about being cockolded later.

The food suddenly lost its flavor, and he pushed it away. Surely somewhere there must be a woman such as he searched for. His father had been successful when he found his mother. The succession of women like Baroness Audrey offered no more than a momentary diversion.

His face softened as he recalled the happiness which had been so evident between his parents. With such an example how could he settle for less?

The night before, he had caught up with his entourage at the Post Inn, where they had spent the night. This morning the restlessness had still been with him, and after a stop for a light repast he had had Diablo resaddled, planning to strike out across the fields and run away from his private devil, preparing himself for the chore before him. He owed it to his father.

The plan had been to rejoin them at the next stop not far from the first assignment. He would arrive at the Wesleys' home in the afternoon, still fresh in his handsome carriage. First impressions were important.

The baron Wesley had two daughters, and he well knew the household would by now be in a flurry of anticipation over his arrival. Vaguely he recalled attending one of the girls' coming outs, but he held no recollection of what they looked like, which did not bode well for the poor girls. Still, it was his duty to inspect them. He had given his promise.

All had gone well until Diablo had struck a smooth rock and stumbled. Wayne had been forced to walk him slowly for what seemed a deucedly long time. Thank goodness he had come upon this inn. He might have to remain overnight to give that leg further rest.

The wineglass was now empty, and he set it down with a thump. Enough of these mental wanderings, he scolded himself. Best check on the horse and see what plans were needed for the night. With luck the boy with those remarkable green eyes had taken proper care of everything.

Strange lad, he mused as he strode to the barn. He had never seen Diablo gentled so quickly. The innkeeper was lucky to have such a gifted stablehand. He had heard of men with a magic touch who were capable of soothing the wildest beast.

Again he felt the startling impact of those green eyes on him. They were not the kind of eyes one would expect in a mere peasant. No doubt the boy came from the wrong side of the blanket.

The boy's loose clothes had given him a certain hungry wistfulness, pathetic in a way. That pale face had a pinched look. Well, if the boy did right by Diablo, he would have to remember to slip him a coin—on the side so that the stable master would not take it from him.

The viscount paused at the stable entrance and glanced over the stalls to locate his horse. The black stallion was not there, and he frowned. It stood taller than most and was usually the first one spotted.

The stableman came to him, properly impressed by so elegant a personage. "May I help yer, m'lord? If yerd sent someone, I'd of had the horse ready. No need for yer to become soiled," he said reproachfully.

"I am Viscount Kingsley, and have come to check Diablo," the viscount said coldly, ignoring his ramblings. "Have you taken care of his leg?"

The man scratched his head as he glanced over the stalls. "Sorry, m'lord. I was not given yer name or that of yer horse. Ken ye see it here?"

The viscount glanced around once more in irritation. "I

handed him to one of your lads. The green-eyed one," he said impatiently. "He had an injury to his ankle, and I left instructions to have it cared for."

"Sorry, m'lord," the stableman repeated, screwing his face while trying to recall such an incident. "I've not received such instructions 'n' don't have anyone working here with green eyes, if y'please."

The viscount's annoyance turned to anger. The devil! Had he been taken in by that lad and handed his priceless horse over to a common horse thief?

He whirled, his riding crop gripped tightly. He'd take it to the twit's backside when he found him! His long strides took him to the road. Perhaps someone had noticed what direction the boy had taken.

The ferry raft was still in. Had the boy endangered the horse by swimming it across the river?

Then he saw them in a little cove downstream. They were standing in the water, the boy's arm across Diablo's shoulder as he rested his head on the curve of the animal's neck. The horse stood patiently, only the twitching of his ears showing that he was listening to the lad's murmured words.

For a moment Wayne was taken in by the peaceful picture, the way the boy's blue-black hair blended with that of the horse. Then fury exploded in him, and he burst forward, his whip rising as he neared them.

CHAPTER FOUR

The whinny of the horse warned Vanessa of the viscount's approach. She stared at him, stunned by the rage blazing in his eyes.

"What," he thundered, "are you doing with my horse? Get him out of there immediately. If you have given him a chill, I swear I'll whip you within an inch of your life!"

Her legs would not move. "I-it isn't cold," she said faintly. "I-I'm standing in it also."

"I don't give a damn about you! Didn't I say put hot fomentations on his leg? Are you so stupid that you cannot follow a simple order?"

Vanessa's only thought was to flee, but hearing his master's voice, the horse moved out of the water, and with her hand frozen on the bridle, she found herself being pulled ashore.

The viscount's eyes were on the horse's leg, watching his walk. "My God, if you have ruined him, I'll strip the flesh from you!" he seethed.

"But, my lord, his ankle is improved," she offered timidly. "I always find that the gentle massage of cool water is the best cure."

She quivered with apprehension. To think this golden god held her in such contempt! Never had she seen anyone so furious. His head was held high in haughty displeasure even as his words branded her.

He ignored her as he bent to examine the ankle. Now was the time to escape, but her legs refused to obey her.

He rose slowly and stared at her. "It appears somewhat improved," he admitted with reluctance.

"Yes, my lord," she whispered, thankful that his anger had abated somewhat. "Now is the time to rub in a liniment and place warm compresses on it. Tomorrow he will be able to carry you without a limp."

An arrogant eyebrow lifted in surprise. "You are giving the orders?" he asked.

"Oh, no, my lord," she replied, quailing. He didn't think the pale face could become any whiter.

His eyes narrowed as he surveyed the youth. "The stable master denies hiring you, yet you profess to know a great deal about such attentions."

Vanessa hung her head. What could she say? The villagers knew about her gift, but a stranger would only laugh, thinking that she was fabricating her ability.

"Look at me when I'm speaking to you!" he commanded coldly. "What is your name?"

"Van . . ." She stopped short. She had almost given herself away!

"Well, Van, answer my question. Did your father teach you?"

She nodded her head. It wasn't exactly a lie. Samuel had worked in the squire's stables.

"Where is your father?"

"He is dead, my lord," she murmured.

"And your mother?"

"The same, sir," she whispered over the tight knot in her throat. *Oh, Mother, help me if you hear me!* she cried inwardly.

"Then you are an orphan. What are you doing here?"

"I-I was seeking work, my lord."

He gave a contemptuous laugh. Anyone so frail wouldn't last long. The boy was hoping to steal something, more likely. He'd scotch that. Still, he could not deny that the treatment had helped Diablo. He stared at the pinched face and reached a decision.

"Come," he said. "Since Diablo suffers your attentions, I will tell the stable master that you are to take care of him tonight." He glanced sternly at Vanessa. "I am Viscount Kingsley. I will see that you are paid for your labors."

Diablo had been cropping grass during the exchange and now lifted his head as the two people moved towards the inn. His action caught Vanessa off guard. His head pushed her, and she stumbled forward.

Wayne would ordinarily have backed away to prevent contact with one who was undoubtedly unclean, but it happened so quickly he instinctively raised his arms to catch the lad.

He was conscious of a slender body and unwittingly thought of his cook's herb garden, then realized that the clean fragrance came from the lad's hair as it brushed his face.

Vanessa's face was scarlet when she stood him up. "My apologies, my lord. The horse . . ."

Wayne made no reply as he strode ahead. The lad's thinness worried him. He would never survive mucking the stables. The work would be too exhausting for someone so slender. He frowned. But there was no reason that this should concern him.

Orders were given, the stall with its bedding of clean straw inspected. The type of liniment to use was discussed, and warm water procured.

"Van, the lad here, will take care of everything," he told the stableman. "I will see about a room and supper. Report to me in two hours," he ordered her upon leaving.

"Glad he gave the job to yer," a stableboy said, eyeing

Diablo's strong teeth, exposed when he came too close. "He'd have me head off in no time."

It was true. Diablo remained docile under her administration but was only too happy to challenge anyone else who came near.

Vanessa was weak from hunger by the time the horse was bedded down. If she went through the kitchen on the way to give her report, she might be lucky enough to find a bite to eat.

She paused by the lantern lighting the entrance, her nose wrinkling with revulsion. Her hands were grimy, and she smelled of the stable. She could not have his immaculate lordship see her like this.

She rescued her bundle and ran to the river. It was night now, and the moon was hidden. The water felt delightful, and she gave herself a vigorous sluicing. The odor of wild thyme hung in the evening air, and she searched out the bush. The crushed leaves offered a pleasant scent which might nullify any unpleasant aroma still lingering.

When she returned to the inn, the landlord was in the kitchen, checking supplies, destroying her hope that a snack could be begged. She sagged, realizing that she would remain hungry.

"Lord Kingsley wishes a report on his horse," she said timorously as the landlord stared suspiciously at her from under heavy brows. "Can you tell me which room he is in?"

"He's in the front parlor with a bottle of my best wine," he growled. "When you come out, let me know if he's finished eating so Rosie can clean up."

She knocked timidly on the door and entered at his command.

He was sitting with his long legs stretched out in front

of him, staring into the small fire in the grate, a goblet of wine at his elbow.

Vanessa did not notice the disapproving look he gave her shabby appearance. She could see nothing but the half-eaten food on the table. There was most of a chicken and several venison ribs, plus a pigeon pie. A bowl of luscious strawberries sat untouched by a pitcher of cream.

She swallowed hard and took several deep breaths to ward off sudden faintness. It seemed ages since she had tasted food.

"Come in, come in," he said with irritation.

She glanced at him with apprehension, and he was again taken by the clear green color of her eyes. They glistened brighter than emeralds.

"Diablo is resting quietly, my lord," she said hastily. She must give her report quickly before she succumbed to this swimming sensation. "He has been fed, and the liniment applied." She backed to the door.

"Come here," he ordered peremptorily. He had been sitting alone, feeling irritable. There was no one in this forsaken place with whom he could converse, and he was bored. Frankly his resentment was building against what lay ahead. He would obey his father, but at the moment he was wrapped in a fit of rebellion. Dammit, this marriage thing was too much like buying horseflesh. At both one went to the various breeding farms and investigated what was being offered.

He wondered what the startled parents would say if he asked for a history of the breeding line or insisted upon checking the teeth or running his hands over the merchandise to see the conformation. Yes, he was in a black mood.

He therefore welcomed the interruption Vanessa offered. This strange boy intrigued him. Should he take him home? He could tell Fentworth to use him as a walker. He need not ask the boy to do the heavy work in the stables.

"You have not told me where you come from, lad," he began.

Vanessa did not answer. She stood by the table, her gaze glued to it. Her hand clutched her stomach as if in pain.

His eyes narrowed upon seeing the pinched face and he recalled the feel of the slender body in his arms. The poor thing must be famished.

"When did you last eat?" he asked sharply.

Vanessa tore her gaze from the food. A faint flush tinted her cheeks. Had she been that obvious?

"Two days," she murmured in embarrassment.

His eyes widened, showing a momentary flash of compassion. "There is more here than I can eat," he said. "Sit down and have some."

He stopped in astonishment. Had he said that? He could not recall ever allowing a servant to eat in his presence.

Vanessa was too hungry to think of anything except that he had given permission, and she sat down hurriedly and ladled food onto a plate.

The whole episode was becoming unreal to the viscount. He had never placed himself in such a position before. He watched with surprise. He had been ready to be repulsed by the lad gulping his food. Instead, the utensils were handled as if the youth were born to manners.

He sipped his wine slowly, and a wry smile formed on his lips. He had wanted to escape his black mood, and he had succeeded. What a story this would make at the next meeting at the club!

He watched critically. Really, the boy's manners were impeccable. Who had taught them to this slim lad in coarsely spun clothes?

The hands were much too slender for heavy manual labor. They were clean, the viscount noticed with satisfaction. The youth must have taken time to scrub them after finishing with Diablo.

The subtle herb garden fragrance reached Lord Larimor again, and he had an astonishing urge to see if that dark, silky hair still smelled of it.

Vanessa paused when her plate was cleaned. Her gaze wandered to the large red strawberries. Did she dare try one?

"Help yourself," he said. "And some cream. It appears fresh. You certainly can stand some extra flesh on those bones."

She ignored his pronouncement as she helped herself to the fruit. A smile of childish delight lit her face as she tasted the creamed berries. "You should try some, my lord," she said impulsively. "They are exceptionally tasty."

"Then serve some," he heard himself say, and again pulled himself up in surprise. The wine must be affecting him. He didn't want to be a victim of a clumsy accident. He had sent a message on to Roberts, but he had no other change of clothes with him. Dare he trust his fine linen shirt to the mercies of the laundry here? If it were pressed incorrectly, it would be ruined. He had never missed his valet more.

Vanessa served the strawberries with care. Wayne noticed that there was a certain grace to the lad's movements, and his eyes grew thoughtful. This was no mere stableboy.

"You say you are alone in the world?" he asked after tasting a berry.

Vanessa thought of her halfbrother, who had left without a word or care. "Yes, my lord," she replied.

"You speak exceptionally well and have learned your manners."

She was instantly on guard. Was he prying or merely making conversation?

"My mother was born a gentlewoman," she confirmed.

That explained a great deal, thought the viscount. So many wellborn families had been reduced to poverty, although evidence of their good breeding remained. He leaned back in his chair as he contemplated the youth. An idea was forming, and he considered it from various angles.

"Last night my page was sent home," he said finally. "He had developed a fever and a bad cough. I am in a position where it may prove beneficial to have someone in attendance. Do you think you would be adept in learning such responsibilities? My valet is a kind taskmaster."

The green eyes were wide on him in astonishment. Now that the lad had eaten, the pinched look was gone. He would be quite comely in the page outfit. The kitchen wenches would be vying for his attentions.

"Th-that is most generous of you, my lord," Vanessa murmured. Inwardly she was thrilled. No more hunger, no more sneaking through the woods or being cold sleeping on the ground. And to be able to serve such a handsome and distinguished personage!

Then the bubble burst. How long could she manage this masquerade? Dare she try it even if it lasted but a few days? He could do no more than dismiss her when he discovered the charade. In the meantime, she would be farther along her way, have a few days of food in her, and be better prepared to continue when shown the door.

He accepted her hesitation as an agreement. "You'll travel with me in the morning. Your first task now is to see that I have hot water for a bath. I cannot sleep with this clinging dust. Also, see if there is anyone capable to do the washing and pressing of my shirt and neckband."

"I will attend to it myself, my lord," Vanessa promised. Her hands were clasped together to prevent their trembling. She had had no idea that the job would entail such personal attention. Heavens, what had she tumbled into!

An eyebrow arched at her offer. Could it be that this lad was already partly trained? he wondered. Perhaps some good would come from this trip after all.

He rose to repair to his room, and she went in search of the landlord to tell him that the room was ready for clearing. She then hurried to the kitchen and filled two buckets with hot water for the viscount's tub.

Somehow she would manage to get through the evening. If it proved too much, she would leave at dawn. Meanwhile, she would repay the viscount for the food he had been kind enough to share. She well knew that she should have eaten in the kitchen, but she had been too hungry at the time to think of anything but the delicious repast spread out on that table.

"'Tis a handsome lord you're serving," Rosie said, coming in laden with dishes. She was a rosy-cheeked country girl, full-bosomed and cheerful. "I'll bring you extra towels in a minute. Let him know I'd be happy to stay, will you, lad? It isn't often we get such fine gentry here."

Vanessa's cheeks burned. She must take a strong hand on her emotions. Would he want the woman's services? It happened frequently, she knew. Dear Lord, how was she to cope?

She pulled the tin tub before the fire and poured in the water. What would be expected of her next?

The viscount was opening a packet placed on the bed, and he uttered an exclamation of pleasure. "I sent a message to the inn at which I had intended to stay to alert

Roberts to Diablo's accident. I could not leave the beast here unattended. He's too valuable a piece of horseflesh. Roberts was attentive as usual and has sent a complete change of clothes. I am not at the mercy of your amateur pressing after all."

Vanessa buried her resentment, reasoning that he had no way of knowing she was accomplished in the work. She was supposed to be a boy and should not possess such knowledge.

"My boots," he said, sitting down and raising one foot. "I hope you have a strong pull."

The long Hessian boots were a snug fit, and Vanessa bent over, intent on her task, exposing the white nape of her slender neck.

The viscount's eyes lingered on the gentle curve. There seemed something very vulnerable about its purity of line. He pulled himself up sharply. At least the neck was clean, he thought sternly. In spite of the deplorable clothes, the creature appeared washed. Thank goodness. There was nothing he abhorred more than the odor of an unclean body.

There was that scent of herbs again. He leaned forward slightly. Yes, it came from the lad. It was surprisingly clean and refreshing. He was struck by how much more pleasant it smelled than the heavy scent of tuberoses which had clung annoyingly to him after he had left the baroness. He couldn't wait to bathe and rid himself of its cloying odor when he had arrived at the inn.

The blue-black hair was a dusky cloud as the lad bent to remove the other boot. It must be silky to the touch. Yes, he mused, the lad would have no trouble with the serving wenches.

A knock sounded on the door, and Rosie entered, the promised clean towels in her hands. She had put on a clean apron, and her lips were curved in an anticipatory smile. Vanessa felt heat rise to her face. Now what should she do?

"Some towels, m'lord," Rosie said, giving an absurd curtsy. "Is there any other service you wish?"

Her eyes were bold, her intention clear. He gave her a cursory glance and turned his back. "My page will take care of things," he said coldly.

She made a face at his back and left, but not before arching her brow coyly at Vanessa. If his lordship wasn't available, the page would do, although he didn't look as if he had two farthings to rub together.

The viscount misconstrued the heightened color flooding his page's white skin and gave a cynical smile. "Let me give you some advice, Van," he said. "Be careful of wenches at these inns. The lice is bad enough, but there are aftereffects discovered later."

Vanessa's face was now a fiery red, and she turned quickly to place the towels near the tub. "Is the water hot enough, my lord?" she asked in a trembling voice. He had started unbuttoning his shirt, and she didn't know where to look.

Her frantic gaze lit on the open packet on the bed, and she grabbed up the clothes like a life line and hurried to hang them in the large cupboard. She busied herself, taking exaggerated care over smoothing the creases.

She heard his sigh of satisfaction as he slipped into the tub and, after finishing at the cupboard, contrived to gather his dropped clothes while keeping her back to him.

"You can wash my back," he said, stopping her before she could leave the room.

Shocked, Vanessa stopped still in her tracks and looked wildly about to see how to effect her escape.

His lordship was leaning forward in the tub, exposing

his back for the expected cleansing. He gave her an annoyed glance over his shoulder at the delay, and she found herself walking to him on shaking legs. She reached for the soap and washcloth and lathered his back with a trembling hand.

"Harder, lad, harder," he said with a short laugh. "Such timorous rubbing! Do I look as if I will break?"

Vanessa stared at the bands of muscle across the broad back. The water glistened on the skin, giving it special highlights. She swallowed with difficulty, fighting the invading weakness in her middle.

She was in an intolerable position and must escape before her legs lost their ability to hold her upright. What would happen when he stood up to be rinsed?

He began soaping an arm, and Vanessa hurriedly placed the towel near him before she grabbed his soiled garments and dashed to the door, fearful that he would rise from the tub and stop her again.

Vanessa found the laundry room and leaned weakly against a tub. This was an impossible situation. How could she have imagined she could manage this masquerade? She must leave at once. She had never suffered through such an ordeal. Her limbs still hadn't stopped trembling.

Not only had she been alone in the room with a man, but he had been undressed, and most harrowing of all, she had bathed his back! She drew in her breath sharply, recalling the sensation of the muscles rippling under her hands.

Vanessa was not one to swoon, but she admitted to a faintness while her heart beat madly in her chest.

She dropped the viscount's clothes on the table and headed towards the door. She paused then as a frown settled on her brow. Her small hoard of clothes was up in his room. She must retrieve them. But not now, no, not now! She would give him time to get dressed.

She sank wearily down on a stool, then rose resolutely. His lordship had been most kind to her by feeding her. The least she could do was repay him by cleaning his clothes and, in the morning, giving that splendid horse one last treatment, if needed. She turned to the tub and began soaking the linen.

"There you are!" a gruff voice exclaimed. It was the landlord, with a thin pallet and blanket under his arm. "Your master said you were to have a bed, and I told him we were so full that there were already three to a bed over the barn, but I could give you a pallet to sleep on the floor. He said in that case you could sleep in his room." He dropped the offering on the floor and left.

Vanessa stared after the man, her head in a whirl. So much was happening to her. She could not assimilate this latest bit. Her heart pounded painfully in her chest. Sleep in the same room with that haughty man? Never!

Common sense returned. Sleeping in his room would be far better than in the dormitory full of snoring men! The inn was already being locked up for the night. If she slept in the wood, she wouldn't be able to get in to iron his clothes before they left.

She hung the handsome shirt and fine linen underwear before the banked fire. These, too, would have to be pressed. She instinctively knew that the unknown Roberts would expect it. He was the one she must impress if there was any possibility of her retaining this employment. The conviction arose that once with this valet she would not be in such close contact with his lordship. Dare she continue her masquerade?

She carried up the thin mattress and found her new

master standing by the fire, resplendent in a blue brocade robe, his coat of arms embroidered over his breast.

He indicated the brass bed warmer by the fire. "You didn't prepare the bed," he said coldly.

"Your pardon, my lord," she breathed. "I will try to anticipate my tasks better."

His features softened. Perhaps the boy hadn't flown the room like a scared rabbit. What could he expect from so green a lad?

She hurriedly scooped some glowing coals in the metal box and placed the warmer under the bedcovers.

"It isn't cold, but I always find these inn beds damp," he said. Heavens, he thought, was there a note of apology in his voice? He drew himself tall as he moved to the bed. It would never do to let this boy think him soft.

Vanessa managed the difficult task of emptying the water from the tub, then straightened the room. When she returned from the kitchen after emptying the buckets, the candles were out and his lordship was in bed.

The banked fire gave a fitful light, and she tiptoed to her pallet at the foot of his bed. Silently she removed her clothes, leaving on the singlet, then crawled under the blanket. Her heart pounded wildly at the sheer audacity of sleeping in a man's room.

Still, how much better this was than the chill of sleeping by the river, she reasoned, becoming practical. She snuggled under the blanket, wondering about the odd sense of security enclosing her. It was as if that arrogant man had somehow offered a protective mantle, and in spite of her worry over her future, she soon fell asleep, a small smile on her lips.

50

CHAPTER FIVE

Vanessa awoke quickly, instantly alert. The sky was just lightening, but already muffled sounds came from outside as early travelers made ready to leave.

She crept into her clothes, then hesitated, while gazing at the still-sleeping man in the double bed. His hair was rumpled, and there was a faint shadow from his beard, but even when he was asleep, one would know him a lord.

Her heart began pounding as she examined him: the outthrust arm; the even rise and fall of his broad chest; the long length outlined by the blanket—all spoke of a strength not to be trifled with.

Suddenly she felt overwhelmed by the audacity of her masquerade. There would be no forgiveness in him when her true identity was discovered. Would he have her beaten or, worse yet, jailed? She shivered in fright.

In her hunger last night the scheme had seemed plausible, but under the calming influence of daylight she could see only doom ahead for her. It would be best to flee now before he awakened.

But first she would do the pressing in payment for his kindness, as she had vowed.

She slipped quietly out the door to the laundry, where a thin, weary woman was already at the tubs. She was only too happy to allow Vanessa to heat the iron.

The cook gave her a thick mug of sweetened tea and some cold meat and bread to eat while preparing a cup of tea to take up with her. Did his lordship take it in the morning? she wondered. She would leave it on his bedside table and perhaps it would still be hot when he awakened later.

Once upstairs, she placed his folded clothes by the packet and carefully set the cup by his bed.

"Is it properly hot?"

Vanessa gave a small gasp, and her heart plummeted. He was awake, and her chances of a quick escape were gone.

"The cook made it from a boiling pot, my lord," she said, her eyes downcast to hide her distress.

"Fine. Now bring me some hot water. I doubt I can trust you to shave me without drawing blood. Then bring me my breakfast here. I do not wish to waste time waiting for service in the parlor. I'm anxious to be on the way and get this beastly exercise over with."

He threw back the bedcovers with an angry thrust. Vanessa flew out of the room. Why was he in such a black mood? He had been almost gentle before going to bed last night. Something was not setting well with him, but then, she reasoned, many men were hard to live with before they breakfasted.

Vanessa hurried the breakfast, and they were soon out by the stable. Diablo whinnied softly upon seeing their approach. The viscount eyed his horse's leg critically as Vanessa walked the animal for his inspection.

"You are lucky your treatment has not ruined him," Wayne said curtly. "You would still have felt the promised lashings if harm had been done."

He turned to the stable master, and she shivered as she stroked the dark head pushing gently against her shoulder. In his present black mood he could well use his whip as threatened.

Vanessa gazed longingly towards the woods. Dare she

make a dash for it now that his back was turned? She clutched her bundle with resolve. A queer feeling invaded her, convincing her that if she did not take this opportunity, her life would be irrevocably altered.

He turned to her to give a command and met the green eyes full upon him in seeming desperation. His chest expanded in response. The lad looked like a wood creature, ready to escape to its normal dwelling. And those eyes. They were now the green of a tormented sea. How odd that they changed every time he happened to gaze into them.

"I have bought a mount for your use so we can be on our way." His voice was colder than he had intended. For some reason he felt on his guard, then shook away the fanciful notion. On guard against this twit of a lad?

His irritation produced more sharp words. "I hope you know something about riding and don't disgrace me by falling off."

The plans he had laid to arrive fresh at the baron Wesley's estate this afternoon had to be abandoned. This whole episode was an irritation, and he was now sorry he had been bewitched last night into suggesting that this ill-dressed boy come along to be trained as a page. At the first sign of annoyance from Roberts he would have the boy dismissed.

Vanessa swung into the saddle. Her decision to escape had been taken from her hands, and with resignation she directed her attention to the horse.

She silently blessed Thomas, the kind head man at the squire's stables, who had taught her to ride years before. As a child she had gravitated to the animals while her mother had been sewing rush orders for gowns for the ladies of the manor.

Thomas had first let her walk the horses, then, seeing

her rapport with the cattle, had let her exercise them. With stern supervision he had taught her the correct posture and handling, had finally even let her jump them. When out of childhood, she had been switched to a lady's saddle, but she remembered the freedom of sitting astride a horse.

She quickly readjusted to the change. This horse was not equal to Diablo. His lordship had looked at the animal with disdain and muttered that it would have to do but would be resold when they reached their destination.

She managed to keep up with him only because he was intent upon preventing a strain to the injured leg of his prized horse.

It was a lovely morning, clear and crisp. It was a joy to ride again, and for a brief time Vanessa was able to throw off the cloak of despondency that had shrouded her for the past days. She was determined to revel in this moment before the hatchet fell when the formidable, unknown Roberts unmasked her.

It was a perfect morning. Her horse, while not of Diablo's caliber, moved with remarkable smoothness and with an eager stride.

His lordship glanced behind to see how she fared. Vanessa was gazing up into a tree they were passing, smiling at the antics of a scolding squirrel. His eyes narrowed as he assessed the lad. The seat was easy, the movement as if one with the horse. Dash it, where had a boy of such poor means learned to hold the ribands with such composure?

After that, whenever he checked back, he assured himself it was only to make certain the youth was not falling too far behind. He had invested money in the horse, hadn't he, although worry over the price of anything had never entered his head before.

When they reached the inn, Roberts came hurrying anxiously to the door to meet them. After first making certain Diablo was attended to, the viscount turned to the hovering man.

"Relax, Roberts," he said as he swept into the inn. "Send word on to the baron Wesley that we were unavoidably detained and will arrive this evening." He waved his hand imperiously as Roberts murmured something. "Yes, yes, I know these country bumpkins eat at an outlandishly early hour, but I do not intend to be so plebeian. Eight o'clock is early enough.

"Meanwhile, I have brought this lad, Van, to replace the one who took ill. I hope he will train easily as a page. Get him out of those outlandish clothes. Surely you can make him more presentable. Then I shall want a bath before considering food."

He glanced back to the door where Vanessa stood, her green eyes wide with apprehension. Dammit, how could a waif appear so wistful and vulnerable at the same time!

"Put him to work as soon as he's decently outfitted," he ordered sharply before striding up the stairs. "We'll see if he's worth teaching."

Roberts was too well trained a servant to let his surprise show. The viscount never allowed a servant near him until he was well trained. He strove for perfection in everything, and nothing irritated him more than a fumbling servant.

He gave the boy a short nod, indicating that he should follow, and hurried to the third floor, where the personal servants slept.

"This is the best I can do at present," he said not unkindly as he tossed an outfit on the bed. "It was fitted for the lad who was much your height but broader. I hope to heavens it does not hang too badly on your thin frame."

He gave a faint shudder over the thought of anyone under his service being poorly attired.

"His lordship's room is below. Come as soon as you are dressed. I must hurry now to prepare his bath. Watch everything I do, and for your own sake do not drop anything or be inattentive, or the heavens will fall on your head." With that dire warning he hurried out, fretting over his lordship's being left so long unattended.

Vanessa stared fascinated at the elegant outfit, then looked warily at the door. She resolutely placed a chair under the knob before removing her clothes with trembling hands.

This was it. The challenge of her position was increasing, but she was held by a fatalistic desire to continue with the disguise.

She poured water into the bowl and washed the dust from her face. Then, because she could not bear dressing in such fine raiment without bathing, she gave herself a quick sponge bath.

On the floor stood a bowl of herbs used to help sweeten the room, and she pulled out the lavender spikes to rub over her body. It was a ritual she was so used to she would not have felt clean without it.

The clothes Roberts had handed her were made for a boy's figure. With a judicious adjusting of ties and a change of buttons she was able to improve the fit. If only her waist was not so narrow!

The shoes presented a problem. Her heavy ones would never do. No matter how tightly she pulled the ties on the slippers provided, they slid off her slender feet. Finally, in desperation, she opened her bundle and tore pieces from her old dress to stuff in the toes before she affixed the silver buckles.

She ran her wooden comb through her hair and wished

that the small metal mirror showed more of the splendor of the outfit. Did she look outlandish? It was a purely feminine craving to wish to look her best for the inspection which lay ahead.

She knocked timidly on the door and took a deep breath. She was well aware that she was now part of a wealthy household, and until she was found out, it was up to her to act a good representative. Her head lifted, and her shoulders squared in unconscious imitation of her benefactor.

Roberts opened the door, and she stepped in, her heart pounding painfully against her ribs.

The viscount was adjusting a long silken robe over his wide shoulders. Vanessa stopped short, immobilized by a trembling within her. The richness of the maroon brocade was accented by a velvet collar. He had been handsome in his riding clothes, but this intimate elegance quite took her breath away.

He tightened his belt as he turned to examine her. His eyes narrowed to hide his surprise. For once Roberts lost control of his facial expression.

The viscount's colors were yellow and blue, the deep blue of his eyes. The outfit Vanessa wore was yellow, piped with blue, and she stood proudly by the door, her slender figure a golden shaft.

Her creamy complexion had a magnolia quality, while her eyes were again the clear green of a well-cut emerald. The raven black hair curling lightly around her face acted as a startling accent.

Never had the viscount seen so handsome a lad. It was incredible what the change of clothes had done. Thank goodness he had not been to a manor born. The ladies at St. James's would have been set on their ears upon his presentation.

He cleared his throat as he sat down. "Turn around," he ordered, his gaze now critical.

Vanessa complied, hiding her apprehension. Something had happened when they had looked at her. Were they displeased with the fit, or did the outfit reveal too much, causing them to suspect? She had checked in the small mirror and had thought the tightened undershirt had effectively hidden her figure under the loose jacket.

"How do they feel?" he asked as she started her rotation.

"Fine, my lord," she murmured, and promptly stepped out of the slippers.

Her face was on fire as he stared at her slim feet with the too large stockings. His hand went over his mouth as he rubbed his jaw.

"The lad needs narrower shoes. Can they be obtained?" he asked his valet. "We cannot have him walking in stockinged feet in the baron's drawing room."

"It shall be done," Roberts said, his face back in its careful mold.

"I shall be dressed shortly," the viscount continued, moving to the bed where Roberts had laid out his clothing. "If you can manage to spread your toes to hold onto those shoes, alert the landlord that I shall be ready within the hour for his repast."

The belt of the dressing robe was untied, and Vanessa flew as fast as her shoes allowed.

She had not realized that being a page would place her in so intimate a position now with Roberts in attendance. The situation was becoming intolerable. Already she could envision his lordship's wrath upon his discovery of the flummery done to him.

"Watch closely," Roberts murmured moments later as he sliced the mutton for the viscount's dinner. "I am usually too involved keeping his clothes presentable to do these niceties for him. I do this only when on the road. He dislikes being waited upon by the locals when at an inn. At home, of course, your labors will be entirely different. You will remain unobtrusively in the background to attend to his fetching."

Vanessa breathed a sigh of relief. The chance of intimacy would be reduced. She had only to contrive somehow to exist through the next few days while he was traveling.

His lordship entered, and Vanessa could only blink upon observing his splendor. The jacket was an unusual rich brown color, and the tight fawn pantaloons molded the long legs, showing their muscular perfection. Roberts had done a magnificent job of tying the snowy neckpiece in intricate folds.

No words were spoken as Roberts served the food. He watched hawklike while Vanessa refilled the goblet with wine and nodded with satisfaction. This was no ordinary bumpkin his lordship had brought for training. The handsome lad had an inherent grace and a quick intelligence. He stifled his sigh of relief. He had entertained doubts about teaching the other boy, who would be better suited as a footman.

Roberts held his responsibilities as *valet suprême* proudly. No one could surpass his lordship on the turn of his clothes. He worked closely with the tailor, both spending sleepless nights over making their fit flawless. If only he wasn't so athletic. It was most difficult to make the set perfect over those muscles. Still, it was better than contending with the unsightly bulge and corsets which other valets shook their heads over.

"You may go, Roberts," his lordship said when his first hunger was abated. "The lad does not seem to have nervous fingers, and I know you wish to get to those boots I wore."

Roberts bowed himself out gratefully. There weren't many masters who were so considerate.

The viscount finally finished and stretched his long legs before him as he sipped the wine. His glance went to the figure standing quietly to one side.

"Have you eaten yet, Van?" he asked in a detached voice.

"Not as yet, my lord," she murmured. She was hungry, but she did not suffer the ravishing pain which had torn at her yesterday.

"Are you expecting to sit at my table again?" he continued more mockingly.

Her cheeks flushed. She lowered her lashes and did not see the glint of amusement in his eyes.

"Oh, no, my lord," she protested. Gripped by acute embarrassment at remembering the unprecedented audacity of eating with him, she gazed up at him pleadingly. "I would never have done that if I hadn't been so hungry," she said. "I should have understood that you did not mean I was to eat in front of you."

He raised an eyebrow, then thought better of the mocking reply he had intended. It might sound coarse to unsophisticated ears. Again he wondered why he should care about a mere servant's sensibilities.

"Just to prove it was not a whim of mine, you may sit down now and help yourself." Dammit, he had not intended to say that. Still, the lad intrigued him, and he wished to examine him further.

Vanessa hesitated a minute, then silently filled a plate before she sat across from him. The situation was decidedly unconventional, but it never entered her head to disobey him.

"You say you are without parents," he said idly, bemused by the boy's fastidious manners. "Surely you did not have to wander off. There must have been a relative or friend who would have offered you a home."

"No, my lord. My half brother took to the sea, and my mother's parents would have nothing more to do with her when she married. I understand they are both dead now."

"And your father's parents?"

"He never spoke of them." She was happy she did not need to fabricate falsehoods. She knew nothing about the parentage of her true or stepfather.

"Surely a lad as adept as you are could have found work in your village."

Vanessa moved uncomfortably in her seat. How much dare she divulge? She had always been a truthful person, and the thought of a verbal deception would only compound her misery. She had better stay close to the truth.

"Yes," she murmured. "The squire offered a position in his household."

He gazed at her as her eyes filled with misery. Those strange eyes were now a smoky green, almost the black of a storm tossed sea.

"And you turned him down?" he asked sharply.

Vanessa was filled with sudden confusion. She could not tell him about the veiled threats. "I-I could not accept the conditions under which I would have to work," she answered in a bare whisper.

She did not see the hard line tightening his firm mouth. She could not know the entirely different interpretation he was giving her words.

Damnation! he thought as swift anger rose in his chest. He could envision the man's lecherous designs on this handsome but peculiarly defenseless lad.

Thank goodness he had decided to take the boy on. A

strong need to protect rose in him, but he shrugged against the sensation. He was just as protective of his horses—was he not?—or anyone in his employ.

He rose abruptly, suddenly restless. "Come," he said, striding to the door without a backward glance. "I wish to examine Diablo to see if he is completely recovered. I intend to do some riding when we get to the baron's estate."

Vanessa followed at a respectful distance. She was becoming accustomed to his mercurial changes. His questions had suggested that he was genuinely interested in her. Now he was suddenly withdrawn, hidden behind that haughty, disdainful stance that she had noticed he offered to the public.

The stableboy walked the horse as Wayne examined him critically.

"I confess I have never seen so quick a cure," he admitted as he gave the animal the apple he had taken from the fruit bowl. "Perhaps I should put you in the stables when we return, instead of dandifying you as a page."

His gaze was aloof as it swept over her. It would be best. He wouldn't find himself checking those incredible green eyes to see what new change in shading they held.

She gazed at him admiringly as she followed him back to the inn. No one, absolutely no one, could be so haughtily elegant, so handsome to the eye, so assertively assured as he.

Was he married? There was so much she had to learn about him, and her chin rose with pride over being even a small part of his entourage. She did not know how much a slender replica she appeared of the man striding ahead of her.

They paused as an elderly woman swept out the entrance of the inn, followed by her abigail. Her face was heavily lined with irritation as she was lifted into her carriage by her footman.

"Hurry up, you lazy lout," she cried crossly. "If you drop one more thing, you can stay here and I won't give you a farthing."

Vanessa looked with sympathy as the harried maid balanced a precarious mound of small boxes while trying to retrieve a trailing shawl. The wind whipped the offending article around her legs. Vanessa saw the imminent accident but could not stop it. The girl tripped over the material and, with a cry of dismay, was sent sprawling.

"That does it!" the woman screamed. "Harris, get my belongings and drive on."

The footman gathered the scattered possessions, then, with a look of apology to the stunned girl, placed them in the carriage before climbing into position. The driver slapped the reins, and the horses took off.

Vanessa was instantly beside the horrified girl, her hand held out to assist her.

"My leg, my leg," the girl wailed, tears coursing down her face. "Dear Lord, what am I going to do! She has stolen my few belongings, and I don't have a ha'penny to my name!"

"Hush," Vanessa said soothingly. "She will return. She only intends to frighten you."

The cries grew louder. "You don't know her! I was warned that she does this all the time so that she doesn't have to pay the wages. What am I going to do? Look at my leg, my leg!"

"The first thing we must do is get you out of this dusty road," Vanessa said, ever practical. She was examining the ankle and saw that it had already started to swell. The poor thing. It would lay her up. The landlord did not look as if he would appreciate being a good Samaritan. Something had to be done, and fast.

Her hands were already beginning their cupping. Her body relaxed into its other-world sensation. She became two people, one watching over the scene, the other suffering with the pain entering her own ankle. Her hands did their slow massage, and gradually the swelling receded.

When the pain left her, Vanessa rose, feeling the deep tiredness which always came after these ministrations.

"Does that feel better?" she asked, and the girl looked at her leg in wonder.

"Healing hands, you have the healing hands," she whispered. "There was an old woman in our village who had them." She gazed in awe at Vanessa, for the first time noticing her rich clothing.

"I can never thank you, sir," she said, scrambling upright and dusting herself off. She looked towards the inn, her face pinched with apprehension.

"Do you think the landlord would give me employment?" she asked. "I have nothing, nothing. What am I to do?" Tears were again running down her cheeks as she realized the full extent of her situation.

Vanessa came too with a start. His lordship! She had done the unforgivable by deserting her post.

He was still standing by the entrance, a foot resting on the first step. He had not moved since the beginning of the episode. He had halted first at the sound of loud voices, then had watched his page's performance with amazement. So the incident with Diablo's leg had happened just as he had noted.

He had, of course, heard of these healing powers, but always under the direction of some old crone, never by one so young and handsome. Should he apprentice the boy to his doctor? The thought did not appeal to him, and he cast it aside. The youth would bear careful watching to see what other potential he possessed. He was indeed a strange but interesting boy.

Boy? For the first time he wondered about his age. There was no sign of shaving on that attractively clear skin, yet some did not start young. The voice was husky enough, as if on the brink of manhood, and there was a certain maturity about him. That he could understand. The youth had been forced at an early age to make decisions.

He realized with a start that the lad was standing before him, the mobile face flushed with embarrassment.

"My lord?"

"Yes?" He gazed down his nose, his eyebrows slightly raised with bored detachment.

Vanessa hesitated, abashed by the forwardness of her intended request.

"Speak up, Van," he said with irritation. Then, seeing her flushed face, he became unaccountably more gentle. "You have a question?"

Vanessa twisted her hands in agitation. "I beg you to forgive me my request," she said, her voice a bare whisper. "Nothing has been said about wages, or if you intend to keep me." She took a deep breath and plunged on. "But if you do, could you give me a forward?"

She quailed, as much from the temerity of such a request as from the astonished anger on his face.

"And what prompts this unheard-of request?" he thundered.

Vanessa closed her eyes as if to make herself invisible. What had come over her? She pictured herself in her half brother's clothes, back on the road.

"T-the abigail has no money and noplace to go," she

quavered. "I would like to give her something to tide her over until she finds a position."

The ensuing silence was profound, and Vanessa could not stop trembling. She did not see the utter amazement which flashed across the viscount's face, in spite of his control.

"You mean that even so handsome a lad as you has to pay for his pleasures?" The words were heavy with derision.

Vanessa's eyes flew wide with astonishment, her face paling with anger at his innuendo. "Of course not," she said, her back rigid with emotion. "I only wish to aid someone in distress. I do not even know her name. Nor do I expect to see her again!"

They stared at each other for a long moment, and Vanessa found her heart beating a wild tattoo against her chest. His eyes became hooded as he turned to examine the abigail, still brushing at the dust clinging to her skirts.

Vanessa found herself breathing hard, as if she had just run to escape the squire. Why, oh, why did she always champion the cause of those in distress? She had only precipitated her own dismissal, and that thought struck her like a knife in her breast.

"Come here!" he called to the abigail, his voice icy with command. The girl stopped her cleaning to look at him with apprehension. Then, seeing his elegance, she hurried over and dropped a curtsy.

"Yes, m'lord?" she asked timorously.

"I understand you are an abigail without employment. How long have you been trained?"

"Two years, m'lord. Madame hired me from my village." She was plainly overcome by his questions, her face pale from fright.

"No doubt there is use for another girl," he said

brusquely. "Go in and see my man Roberts. He should be able to find plenty for you to do until we return home."

The poor girl's mouth fell open. She managed to bob another curtsy before scurrying inside, her face alight with hope.

"Thank you, my lord," Vanessa murmured happily. Her eyes were like stars as she gazed up at him, bright, shining green stars.

He turned sharply and strode into the inn, incensed over his action. Fustian! He had never done such a lowly thing as hiring someone, and here this creature had him doing it twice in as many days.

CHAPTER SIX

"My lord." Roberts was waiting for them as they entered the inn. "Mr. Brooks has just arrived and wishes an audience. He is in the private dining room."

"Good," the viscount said with satisfaction. "I was hoping he would come before I reached Baron Wesley."

Vanessa hesitated, and Roberts indicated for her to follow. "He is his lordship's comptroller and secretary," he murmured in an aside. "They may need you to fetch something."

Mr. Brooks was middle-aged with a touch of grey in his dark brown hair and a comfortably expanding waist. His tall frame was bent, suggesting long hours spent over books, some of which were on the table before him.

"My lord," he said, bowing respectfully.

"It's good of you to come, Brooks," Wayne answered cheerfully. "I assume this promptness means you have good news?"

"Yes, my lord. Your predictions were correct as usual. You have made two successful acquisitions, and the property you wished has been obtained at a much lower price than anticipated."

The books were opened, and the two sat down to pore over them. Vanessa retired to a seat in the corner. The room was small, and she could not help overhearing the conversation. She was soon dazzled by the intricacies of his lordship's holdings. His was wealth beyond imagining.

Aside from mourning over her mother's death, Vanessa's greatest loss had been that of the manor house library which was no longer at her disposal. When not with the beloved horses, she would curl up with a book in the seldom-used room. Early on she had found a hidden nook in a window seat behind a heavy drape. There she would read by the hour until her mother would come for her, her eyes weary from the close work required of her sewing.

The squire's father had amassed a surprisingly diverse selection of books, and Vanessa was certain that she was the only one now reading them. The *Gazette* delivered from London was all the news those at the manor were interested in. Vanessa read the paper thoroughly, hungrily following the conditions around the country, the market, the people.

One shelf of books she had particularly enjoyed were the old farm ledgers. She had a quick affinity for numbers, and nothing pleased her more than to find a mistake in the columns. It had also given her an understanding of the many facets of running an estate, though nothing as extensive as what was heard exchanged between the viscount and his secretary.

She therefore could grasp much of what was being discussed. The two men would have been amazed at the intelligence of the page sitting quietly on the stool.

They finally sat back, satisfied with their transactions, and Vanessa was sent for wine and a light repast, for Mr. Brooks was anxious to return to the viscount's house in London. These new decisions must be acted upon immediately.

The man eyed her questioningly as she poured the wine, and the viscount explained. "Place Van on the payroll," he said. "He is my page. Also, Roberts will tell you about an abigail I seem to have acquired. When we return, they are to have an allowance for the necessary clothes." His glance was sardonic even as a faint twitch moved his lips.

A quickly suppressed glint of surprise crossed the secretary's face. This was very odd indeed. His glance lingered on the youth, noting the comely face, the inherent gracefulness, and he suppressed a sigh. Like the viscount, he wondered if the lad came from a titled family in poor straits. Such cases were more and more common. Noble families and their estates were falling into bankruptcy from poor management or unwise gambling debts.

Brooks's thin shoulders straightened with a quiet pride. How different it was working with the viscount. Their minds meshed like a matched pair. What one didn't think of, the other did. He had had many surreptitious offers with stupendous bribes, but they offered no temptation. None could match the sheer enjoyment of being in the viscount's employ.

"Your family is well?" the viscount asked as Brooks gathered together his papers before departing.

"Very much so." The man smiled. "Beatrice, our oldest, is betrothed, and the house is in a constant upheaval."

"Can Beatrice be so along? I remember her as a mere chit!"

"She was seventeen this spring," he answered with a tinge of pride. "She has turned into a lovely lass, much like her mother, and is very much in love with the lad she is to wed. He is a good boy, too."

A bitter twist came to the viscount's lips. "You mean there are still those who believe in that fairy tale?"

The elder man did not answer. He was well aware of the reason for this trip.

"We will have to augment Beatrice's dowry," continued the viscount. "Draw one hundred pounds for her, Brooks. It should help set their life in order."

The secretary's face beamed with appreciation. He gave a deep bow. "Many thanks, my lord," he murmured. "Your kindness will indeed make their way easier."

"A little more wine, Van. Then I must dress to finish the rest of this journey," the viscount ordered with a sigh after the secretary left. A frown creased his brow, and hard lines deepened along his mouth, making her wonder why he always seemed displeased when he mentioned the trip.

She hesitated after pouring the wine, remaining by his chair. "My lord?" she began tentatively.

His eyes were heavy in thought, and he glanced at her with annoyance at the interruption.

"I beg your pardon, my lord, but may I say something?" Her hands were clutched tightly around the wine bottle. Why didn't she keep her mouth closed, her doubts to herself?

He lifted the goblet to his mouth, then replaced it before answering. "Proceed," he said. "I do not see anyone lying on the floor, so I can assume I am not to rescue someone else for you."

Vanessa bit her lip in consternation. Was he teasing her or angry? She took a deep breath before continuing.

"I could not help overhearing you speaking about the land you recently acquired. I know something of the area since it is near my birthplace. Mr. Brooks suggested planting fruit orchards there, but I would strongly advise you not to do so."

There was no change in his expression as he stared at her, but she was aware of the anger rising in him, and she hurried on. "There is a deposit of lime nearby, and it tends to stunt the trees."

"Are you telling me you know more than the land surveyors?" he asked, incredulous at such audacity. "I hired the best in the field, yet a mere lad wishes me to obey him over their verdict?"

He rose from his chair to tower over her, filling the room so that it was difficult to breathe.

"I assume you base your wild assertions on solid fact?" he asked in a deceptively quiet voice.

Fear rooted her to the spot. Her mind urged a rapid escape, but her legs were incapable of following the edict. She shivered at the menacing thrust to his jaw now too close for comfort.

"N-no." Her husky voice was a bare whisper. "B-but I have overheard the farmers from that section speak as they passed through with their produce. The deposit is only local knowledge, and I'm certain they would not impart it if wishing to help the seller."

"And pray, what was their gossip?" he asked coolly. She was not deceived. Her audacity had infuriated him.

"T-they are always fighting the lime encroachment which fortunately lies deep under the soil. Vegetables can be managed, but trees whose roots go deep are especially susceptible."

"So I am to become a vegetable gardener under your advice." He straightened, breaking the disturbing eye contact.

Thoughtful, he took a sip of wine, then replaced the goblet with a hard thump. "Fetch my writing pad from Roberts. I must get a letter off to Brooks before he starts buying those damn trees."

The timbre of his voice softened only slightly. "You may have saved me hundreds of pounds. But if not, you will feel my wrath."

She flew to do his bidding. She had been perilously close to a dismissal. How much more of her audacious behavior would he tolerate? She must hold her tongue before he carried out his threat.

The next morning Vanessa managed to gather some information about where they were going, and why, in spite of Roberts's preoccupation with the proper folding of the viscount's garments and the restrapping of trunks in the baggage wagon.

"I managed to find a smaller pair of shoes," he said, handing her thin black sandals while indicating a small trunk filled with changes of uniforms from the previous page. She quickly pushed her bundle of clothes into a corner and strapped the trunk. She should throw them away, but one part of her cautioned that she might need them again, and shortly.

"Is the baron Wesley's estate large?" she asked, watching him carefully wrap the riding boots, now in a high state of gloss from his rubbing of champagne and blackening.

"He is reputed to have money and breeds blooded horse stock," he answered, his demeanor indicating that although this was so, the viscount's stable was far superior.

"Is that why we are going there?" she persisted. Buying horseflesh should not give him these black moods.

"Heavens, no, although if one appeals to him, he will no doubt purchase it. His father, the earl, is insisting he find a wife and has set up a program for him to inspect the women from which he deems it acceptable for him to chuse."

Vanessa's mouth opened in surprise. Could his lordship be so coerced? How could he go searching in so coldblooded a way! She then reasoned that it should not be surprising. From her extensive reading she had learned the importance the nobility put on keeping the lines of descent pure. Estates survived more certainly if money married money.

But surely he did not need more? She had just heard of the fantastic fortune he was amassing above what he had inherited.

Yet this could explain his dark moods. Did his father, the earl, have such a strong hold over him, forcing him even though he rebelled? Was there perhaps some other woman he preferred, someone who did not meet the earl's strict requirements?

She shrugged against the tightening in her chest. It was no concern of hers. Marriage, she despaired, was something she would never experience.

The hansom coach drew up, the matched chestnuts eager to move on. Vanessa handed the viscount his soft leather gloves, and he placed his high hat on at a rakish angle, effectively enthralling her. Yes, he was of the first stare of fashion.

"Let's proceed," he said grimly. Then, glancing at her, he saw the mobile face full of admiration over the figure he cut. He could not help giving her a smile at the naïveté of her expression.

She was immediately transfixed. She had not previously been the recipient of his smile or seen the shattering charm usually hidden by his haughty mien.

Quickly averting her gaze, she concentrated on the splendor of the awaiting company. The two footmen and driver as well as the two postillions were dressed in uniforms sporting his colors of yellow and blue. Spying all this, the waiting maid should be properly impressed!

"You will ride with me," Wayne ordered as the footman pulled out the steps.

The cushioned seats covered in the softest of leathers were unbelievably comfortable, and the special springs made the ride dreamlike. She had been exposed only to the bouncing of farm carts, and this luxury was beyond comprehension.

Her eyes brightened with excitement, and Wayne hid his glint of amusement. How like a child the boy could be! he thought. It was almost fun to expose him to new things to see his reaction.

They headed north. There was twenty miles to travel, and while Vanessa's head kept swiveling to take in the sights slipping by, the viscount was soon bored.

"The road is in remarkably good condition," he said. "Hand me the book in the box by your side. I started it on the way but have not finished it."

Nested by her seat was a fitted receptacle, and she removed the slim volume. There were also journals, and when they reached a stretch of woodland, she found her gaze going to them. Dare she read one? Somehow it did not seem the proper thing to do. Yet she longed to glance at one. She had not had much opportunity to explore new reading matter since her mother's death had closed the squire's library to her.

His lordship was deep in his book. Surely if she were quiet, he would not notice. A finger moved surreptitiously, and she exposed the first page. If she left it on the seat beside her, it wouldn't look as if she were reading it.

It was a story about sheep ranching in Scotland. Since she suspected her father came from somewhere near the border, anything pertaining to that country intrigued her. The author had a gift with words, and she was soon deeply immersed.

"I see you can read, but surely you have no interest in something so technical."

She looked up with a gasp. He had finished his book and laid it down. How long had he been watching her?

"He is an exceptional writer," she murmured apologetically. "He makes raising sheep seem like an interesting and profitable pursuit."

His faint smile curled with derision. "I will have to take you to my castle in Scotland when I go for the pheasant shooting. My herdsmen say there has been an excellent crop of droppings this year. You will see all the sheep you wish."

"Do you really own a castle?" she asked wistfully. She had had many childhood dreams in which she lived in one.

He nodded gravely, amused at her obvious enchantment.

"Upon my mother's father's death, as the only male heir, I inherited Ferncliff plus several other pieces of land."

"Then there is Scottish blood in you."

"Yes, though many do not admit to it with the ravings of politics being what they are. There is little love shared between many Englishmen and Scots. Does that annoy you?" His amusement was now apparent.

"It's just that I believe I have some Scottish blood also." She averted her face immediately. What had possessed her to make such a confession? She had never intimated to anyone anything about her possible parentage. Still, she need not be apprehensive. He knew nothing about the stepfather and would not take exception.

He returned to his original question. "Who taught you to read well enough to understand this journal?"

"My mother," she admitted. "When she taught all she knew, she would borrow books from the squire's library." Her expression brightened as she thought of all the happy hours spent with them. "I became insatiable. It was the opening of a whole new world for exploration."

Her smile widened, and he found he was answering it.

"You like the idea of traveling?"

Her hands were again clasped in a childish gesture. "It is my most fervent dream," she admitted with a sigh.

He shifted, lifting several papers from a leather case that Brooks had left for his perusal. "I plan to visit France this fall, if it still remains calm with Boney out of the way. Perhaps you can come along," he said as he bent to the sheets.

Vanessa's heart soared before she rejected the tantalizing possibility. She would be long gone from his employ by then.

He sorted the papers, and she noted that they were itemized accounts. He ran rapidly down the list, adding as he went. The carriage gave a lurch upon hitting a pothole, and he lost his place. He muttered under his breath and started again.

When it repeated, he cursed in disgust, not noticing that one paper slid off his lap and onto the floor. Vanessa picked it up and glanced at it. She paused to admire Brooks's fine hand, then automatically began the addition.

"Well, does it add correctly?" he demanded coldly.

She flushed as she hurriedly replaced it on his lap. "Yes, my lord," she answered apologetically. "I see no mistake."

His gaze pierced her for a long minute before he returned to his work. But she noticed that except for a cursory glance, he did not recheck the list she had added.

Dusk was descending when they rattled through a pair of imposing posts and up a long driveway to stop before a handsome stone manor house. They were plainly expected. The windows were ablaze with light, and a footman hurried down to adjust the steps and open the door.

Vanessa hesitated, not knowing what to do. His lordship's face was grim, and his eyes were cold as he looked at her before stepping out.

"Now I shall see if you are worth your hire. You are to stick to me like a leech. You could even call yourself my chaperon."

He gave a hard, bitter laugh and stepped out, while the unbelievable announcement whirled in Vanessa's head. Bewildered, she followed, handing him his hat. He set it on at a rakish angle, accepted his gloves, and followed the footman up the steps. His hard anger of a minute ago was now replaced by haughty boredom. Only Vanessa suspected his true feelings boiling beneath the calm surface.

CHAPTER SEVEN

The butler bowed the viscount in, and a flunky took his hat and gloves. They followed him to the drawing room.

"Lord Larimor, the Viscount of Kingsley," he announced grandly.

Vanessa took in the tableau as she stepped inside. It was a handsome room, a little too ornate with heavy draperies and gilded furniture, but the people gathered by the intricately carved fireplace held her attention.

Baron Wesley was a short, heavyset man, his florid face indicating a predilection for port. The baroness was also plump with flesh bulging around her tight corseting. The two daughters were standing beside them, also showing an inclination to the weight problem which afflicted their parents. Vanessa could imagine his lordship's reaction to this first inspection.

"Wainwright, my boy, it is good of you to come!" the baron cried heartily, coming forward with his hand outstretched. "And how is my dear friend the earl?"

"When my father heard I was traveling this way, he insisted upon my stopping here and bade me give you his warmest regards," the viscount replied smoothly, giving no indication of his bending of the truth.

A spasm of uncertainty crossed the baron's face. Had they misconstrued the reason for the visit? But of course, Lord Larimor would not declare himself immediately. The baron's jaw firmed. It would be up to the women to conjole him into doing the expected. He had full confidence in them.

"While we have met in London, I don't believe you have been introduced to my dear family." He drew the viscount to the waiting women.

He bowed over the baroness's hand, and she gave a little titter. She was acting coy, but Vanessa saw avarice sharpen her face before his lordship straightened and gave her his attention. She would do her utmost to trap this prize plum, and for the first time Vanessa realized the delicate yet perilous situation the viscount was in.

"And my two daughters, the apples of my eye." The baron smiled facetiously. "The ladies Susan and Marie."

The viscount bowed to each, murmuring their names while the girls curtsied prettily.

There was barely a year's difference between them, and they looked as alike as two peas in a pod. Both were short like their parents, fair-haired, with round blue eyes and smooth country complexions. They were young, the elder barely eighteen, and having lived in the country, they lacked town polish. The expensive gowns they had bought hurriedly in London for this occasion were too sophisticated to be appropriate and made them look like children dressed in their mother's clothing.

Still, they were wholesomely attractive. Vanessa had stepped to one side after entering the room to blend against the wall, and now she glanced at the viscount to see his reaction.

His expression remained unchanged, and its haughty boredom effectively tongue-tied the girls. After an initial glance he turned to the baron.

"I have heard interesting tales about your stables and would enjoy inspecting your stock," he said politely. "I am always alert to the chance to improve my stable."

The baron was off on his favorite and, indeed, only subject of interest. But upon meeting his wife's icy stare, he returned to what they had hoped was the reason for the viscount's visit.

"I am sure his lordship would like to change after the arduous trip," the baroness said, giving her husband a frigid glance before smiling beguilingly at the viscount. "I am certain you are hungry, and supper will be served when you are dressed. But perhaps first a drink?"

His lordship demurred, saying his first need was to effect a change. He offered his humble apologies for being introduced to them in so dusty a condition.

They were so evidently overwhelmed by his present sartorial splendor they could only acquiesce while wondering how he could surpass this elegance. The bell was pulled, and the butler was ordered to show his lordship to his room.

An evening suit had been laid out on his bed. Fortunately Vanessa found herself assigned to unpacking his trunks while Roberts assisted him with the change. She buried herself in the large clothes closet to hang up one magnificent suit after another.

"Vapid! Bovine! Did you see them?" The viscount was exploding, his voice taut with fury. "Change the color of their eyes, and I would swear I was looking at a pair of calves. My father must be approaching senility if he thinks I would even consider either one of them. I can only hope the others are an improvement. They can't be much worse."

Roberts's voice came in a soothing murmur, but the viscount was too incensed to heed it.

"Oh, yes, they appear to be innocent, but I would rather bed with someone who had the experience to give me pleasure than such innocuous creatures. Gad, I'd have to hide them in one of me lesser estates so that I could escape to my bachelor life in London. That is the only way I could tolerate a liaison with either one!"

Again the soothing voice of the valet attempted to mollify him. Roberts had evidently filled this role before.

"The one to be on guard against is that mother," his lordship continued irately, refusing to be placated. "Did you ever see more rapacious eyes? She will stop at nothing to trick me into a declaration. I have seen her type before. She is the one I must outsmart."

"Van!" Roberts called. "A handkerchief for his lordship!"

Vanessa left the wardrobe with a snowy square edged in fine lace, only to become instantly dazzled by the tall figure before her. The viscount's cutaway jacket was of a wine-colored velvet; the skintight breeches were of a pale yellow satin. Roberts was busy tying the neckpiece in an intricate *Osbadestone*.

The deep blue eyes were still stormy, and he glanced at Vanessa for a moment, then gave a hard smile.

"Van, remember what I said before. Get something to eat while we are at supper. I will have no need of you then. But when we return to the drawing room, you are to stay with me even when I am sentenced to walk in the garden. That harridan will inveigle me into it some way."

He gave a bitter laugh upon seeing her astonishment. "In this marriage game one learns to outfox the opposition. How do you think I have remained in this blessed state for so long? I have heard some of the tricks used to ensnare the more luckless of my friends, but I have too much pride to let the final decision be anyone's but my own."

He checked his image in the mirror before turning to Roberts. "I have thought of another way to lay a screen.

I understand Van is to sleep with you. See about having a cot placed in this room for him. Keep it undetected if you can. The wily baroness is apt to attempt something desperate when I inform her that I plan to stay but the se'ennight, instead of the fortnight my father indicated in his letter."

A hard gleam had come to his eyes, and Vanessa realized that he was beginning to enjoy the battle of wits. "I have never seen so comely a chaperon," he continued, glancing at his page. "I am sure the maids below will curse me for keeping you away from them through the night. I begin to wonder who is chaperoning whom!" His smile was devilish, and Vanessa caught her breath as he placed his arm across her shoulder in a quick squeeze.

"I have but one request," he added. "Keep your ears tuned for any trap. You have a strange quality about you, Van. I find myself talking to you more than I intend. Get the maids to do the same."

He paused as Roberts opened the door. In that second he eschewed his sarcastic humor and retreated behind his mask of polite boredom, which was the despair of the ladies in London society.

Vanessa was in a quandary, caught in a trap of her own making. The viscount was right. The kitchen maids were making sheep's eyes at her, the more adventurous making outright proposals.

At first she thought to imitate the viscount's haughty demeanor, then realized that if she hoped to garner any information, she must be friendly.

Help came in the form of the abigail she had rescued. The girl hurried over upon seeing Vanessa and practically kissed her hands in gratitude for making this employment possible and saving her from the streets.

She was in her early twenties and astutely recognized

her benefactor's uneasiness. "Act as though I'm your special girl, and they'll leave you alone," she whispered with a knowing wink.

Vanessa was only too glad for the solution, so placed her arm around the girl's waist as if in affection.

"I don't even know your name," she whispered back, and the two giggled like conspirators.

"Polly. Plain Polly, I'm called."

It was painfully true, but the brown eyes held a merry twinkle, and Vanessa realized regretfully that under other circumstances she could have become good friends with this lively girl.

As a rule, the servants did not eat until the gentry had finished, but Vanessa explained her position to the cook, and he gave her a large wedge of pigeon pie and a mug of sweetened tea. She would be on duty until the viscount went to bed—and later, if his dire predictions held true. So far she had survived with her masquerade, but she was not happy about spending more nights with so spectacular a man. What if he discovered that she was not a boy? The thought sent a shiver through her, causing her heart to pound painfully.

"The servants are excited, wondering when the wedding will be," Polly said conversationally, joining Vanessa at the table. "Which one does his lordship plan to marry? I swear it's hard to tell one from the other."

"They are a bunch of silly peageese," Vanessa said with disgust. "You should not listen to such gossip." Then the idea came to her. Polly would be the logical one to hear what was afoot. The baroness might think her plans would go undetected, but little escaped the servants. Polly would act the spy for her.

Quickly she explained the viscount's request. At first Polly was appalled; then she was soon chuckling over his adroitness at realizing the necessity in planning countermeasures to the wily baroness.

Polly's assistance was quickly pledged. She had been saved by the viscount, and there was no doubt where her loyalty lay.

"It should not be difficult," she said with a laugh. "I never saw a bigger nest of gossips. I shall cosy up to the baroness's abigail, and I'll have the latest before it gets out of her ladyship's mouth!"

Vanessa left the kitchen well content that there would be a quick relay of any conniving. She hurried upstairs to change. Dust still clung to her uniform after the long ride. The honor of the viscount's name had to be upheld. She, too, must appear resplendent.

The women were repairing to the drawing room for coffee when Vanessa returned to the hall. As usual, the men would have their port before joining them. They did not see her, and Vanessa, watching them, noted that the determined set to the mother's face was reflected on her elder daughter's as well. She had been well instructed, and the battle was on.

Vanessa waited by the dining room, catching snatches of the conversation. She marveled at how smoothly the viscount kept the conversation on the subject of horses. The baron went willingly along with him. The fact that his wife had given strict instructions to pump for his intentions was quickly forgotten for the more pleasant topic the viscount wished to pursue.

The men finally entered the hall, a harried expression on the host's face. He could well imagine the baroness's anger for keeping her waiting so unconscionably long.

The viscount gave Vanessa a sly wink, and immediately her pulse jumped. He had deliberately kept the subject on horses, denying the baron the opportunity to question him on his reason for coming. He would be a formidable opponent in any game they wished to play.

The baroness's gaze fastened on her husband, and she gave him a venomous look, then firmed her chin. He was evidently hopeless at this game. She would have to handle matters in her own way. She smiled benignly at her guest.

"Shame, my lord, for depriving us so long of your presence, especially after the delay of your arrival. Was the port so enjoyable?" She looked archly at the viscount. "Poor Susan has been beside herself since the message arrived saying you were detained. The dear, sweet thing was afraid you had come to ill fortune. She was waiting to entertain you with questions about London. We have been toying with the idea of presenting her but wondered if it is best to refrain and keep her sweet innocence intact. One hears such *distracting* tales of the morals of today's society."

Vanessa had inched along the wall so that she could lean against a chair. Standing up the whole evening could be tiring. As she listened to the simpering dialogue, her sympathy went to the viscount, who was being forced to answer such drivel. Black mood indeed. He had full reason for one. How much wiser it would be for the woman to let things develop naturally!

"I agree it is a warm night. I would be most happy to have the lovely Susan show me the garden," the viscount said, rising.

Vanessa pulled herself from her musings. She had missed the turn the conversation had taken and was immediately alert. He had said she must stand guard. How was he going to get her to go along?

"But I insist the just as lovely lady Marie accompany us," he continued. "Nothing would appeal more than having two such charming young ladies show me about."

It was done so smoothly that the baroness was momentarily taken aback.

"Marie is sensitive to the cold. It is best she remain behind," she said quickly. That robust young lady quickly hid her pout.

"Certainly no harm will befall her on a night like this," his lordship protested. "As you have mentioned, it has been exceptionally warm for June. I intend to take my page as well. He can carry their shawls in case they feel a chill."

The baroness had reluctantly to concede that she had been outfoxed, and she kept a fixed smile on her face while sending for shawls for her daughters.

Vanessa paced decorously behind them as they walked the paths of the garden. In the moonlight the two girls seemed like squat dwarfs on either side of the viscount's tall, elegant figure.

He strides like a cat, she thought. At home there had been an arrogant tomcat whose gliding, muscular walk had often intrigued her. He had moved as if king of the hill, and this lithe man had a hint of that same aloof swagger, as if no one should dare defy him.

Marie lagged behind, but Vanessa hurried her steps so that his lordship was never alone with the scheming elder sister. How well the mother had trained them!

They circled the garden. She only half listened to the thin, affected voice as Lady Susan continued her monologue about the trouble in matching the right shade of silk for her embroidery, the expense of French lace for the handkerchiefs she was making for dear, dear Papa, and, with a huge sigh, how she would *desperately* love to live in London.

It proved a trying evening, and his lordship's patience was sorely strained by the time they retired.

"Van, hunt up the butler and see about some wine," he said in exasperation. "Make certain it is the best. I deserve some consolation after putting up with this nonsense."

She hurried to comply as Roberts helped him undress. He was still muttering angry imprecations.

When she returned, he was in a dressing gown sitting in the large easy chair and staring moodily in front of him. Vanessa poured a glass of wine for him.

The window was thrown open to the warm summer breezes. The moon shed a reflective glow on the floorboards, and candles by the bedstand offered a fitful light, creating an atmosphere conducive to quiet talk and introspection.

Vanessa sat on her cot as they talked, her arms around her legs with her chin on her knees. When his glass was empty, she rose to refill it.

"How old are you, Van?" he asked, gazing on her face as she bent to her job. "You look sixteen but speak on many subjects better than many of my peers. If only that insipid creature I'm here to inspect showed half your intellegence, I could swallow my revulsion and consider her."

"That is because I have always enjoyed reading," she answered, deliberately avoiding his question. If she told him she was nearing twenty, he would undoubtedly question her further. At sixteen many boys had not started shaving. Twenty was a different matter.

"Roberts told me of the extensive library you have and how your custodian keeps it up to date. I was going to ask your lordship if I might have the privilege of reading some when we return if I am very careful."

In this relaxed mood it was possible to ask so unheard of a question.

He gave a small smile, "It would please old Damon's

heart to have someone besides myself examine his treasures. They are at your disposal as long as you do not permit reading to interfere with your work."

Even in the uncertain moonlight he could see the delight shining in her eyes. The boy had done something to his uniforms; they fitted much better this evening, outlining the graceful, slender figure. He was a very comely lad, a fine acquisition, whose grace was visible even now in his curled position. Wayne's jaw hardened as he thought of the squire who had frightened the twit into running from his unwanted advances.

"You should be out of your uniform," he said. "I know how these fashionably tight clothes can become deucedly uncomfortable when one wishes to relax."

This was what Vanessa had feared. "Think nothing of it, my lord," she answered quickly. "I shall wait until you retire. You might wish something to be fetched."

"There is nothing," he began. Then realization dawned. "I picked you up with no trunk. Do you have nightclothes?"

"No, my lord," she murmured, unbearably embarrassed.

He waved his hand imperiously towards his wardrobe. "Take one of mine until we can procure one. It will be too large, but I am the only one who will see."

She was thankful for the relative darkness; he could not see her crimson face. She had unpacked the nightshirts and admired their fine, thin cotton. He was wearing a robe over his, but she would be exposed, barely veiled by the fine material. She went to obey, as she must, but when she returned, she left the nightshirt on the cot besides her and adroitly changed the subject.

He spoke about his town house in London and, because he knew she had seen some of his estate figures, touched on some of the enterprises he was involved in. At first he was amused by her interest, but when he heard her intelligent questions, he went into more detail until he realized he was telling this chit of a lad more about his private concerns than he had told anyone except Brooks.

"You are too good a listener, or this wine is more potent than I realized," he exclaimed with exaspiration. "If you repeat anything I have said, I will have your head. Fortunately few will believe you. They believe me the usual fop at St. James's."

"You cannot believe I would do such a thing!" she protested, leaning forward in her earnestness.

To avoid meeting her unusual eyes, he glanced at the clock, noted the time, and rose with a yawn.

It was strange how that husky voice and expressive face clung to the back of his thoughts as he welcomed sleep.

CHAPTER EIGHT

Vanessa awakened at the crack of dawn. The viscount had made arrangements with the baron to inspect his stable in the morning, but he planned first to take Diablo for a prebreakfast ride.

Vanessa sneaked into the adjoining bedroom. She knew it was not used and had planned her deception the day before. She hadn't been able to carry up much water to place in the tub. Now it was a refreshing room temperature, and she sank gratefully into the water.

Polly had spied her preparation and had promised to clean up after her later. Vanessa scrubbed with the delicate French soap, so different from the harsh ones at home. When she poured the rinse water over herself, her gaze traveled over the soft curves of her glistening body. Several times she had rued its slenderness, but now she realized that the small breasts, the narrow hips and waist were her salvation, making it possible to carry off her masquerade.

Quickly she dried, then reached for lavender she had picked from the garden. The scent from the crushed leaves filled the air. She sniffed appreciatively as the warmth of her body enriched the oils.

Her riding suit was also in the viscount's colors, but now the deep blue predominated, the yellow carried out in the braiding. The deeper color accented the magnolia smoothness of her skin and made her green eyes all the more startling.

The viscount had insisted that she ride with him. "If we are to foster the idea that you are indispensable to me, you must always be in attendance," he had said with some humor the night before. "You will find that riding is something I enjoy doing daily. The baron promised a better steed so you will be able to keep pace with Diablo."

Upon hearing Roberts conversing with his master, she finished her toilet and hurried into the next room.

"Where did you sneak off to?" the viscount demanded coldly as she entered. When he had awakened and seen the empty cot, he had experienced a moment of loss. He immediately berated himself over the foolish reaction. Still, he had enjoyed last night's exchange and had entertained a vague desire to continue it before the day's events crowded in.

The faint scent of lavender came to him, and his face softened upon realizing what the lad had done. "It seems, Roberts, that we have a fastidious page," he said drily. "That is one thing you do not have to take him to task about."

Lavender. He didn't know if he liked it better than the wild sage or thyme he had sensed before. They all were clean-smelling, their faintly clinging odors refreshing, a pleasant change from the heavy, cloying scents admired by the women he had pursued.

When they went down to the stable, the groom holding Diablo was properly apprehensive. The horse danced nervously at the end of the lead, his eyes rolling and his large white teeth menacingly exposed.

There was a grey spotted stallion for Vanessa, almost as powerful as Diablo, and the viscount compressed his lips in anger. He had asked for a horse for his page. Were those slender wrists capable of controlling him? Or—and the thought dangled darkly—was there mischief afoot? If the boy met with an accident, it would eliminate the problem of his attendance. Would the baroness sink to such a depth in her pursuit? The thought made him angry, and he turned to the groom curtly to demand a different horse.

Meanwhile, Vanessa had already assessed the animal's power and had at first quailed at the thought of sitting him. But she took the reins and rubbed her hand gently along the fine nose, her crooning voice a soft lullaby which quickly mesmerized the horse.

Silver Ghost was his name, the groom told her. Now that he saw how slight the page was, he, too, wondered why so strong a beast had been ordered. He would see that a cart was ready in case the call came for an injured rider to be brought back.

Vanessa ordered the groom to set his hands, and he helped hoist her into position. The viscount regarded the mounted figure, then gave a faint shrug and turned his horse towards the field.

Both horses let their riders know that they anticipated a run, and when they reached the open field, they were let out on a gallop.

The viscount had at first glanced behind at his page with concern, but the quiet assurance the lad projected soon convinced him there was no need for alarm. Besides, it was a perfect morning for a run, and since Diablo was demanding his full attention, he turned to the job at hand.

Vanessa's heart was pounding. She might look self-assured, but it was a façade she was copying from her master. She had never ridden so powerful a beast. The squire's stableman would never have allowed it. Frantically she struggled to recall the wisdom he had imparted. "Never let an animal know yer to be afraid," he had said in his flat voice. "He then becomes yer master and will take his head. Yer hands, yer knees, yer whole self must be firm and show control."

Vanessa now steeled herself from the trembling which threatened to take over. She had managed Diablo, she assured herself. With luck this Silver Ghost would be no more difficult.

She must control herself before she could the horse, and because she was concentrating deeply, the beast soon responded to her direction.

By the time they reached the field she was enjoying herself thoroughly, and when the viscount urged Diablo into a gallop, she leaned over her mount and did the same.

What incredible fun! The long, eager strides ate up the distance. Then, because her horse was begging for it, she urged him to a fuller speed until they were racing the viscount.

He glanced over his shoulder as the pounding feet came closer. He took in the eager face, flushed with excitement, the lips parted in a smile of pure joy, and the sparkling eyes which laughingly challenged him.

He raised his riding crop in acknowledgment and leaned over his horse. The race was on!

The beasts were fresh and eager, and although Diablo was stronger, Silver Ghost had less weight to carry.

They raced nose to nose, one gaining a yard, then the other. Not until they reached the forest where the path narrowed did they slow down.

"Magnificent!" he exclaimed. "You ride exceptionally well. I will have to see about having you as jockey for one of my entries in the next races!"

They were grinning at each other, their exuberance overflowing from shared happiness. He took in her radiant face, her dazzling green eyes, and a strange tightening again invaded his chest. He breathed deeply against the discomfort, wondering why the exertion had caused this reaction.

They held the horses to a walk to cool them down and, when they reached a stream, dismounted so that the animals could take a drink.

Vanessa pulled some grasses to rub down the lather on the horses. The viscount sat down on a fallen log, and she was uncomfortably aware that he was watching her from hooded eyes. Had he penetrated her disguise? Fear shot through her like a knife stab. Never had life held so much interest; never had she enjoyed talking to someone as she had last night. The possibility of her adventure's ending was almost too much to endure.

"Sit down and relax," he ordered when she tossed away the grasses. "Let us enjoy this moment before going back to the lion's den." The bitter curl returned to his lips, and she hurried to his side, anxious to prevent his black mood from returning.

Something breathlessly unique had quivered between them at the end of the race, and she ached to recapture it. Immediately abashed by the temerity of the thought, she backed away quickly from so silly a desire. This was romanticizing, letting her girlhood dreams resurface!

"I have decided that when we return, I shall inform them of my decision to stay only this se'ennight," he informed her as she struggled to overcome her confused emotions. "I shall then send a message to the next place on the agenda, alerting them that we shall arrive earlier than planned."

His mouth firmed, and a muscle worked along his jaw. "Sir Bartongale lives farther north. After that visit I think I shall visit my estate in Scotland. You will then see the sheep I spoke of. Does that appeal to you?"

His face softened with amusement at seeing her obvious

delight. "Indeed, my lord!" she cried, then added with a hint of mischief, "Do you think the baroness will let you escape so easily?

He gave a short laugh. "I have been in training since before leaving Oxford. My dear innocent, when introduced to society, one soon learns how to escape the traps which are set by conniving mammas. To fail means one hasn't been alert enough!"

"I did not realize it was one of the lessons offered at the university!" she exclaimed mockingly.

He grinned, flicking a pebble at her. "It is an unofficial but popular subject, with freedom the reward for those who pass. The first rule is never to be caught alone with an ambitious young girl. That is why your page duties have been expanded. You must cling to me like a shadow."

He rose, she with him. As before, his arm went across her shoulders, and he gave her a squeeze.

"You have become invaluable to me," he murmured as his hand ruffled her curls. Then, realizing that he had again exposed his inner self to her in an unheard-of way, he turned abruptly to the horses. In an instant he was on Diablo and cantering off, leaving Vanessa immobilized by the confusion of sensations racing through her.

She finally mounted Silver Ghost and pounded after him. Not until she reached the outskirts of the forest did she see him a half field ahead, again racing Diablo. Did he still need to clear his mind for the unpleasantness ahead?

She waited for him after breakfast, when he and the baron were to inspect the horses. Following his orders, she followed them into the stables.

The baron became expansive as he pointed out the fine

points of his stock, enjoying talking with someone so knowledgeable.

"My wife tolerates my pastime," he said finally, "as long as enough blunt remains for a proper dowry for our daughters. I assured her they were handsomely provided for." The little eyes peered slyly at the viscount. No matter how wealthy a man was, surely the chance to acquire more would interest him. "I might even gift the fortunate gentleman with the pick of my prize stock."

The viscount did not look properly impressed with so magnanimous an offer, and the baron showed his irritation.

"I hope you find such a fortunate gentleman," his lordship replied, showing negligible interest. "My desire at present is that mare over there. I might wish to buy it for my page."

The baron looked nonplussed. He had given the viscount every opening to declare himself, only to have the door closed in his face. Was his wife perhaps incorrect in assuming that he was here to chuse a bride? He hesitated over the prospect of informing her of his conclusions. She was determined to have Susan declared for before his lordship left, and he heartily wished the same. From experience he knew life would become unbearable if she failed to get her way.

The horse was large for a mare but prettily marked, creamy white with grey marks on her flanks and a darker grey mane and tail.

"Silver Ghost is her sire," the baron said proudly as the stableboy walked her for inspection. "All his offspring inherit his swiftness and stamina."

The viscount ran an experienced hand over the horse, checking her fine points.

"Will you saddle her, please?" he asked. "I wish to see her gait."

It was quickly done, and he turned to Vanessa. "Ride her so that I can examine her more thoroughly."

The baron was annoyed. He had a groom who did this job well, being adroit in bringing out the good and hiding the weak points. Still, he did not have to be concerned. The page certainly did the horse proud. He was a fine rider, handsome, too.

Vanessa dismounted after the demonstration, and the viscount turned to the short man. "I'll take her. I need an appropriate mount for my page. I could not have him ride so huge a horse as you offered this morning. He was far out of proportion to the rider." The deep blue eyes were steely as he looked down at the baron, causing him to shift uncomfortably under the icy condemnation.

"Your pardon," he muttered in embarrassment. "I was thinking primarily about a horse capable of keeping up with so magnificent a beast as Diablo." Had the viscount guessed what had been plotted under the baroness's prodding? Not that he wished to harm the youth. Only perhaps a sprained ankle to keep him out of the way.

The baroness was waiting for them when they returned and was quick to suggest that the viscount might like to see another section of the estate. "Our Susan is an accomplished rider. She can show you some different paths for your enjoyment," she said with a meaningful titter. "You might like to explore them further in your morning rides. She would have enjoyed riding with you so early in the day, but I firmly believe that it isn't ladylike to go abroad at such an early hour." The simpering increased. "We girls have to think of our appearance."

"My dear baroness," the viscount replied with barely

concealed sarcasm, "added rest could not add to your appearance."

Vanessa smothered her grin. Her ladyship, intent upon her plot, had not caught the underlying implication.

"I know what I shall do," she said brightly as if the idea had just occurred to her. "It is such a lovely day that I shall have a picknick basket made up for you two and have the groom take it to a lovely place we attend by the river."

"You must make it for three," he replied suavely. "I could not bear to separate your two daughters; they are so charming together."

She paused for a second, intent upon inventing an excuse. She would have to instruct Marie to find a way to leave the two alone.

"And perhaps you could include a morsel for my page?" he continued blandly. "I have just bought a horse from the baron for the lad's use, and I know he wishes to test it."

Her eyes hardened. That page was becoming a nuisance! She had heard of the custom of having a page in attendance, but surely the practice was an affectation not needed here in the country. Something had to be done about the youth, and soon.

"Incidentally," the viscount continued, flicking an imaginary particle of dust from his sleeve, "I wish to inform you, my lady, that I shall be leaving this Monday. It occurred to me that my property in Scotland is a mere three-day ride from here, and now that I have enjoyed a taste of the country, I decided it wise to put in an appearance there. The trip is long and exhausting from London, so I have not attended the estate in several years. It behooves me to see how my bailiff is managing it."

The baroness almost swooned from an attack of the vapors. Instead of the month's visit indicated in the earl's letter, she now had but a few days left in which to accomplish her work. Susan would never again have such an opportunity to attract so important a title.

Her mind darted feverishly, devising ways to ensnare the aloof visitor. He could not have reached his present age and remained a bachelor without being aware of the usual snares. She had one plot which would force him to do the expected. He would then have to offer his name, or society would ostracize him.

The baroness smiled grimly at her guest. "You fain take my breath away, my dear Wainwright. We have prepared various entertainments for you. It is too bad this is not the season so the baron can offer hunts for you. Our partridge, I hear, are plentiful this year."

"Perhaps another time," Wayne murmured. "Now, if you will excuse me, I will change from my riding clothes and meet for breakfast."

He moved to the stairs. Only Vanessa saw the look of frustration on the baroness's face.

After a leisurely meal the men retired to the library. The baron was anxious to show the pedigree of some of his cattle.

Vanessa repaired to the kitchen where the preparation for the picknick was in progress. She watched with amazement as a cart was loaded with a table and chairs. Hampers were filled with roast chicken and veal tarts, apple pie and frosted cake, fruit and cheeses. Chilled bottles of wine for the viscount and lemonade for the daughters were nestled in straw to keep them cool. Scalding coffee was poured into another container and carefully wrapped in flannel to keep hot for his lordship's pleasure. All was set on a bed of straw, and layers of the material were placed over the hampers in an effort to keep the contents at the proper temperatures.

The butler then placed in the cart a box containing a fine linen tablecloth and china, as well as silver and crystal goblets, and the groom drove off with a footman who would wait on the party.

Vanessa had to smile with amusement at the preparations. In contrast, the picknicks enjoyed in her village consisted of loaves of bread and cheese carried in squares of cloth and a jug of wine kept cool in a stream.

The horses were brought to the front door after the first heat of the sun had begun to subside, and the four started off.

The viscount gallantly rode between the sisters, with Vanessa a proper distance behind. When the path narrowed, the younger girl dropped back as if on signal.

Vanessa didn't know whether to be amused or annoyed. The sister had begun an outrageous flirtation with her as if to keep her attention from the other two. She kept slowing her horse, obliging Vanessa to do the same.

When the path widened, Vanessa urged her mount forward, forcing the girl to hurry to catch up with them. Her mouth formed a pout, and Vanessa could well imagine the instructions she had received from her mother and the displeasure she was certain to incur when her parent found out that the obvious ploy had not worked.

Even though the viscount's countenance did not change from its detached boredom, Vanessa knew he was alert to the trickery the sisters were attempting.

By the time they reached the picknick area both girls were hard pressed to hide their sullen expressions. It had seemed so easy when rehearsed by their mother on how to give Susan the opportunity to be alone with the viscount.

"You did very well," the viscount told Vanessa when

they were again alone in his room that night.

"At first it was amusing," Vanessa admitted. "Then I almost felt sorry for them. To think they imagined they could outwit you! It was most pitiful."

She filled his goblet with wine and returned to her cot to sit with her arms around her legs.

"Pity is one emotion I do not possess," he said, then smiled cynically. "I was thinking what the bovine Marie would do if you had followed through with her flirtation."

Vanessa shifted uncomfortably. "Girls do not interest me," she murmured.

He gave a knowing laugh. "You must be a late bloomer, for which I should be thankful. Your time will come, Van. Let me warn you that nothing compares to the sensation of a soft, giving woman in one's arms!"

She bent her head so that all he saw were the silken curls on top of her head. Her face was flushed as she struggled to answer.

"Roberts has said you are much sought after in London," she commented. "You have been feted by the *haut ton,* yet you must search for a wife. Surely you must have found someone you could love?"

It was a daring question from a page, but their moonlight conversations were becoming more and more intimate. The viscount was indeed a different person at this time. His mask of indifference was shed, and she discovered an enthusiastic and intelligent, even witty man with a searching mind. She was certain few people were privileged with so intimate a disclosure.

He was silent for so long that she finally glanced at him, to see him gazing with a deep frown into his wine goblet.

"Love?" he said at last. "What does love mean to you, Van?"

Her eyes grew dreamy. "It is the beginning and the end.

A sharing between two people who cannot bear to be apart. It is an ultimate happiness."

His eyes were hard on her in surprise. "How can a young chit of a lad, one who admits to not having been with a woman, come to that discovery?"

She retreated in confusion. His question had caught her off guard, and she had spoken from her heart.

"I-I do not know," she confessed. "It is but a feeling I have."

He again stared into the goblet as he twirled it with long fingers. "Still, you speak of something I once felt. I've searched until I have decided it is only romantic nonsense. When my father said I must start thinking of begetting an heir, I did not argue.

"Yet I keep searching," he said, as if to himself. "Whenever I leave a woman's bed, I find myself asking: Was there any of the special magic I expected? The answer is always that she was delectable and I might return for more. But I do not deceive myself; women can fulfill only a physical need."

He sat up straight, squaring his broad shoulders with a shrug. "You have done it again, Van," he said with a mocking laugh. "You encourage too much introspection. I do not know if I care for it!"

He glanced with annoyed amusement at this extraordinary page and immediately became sober.

The face was a pale blur, but those eyes, those haunting green eyes, were wide as they gazed at him. They seemed to shimmer with their own light as they looked at him, into him, through him, causing him to be transfixed by their luminosity.

"Do not stop looking," she said in a soft voice which seemed to come from a great distance. "You will find her, and she will be all you are searching for."

What kind of moonlight madness was this? He felt the hair on his arms prickle, and he recalled the page's supernatural soothing of the swollen limbs. Was this another of the youth's sorceries?

Vanessa's eyelids felt heavy and drooped. An indescribable weariness crept through her, similar to that she felt when she did her healing. What had possessed her to speak such outlandish words? They had come out unbidden, as if spoken by someone else.

"I only hope you are right," the viscount said, rising abruptly. "But it had better happen quickly because I have less than six months until I reach the deadline imposed by the earl."

There seemed nothing further to say, and they prepared for bed, Vanessa waiting, as usual, for him to snuff out the bedside candles before undressing and donning the borrowed nightdress. She was conscious of a strange sensation after the gown was on. It was as if she were enclosed in a protective wrapping. Peagoose, she berated herself. But the comfort remained as she settled into sleep.

CHAPTER NINE

"We have but one more day," the viscount said with a protracted sigh of relief. "I intend to leave early the day after tomorrow."

They had just returned from their morning canter, and he moved reluctantly to the house after the groom had taken their horses.

Vanessa could understand his attitude. The days had developed into a depressing routine. The baroness would alternate between unbecoming coyness and grim relentlessness. Lady Susan always appeared in close proximity at every move he made. His only escape was the stables or his room.

"And there is a limit to how much I wish to ride," he admitted sourly.

After changing from his riding clothes, he went to have breakfast. The meals, at least, were acceptable.

When he finished eating, the butler presented him with a packet of mail. "Perhaps you would like to peruse your letters in the privacy of the library," the baron said.

The viscount accepted the offer gratefully and retired to that room. Vanessa posted herself as a guard outside the door to insure that he was not disturbed. She had recognized Mr. Brooks's fine script and knew his lordship would resent an interruption while he investigated his mail.

She was idly examining a large painting in the hall

depicting a pastoral scene when the baroness came from the salon.

Vanessa became instantly alert. The insolent stare the baroness gave her was full of malevolence. She paused before her, and Vanessa gave a restrained bow, already tense, knowing the baroness would not have stopped unless she wanted to pour her frustration upon her.

"Still guarding his lordship?" she asked sneeringly. "Tell me, has the viscount always had a predilection for young boys? I understand he found you on his way here."

At first Vanessa did not catch the innuendo. But her life had not been sheltered, and reading had exposed her to matters not usually considered proper for young ladies.

Her face flamed, and the baroness glared at her with satisfaction. "He will no doubt toss you aside in time," she said. "I am surprised, though. We heard that he preferred the beds of the more enticing women frequenting St. James's." Her eyes narrowed in cold disgust, and she swept away.

Vanessa could barely stand, numbed by the horror of the woman's implications. Is that what they thought about his lordship? She felt ill but remained at her post while the words reechoed through her mind.

Should she alert the viscount about the baroness's vicious words? She drew in a long, shuddering sigh. She could imagine the extent of his fury. It would be best not to. They would be departing shortly in any case.

Her decision was made. She would leave him. Her masquerade must end. She could not be the reason for a black mark placed on his name.

A desolation invaded her. In spite of the hovering threat of discovery, she had enjoyed her employment. His lordship had been a kind master, and therefore, she must leave to protect him.

With that resolution firm she managed to get through the rest of the day. However, upon retiring that night, the viscount took matters into his own hands.

"You seem perturbed," he observed quietly.

Vanessa did not reply. Instead, she concentrated on turning back his bedsheets. She was heartsick over what had transpired that afternoon and still struggled with the urge to warn him. If she did, he would rightly terminate her employment, and she did not wish their separation to come in anger.

"Come here, Van." His order was firm.

She came to stand before him, her face averted.

"We have become exceptionally close through this," he said gently, observing her distress. "Something untoward happened this afternoon, didn't it? I sensed your withdrawal after I was finished with my mail in the library."

Vanessa wrung her hands.

"Where is my page, whom I rely upon to get me out of a black humor?" he chided. A long finger lifted her chin, and his deep blue eyes searched her green ones.

She quivered under his touch, the sensation causing her to blurt out in agony, "You must discharge me, my lord! It is best I leave when you go to your next visit."

He looked at her in astonishment. His hand was heavy on her shoulder, and he pushed her down on the stool at his feet.

"What nonsense is this?" he asked sternly.

"I'm afraid you did not realize the picture we made with you keeping me in close attendance." She gazed beseechingly at him.

"Explain your remark," he said coolly, his face hardening, as if he had sensed what was coming.

"Wh-when you were in the library this afternoon, I posted myself by the door." She began hesitatingly, then rushed, agonizing, into the story. "Her ladyship came into the hall and saw me there." With bent head she continued her tale.

The viscount heard her out, his face frozen in fury.

"So you see, my lord, I must leave before she darkens your name beyond repair!" Vanessa cried.

"Don't be a fool," he said coldly. "My friends would laugh at such an idea. The rest do not matter."

He was striding the length of the room as Vanessa sat unconvinced on the footstool. She knew how gossip spread, magnified with each telling.

She had been shunned by the village women simply because she looked as if she might lure their men. She was certain gossip had embroidered it into more.

He stopped beside her and saw her misery. His face softened as he laid a hand on her shoulder.

"You are not to worry," he said with forced assurance. "In spite of the baroness's crass assertions, I intend to continue as before. At least until we are quit from this abominable place!"

Wayne sat down and examined his page. The roles were now changed. He was the one who must pull this sensitive youth out of his depression. He could not let the poor lad remain in so unhappy a state. He was well aware of the gentle persuasion of the boy when his own humor was strained. There was something pathetic about the unhappy face, the despondent droop to the shoulders that brought forth a strong protective instinct.

"Look, Van," he began earnestly. "We can live through this farce one more day. I hope we will not have to continue this way at Sir Bartongale's. You'll be sleeping with the servants, and there will be no need to concern ourselves further with her words."

Vanessa's heart plunged. All she heard was the fateful

words telling where she was to sleep. Servants seldom rated a private room. This would then be the end. Her masquerade would be uncovered the first night.

"I-I think it best if I leave," she repeated doggedly.

He took in the stubborn thrust to the jaw, and a strange coldness clamped over his chest.

He stared angrily at her. "Is this all the thanks I get for giving you employment when you were in need?" he said bitingly.

She hunched within herself but stubbornly persisted.

He stood up abruptly to loom tall over her. "I want your promise that you will not leave until I give permission, do you hear?" he shouted, then stopped short, aghast. Why was he yelling?

"I'm waiting, Van," he said in a quieter voice. "I demand a promise."

"I-I promise," she agreed reluctantly. Something in her warmed at the reprieve.

His hand was on her head, and he ruffled her hair. "Remember, I'm holding you to it. Now go to bed. It's late," he said gruffly as he withdrew his hand.

Such silky hair! he mused, then quickly rubbed his hands as if to banish the memory.

The kitchen maids eyed Vanessa speculatively the next morning, moving away when Polly sat down beside her.

"What did you do to warn them off?" Vanessa asked, spooning out her porridge. The usual flirtatious glances were absent.

Polly's face reddened. Then she tossed her head and looked at Vanessa defiantly. "The news is that his lordship has a special interest in you, and that's why you are always with him."

Vanessa fought a sick feeling. The baroness's assertions must have been overheard.

"That's nonsense!" she said sharply. "You know the reason. It was to protect him from that woman's schemes. I explained it all to you!"

"Don't bite at me," Polly returned. "I'm repeating what was overheard in the baroness's bedroom last night. There was an argument between the baron and his lady. They were not careful of their voices. It ended when he shouted that she would be lucky to capture a prospective earl and a wealthy one at that. She subsided then and put her mind back to how to get him to declare himself since he was leaving tomorrow."

"Did you hear anything else?" Vanessa asked, closing her mind firmly against the insinuations. If the baroness made one last effort, she would do it today. She had best forewarn the viscount.

"No, but if there is anything afoot, I'll let you know. I'm bosom pals with her abigail." She gave a sly wink and bent to her porridge.

Vanessa's appetite had disappeared. She could imagine how the servants relished the latest gossip, embroidering upon it in the retelling. It was as if everyone were leering at her, even the men. It was an impossible situation, and if she hadn't given her promise to his lordship, she would be making plans to disappear when night came.

They had both woken up late in the morning, having overslept after talking late the night before. Vanessa had been acutely aware of the viscount's turnings in bed. Before, she had always succumbed quickly and had assumed he did the same.

The viscount had shrugged at her apologies over the late rising. "We'll have our ride after breakfast. Since the ladies sleep the morning away, it will make no difference to them," he had said.

When dressing the viscount, Roberts ordered her to get the boots he had polished. His command was cool, and she wondered despondently if he thought there a grain of truth to the rumors which he also must have heard. Surely he knew the reason for the cot in the room! More likely he was resentful about the slur to his master's name. It was an unhappy situation which she hoped would end when they departed from this horrid house.

How little she had foreseen the tangle she could create in other lives when she had started her deceit! The viscount was too outstanding a man, too kind and decent, to have any doubt cast upon his reputation.

He had given her employment, had clothed and fed her, and, most of all, had given her the rare and thrilling chance to share his innermost thoughts.

How he would hate her when her masquerade was uncovered! The feeling of approaching doom was strong. She should depart, but her promise to him was an effective block. Perhaps when it was all over, he would at least remember that she had kept her promise. It was a small consolation.

Surprisingly there was no attempt to trick the viscount into being alone with Susan that day. The baroness had evidently admitted defeat, their countermeasures having proved effective.

"I do not understand her ladyship's not making one last try," Vanessa confessed as they sat in the bedroom that night. "She has hitherto been so determined. Perhaps she does not wish her daughter to associate with you now after her assertions."

"If that is so, I shall be happy to have my name greyed for the duration," he said with a cynical smile. "But like you, Van, I have been doubly alert and somewhat surprised that they have not offered further trickery."

Vanessa went to the kitchen to fetch the decanter of wine the butler now left out for the viscount's use.

"Van!" The call came in a muted whisper.

It was Polly. Roberts had given her the job of laundering and ironing the viscount's clothes, and since they were leaving shortly after breakfast, she was hard at work.

"I was hoping to catch you," she said, wiping her soapy hands on a cloth. "I have something to tell you, although I know not what it means."

Vanessa looked at her questioningly. The kitchen was empty this late in the evening, except for a young girl scrubbing the floor. Polly led her into the laundry where she was working alone.

"Everyone has long flapping ears," she said in disgust. "I never heard such gossiping as goes on here. I overheard a footman discussing it with one of the flunkies."

"Discussing what?" Vanessa asked with some impatience. She did not like leaving the viscount alone for so long.

"He was wondering why her ladyship had ordered him to stand watch outside Roberts's room tonight after he finished with the viscount." Her gaze was questioning. "What has Roberts done that he needs guarding?"

Vanessa looked bewildered. "I haven't the faintest idea. What else did he say? Was he to use force if Roberts left the room?"

"No. He was just to run and tell her if anyone left the room."

"Anyone? Don't tell me our proper Roberts is sneaking in one of the maids!"

Polly averted her flushed face. "I can't believe it. I would have heard if he was making eyes at anyone. Besides, she wanted to know when anyone left, not who went into the room."

Vanessa admitted it made no sense to her either and shrugged her shoulders before reaching for the wine decanter. "You must have misheard, Polly," she said. "After all, I was assigned to share Roberts's room. Perhaps she is suspicious that I have a rendezvous with one of the maids. She would like to discredit me. Roberts fetched my cot from the attic, and maybe she isn't aware that I sleep in the viscount's room."

"I wouldn't know," Polly admitted, and Vanessa returned to the viscount with the wine.

"Now what gives you concern?" Wayne demanded. His gaze was sharp on her thoughtful face as she poured the wine.

"I-I don't know," Vanessa admitted. "Could the baroness strike at you through Roberts?"

His eyes became instantly wary, as they tended to do whenever the baroness's name was mentioned. "Her devious mind could contrive anything," he said sourly. "Why are you asking?"

Vanessa repeated her conversation with Polly. "She was certain the footman stressed that she be notified only if someone left the room and not if someone entered it."

He frowned in concentration. "I confess I have not the vaguest notion what is behind it all," he admitted finally.

They talked on other subjects, but Vanessa could see that the problem still nagged him. He did not like unsolved riddles, and they had learned not to trust the baroness's actions.

Was this part of her last attempt to get the viscount to declare himself? Vanessa could not see a connection, but she vowed to sleep lightly that night.

* * *

They had left the casement window open to the warm June night, and a cooling breeze blew in. Vanessa pulled at the sheet to cover her shoulder and became instantly alert.

She had not meant to fall asleep, but now a warning ran through her. She opened one eye cautiously to see a faint flickering light. The bedroom door was opening slowly, and the taper in the hall sconce cast a dim glow on the carpet.

Vanessa sat up quickly. From the far side of the room she could not be seen on her low cot, hiding in the shadow at the foot of the big bed. She watched in fascination as the crack widened and the figure of a woman appeared, outlined in the doorway.

Lady Susan! The back light showed the short, pudgy figure through the thinness of her peignoir. The girl hesitated, apparently adjusting to the poor light in the room. Her face was turned to the master bed, and she took a careful step forward.

Vanessa was instantly on her feet. For one panicky moment she realized that she, too, was in a thin nightdress. She grabbed the viscount's robe, which was draped over the chair, and pushed her arms through the sleeves.

"Is there something I can do for your ladyship?" she asked, blocking her path.

Lady Susan gave a frightened squeal, her round blue eyes bulging.

"You!" she cried in disbelief. "But the footman swore you were still upstairs!"

"I assure you, I am here," Vanessa returned, her voice surprisingly cool, considering the circumstances.

"Y-you are in his bathrobe!" Her voice went up an octave in horror. "Mamma, Mamma!" she wailed. There had been no instructions to cover this.

The square figure of the baroness loomed behind her daughter. Vanessa saw with surprise that she was still dressed in the clothes she had worn that evening.

"So!" she cried in righteous indignation. "It is as I expected! You are sleeping with the viscount. Oh, to think that my pure daughter has been exposed to such despicable morals!"

Her arm went about the quaking shoulders of the now completely bewildered girl, and the baroness led her loudly sobbing daughter away. The broad back was stiff with virtuous wrath.

Vanessa closed the door and leaned against it, needing its support. A sound came from the bed. Of course, the viscount would have awakened with so loud an exchange! The sound increased, and she realized that he was laughing.

"Van!" he cried, wiping his eyes. "You were priceless! I never expected to see such an avenging angel draped in my robe! Come here, lad, and light the candle."

She forced her truant legs to obey and lit the candle by his bedside.

"Sit down, sit down," he said impatiently as he shifted in the bed to make room, patting the space next to him. "How did you know she was there? I thought myself a light sleeper, but she opened the door so silently I'm certain she would have been in my bed before I awakened."

Vanessa shivered and pulled the robe closer. Dare she sit so close to him? The thought increased her tremors.

"Are you cold?" he asked sharply. "Keep the robe on, but tell me your tale."

She moved to the foot of the bed and sat gingerly at the edge.

"It was the breeze, my lord," she explained. "When she

opened the door, a draught came from the open window, and I felt a chill. Then I saw the light from the doorway."

It had been a near catastrophe. To have been discovered with Lady Susan in his bed would have put his lordship in an intolerable situation. He would have had to marry her or face ostracism by society. It was acceptable to have discreet liaisons with married women or have a charmer for a night's pleasure, but society frowned heavily upon compromising a virgin, especially a daughter in her own house, and he a guest!

"My father almost had his problem solved, and I would have been shackled to that cow for the rest of my life!" he said bitterly. "My debt of gratitude to you is increasing, Van."

The viscount gazed at the slender boy wrapped in his large bathrobe. The youth looked ridiculously vulnerable, yet time and again he had proved his resourcefulness, his quick mind. Tonight could have ended in a tragedy. The viscount could not have accepted the sentence of marriage to Susan, who now completely repulsed him. He would almost have preferred escaping to Europe to become one of the wandering nobility, a man without a country, hoping the scandal would abate in time.

"Now we know why Roberts's room was being watched," Wayne said thoughtfully. "This is not a large manor house, and if you remember, you were billeted with him until I decided, luckily as it turns out, to have you sleep here. Somehow the baroness's spy system missed up on that piece of information, and her twisted imagination had you sneaking down for a rendezvous with me. She wanted to make certain I was alone so that her scheme could work."

Vanessa's cheeks flushed as the full import of his words struck her. She gazed across the room, her green eyes clouded with consternation. What a despicable trick the baroness had attempted! Was she herself in some way to blame?

A breeze found its way through the open casement, causing Vanessa's curls to flutter against her cheek. She brushed at them with an absentminded flip of her hand. The action released the outside robe she had clutched to her, and the front fell open.

The viscount's eyes widened. An expression of disbelief crossed his face as he observed the soft swelling of breasts outlined by the thin nightshirt.

He muffled an oath while staring incredulously at his page. What devilment was going on here? Certainly the half-light was playing tricks on him! This was not a youth!

Anger blazed through him in an explosive heat. How dare any cheap bit of muslin think she could flummox him with such atrocious behavior! Cutting words of denunciation rose to his lips.

He hesitated, struck by the innocent picture she made huddled on his bed, and the words died in his throat, unsaid. Wrapped in his large robe, she looked like a child playing in her elder's clothes.

Pictures flashed in the viscount's mind—of green eyes bright with laughter; of a sensitive face bent eagerly towards him while in discussion; of silky hair soft to the touch. They were quickly smothered as his irritation rose.

Great bodkin! How could this have befallen him? How stupid he had been not to have recognized the obvious. Had he become so addlepated as not to recogize a doxie when one was sleeping in his very room? He'd be the laughingstock of the *ton* if they ever found this out!

The thought gave him pause. What an embarrassment! What was this Van whatever-her-name's reason for the masquerade? What trick did she have up her sleeve? If he dismissed her now, would she demand recompense or threaten to expose her fraud?

Blackmail! The notion repulsed him. This problem must be given careful thought. The situation could become damned uncomfortable.

How could he not have noticed the disguise before? His whole attention had been concentrated on this distasteful mission his father had fostered on him. No wonder he had been so gullible and not seen what was now so evident.

The viscount leaned back against his pillow, his eyes narrowing as he examined the girl. His first heat of anger was over, and he must consider his next move.

He had resigned himself to six months of boredom while searching for a bride. Yet ever since he had hired this green-eyed wench, his spirit had lightened. Her wit had been enjoyable, and she had been adroit in easing him out of his fits of depression. A faint sneer tightened his mouth. Now that he had uncovered her masquerade, he would be doubly entertained.

He was not one to enjoy being made the fool, as this chit almost certainly had succeeded in doing. His anger had not completely abated and was now joined by the desire to inflict punishment. No, he would not unmask her now. He would contrive more subtle ways to obtain his revenge.

The assessment of her incredible deed had taken but seconds. The viscount forced his tense body to relax while he coolly examined the girl. She was still staring abstractedly across the room, unaware that he had pierced her disguise. All the better!

"I daresay you will find it difficult to court sleep after this adventure," Wayne said in a soft voice which only partially hid his malice. "Do share my bed. It is delightfully comfortable and more conducive to sleep than your hard pallet. We need the rest. The trip tomorrow will be long and tiring."

Vanessa's eyes widened in alarm as she scrambled from his bed. "N-no, my lord!" she cried, feeling a crimson tide rush to her face. "I am perfectly content on my cot. I-I might be restless getting back to sleep and would not wish to disturb you."

"I'm certain I would not be conscious of your tossing in so large a bed," he continued, enjoying his teasing. "Certainly a night spent on this soft feather mattress is more appealing than one on your thin straw pallet."

"I-I am comfortable, my lord," Vanessa stammered, quaking at the thought of sleeping with him. She quickly slid under her blanket. "I-it would never do for a page to sleep with his master."

The viscount gave a mocking laugh. "Perhaps you are right," he admitted. "I am certain we will not be disturbed again, but we must guard our reputation. The Wesleys would far more easily accept finding a girl in my bed than a youth."

The words held no amusement for Vanessa. She was bewildered by the taunting evident in his mocking laugh. Was he blaming her for this latest affront by the baroness?

It was a long time before the trembling left her, and she could recapture the sleep interrupted by the warning breeze across an exposed shoulder.

CHAPTER TEN

"Gad, how I wish I had my phaeton!" the viscount said with irritation, brushing at the dust settling on his sleeve. "At least I would be out in the air and not in this beastly shell. I had no idea it could be so hot in a coach even with the windows removed."

They had been several hours on the road, and the sun was beating down with unseasonable heat. The fields were dry, and dust rose in engulfing clouds.

Their departure had been inauspicious for so titled a guest. The baron had appeared at breakfast, his embarrassment so acute that it was evident he had not had prior knowledge of his wife's infamous exhibition the night before.

The viscount's air of haughty disdain had increased tenfold, and the baron was thankful that the conversation remained on the relatively innocuous subject of the prospective weather.

The baron was most humble when he bid the viscount and his entourage good-bye. He knew that his family would be persona non grata at the earl's residence should the viscount choose to make his report. He admitted sadly he would miss the old friendship. Damned scheming women!

Neither the baroness nor her daughters made an appearance before the viscount's departure. Vanessa could well imagine their embarrassment, as well as the mother's fury, which kept them to their rooms.

The horses were now turning north on the post road. It was a two-day ride to Sir Bartongale's estate, the next stop on the viscount's agenda. They lived close to the Scottish border, he told Vanessa.

The viscount had slept poorly the remainder of the night before. The baroness's fiasco had been dismissed for the pitiful scheme it was. But he could not dismiss from his mind the implications of his discovery about his page.

He had found himself vacillating between an angry resolution to dismiss the chit immediately and a desire to keep her near until he could devise a suitable revenge for the affront to his sensibilities. He was not one to suffer gladly such villainy directed against him. His pride was sorely pricked.

They were driving through a small copse of trees beside a brook when the viscount knocked on the front of the carriage. The horses were immediately brought to a halt, and a footman leaped down to look questioningly through the open window.

"It is time to rest the horses," the viscount said, still vexed. "Bring the basket Roberts packed. I only hope the wine is palatable after this jouncing."

The footman carried the wicker basket, and Vanessa spread a blanket on the ground by the brook. The water was low, but it offered a cool spot to pause while eating.

By the time the viscount returned from stretching his legs their repast was ready. The wine was still chilled, and he emptied his goblet in several long draughts.

"Do you think it likely you will encounter the same trickery again, my lord?" Vanessa asked, offering him a meat tart. She gazed at him timidly. His attitude towards her today was cold, and his commands were abrupt.

The viscount gave a deep sigh. "Let us hope not, Van," he said grimly. "It is enough to try a man's soul. I'm sick of this whole operation, and if Sir Bartongale's daughter is the least presentable, I'll end this farce at once by offering for her."

He chewed reflectively. "In spite of your prediction the other night, I don't think there is a woman made in the mold I seek. If there is, she is no doubt married by now. So perfect a creature would not have escaped male eyes."

"Most men desire a docile, uncomplaining wife," Vanessa murmured, "one who will give them an heir and perform her obligations. Few men would want one with the intelligence you seek. It would be disconcerting to them."

"True," he said, offering his goblet for more wine. "I will then have to keep you by my side. I find our verbal duels each evening most stimulating." His eyes mocked her as he reached for an apple. "I can envision my wife waiting patiently for me while I first spend an hour or two with my page!"

His laugh held derision as he bit into the fruit. His glance went to the chit repacking the basket.

Vanessa looked up, laughter dancing on her face at his words. She was unable to move as their eyes met and held. A roaring filled her ears as her heart beat unevenly under her breast.

The viscount rose abruptly and threw away the barely tasted apple. He strode swiftly to the waiting carriage, a frown dark on his brow. The footman came for the basket, and Vanessa followed, her trembling legs barely holding her erect, dazed as she was from the effect of that silent locking of their eyes.

By the time they reached the posting inn it was late in the afternoon. "I wish a bath to rid myself of this confounded dust before I even think of food," the viscount told Roberts, and Vanessa hurried into the kitchen to relay the order while Roberts led his master to his room.

Polly was there checking the laundry facilities she would make use of later for the viscount's clothes.

"I heard there was a big to-do last night," she said eagerly. "I had so much to do before we left I did not hear the full story. What happened, Van?"

"I'll tell you later over supper," she whispered back, wondering how much of an edited story she would give. She did not like gossip, but Polly's warning had alerted her and his lordship might have need of her once more.

Again she thought sadly how Polly might have become a friend under different circumstances. There was an easy companionship between them. She had not tried to flirt like the other maids, intent upon attracting the handsome page's attention.

Vanessa would have been surprised upon learning the extent of Polly's devotion. She regarded her benefactor with respect, ever aware that she would have been left abandoned except for the page's intervention.

Eager to make a good impression, the landlord hurried a half-witted boy with the hot water. He was not on the direct road from London and usually missed such trade.

Vanessa tarried, and the viscount was dressed by the time she returned upstairs. He went to the parlor while Roberts left with the clothes with directions for Polly to clean them.

The viscount said he would relax with a glass of wine, intending to give Vanessa time to change before coming to serve him. He was fastidious about his meals and saw that the dust on her clothes was as bad as his had been.

Vanessa hurriedly opened her small trunk to remove a clean outfit, then looked longingly at the bathtub still in

123

front of the fireplace. There was still a half pail of rinse water. Did she dare?

She stripped hurriedly and stepped into the tub. She soaped herself, then let the water cascade over her slender body. It was worth the risk to feel clean again.

She leaned over to reach for a towel when a loud gasp came from the doorway. She looked up in horror to meet Polly's astonished gaze.

They stared at each other for what seemed an eon, both white-faced and unable to move. Polly pulled herself together, quickly stepped inside, and closed the door.

"Van?" she questioned uncertainly. "What is this all about?"

Vanessa recovered from her shock and pulled the towel around her naked body. Her secret was out! But then, hadn't she expected it would happen soon?

"Roberts sent me for the stockings he forgot," Polly continued, her expression a mixture of surprised confusion and suspicion. "You are Van, aren't you?"

The only solution was to disclose the whole story. Vanessa's fingers trembled as she began dressing, using the action to hide her agitation.

"The viscount must be enjoying your masquerade," Polly said when the tale was finished.

"But he doesn't know!" Vanessa hurriedly exclaimed, appalled that Polly should imagine such a thing.

"But you've spent every night in his room," Polly said slyly.

"It is not as you assume!" Vanessa protested, her cheeks flaming. "Roberts took care of him. I was used as a guard and slept on a cot." Quickly she explained how the practice had paid off the night before. "The baroness's scheme would have succeeded if I hadn't been there."

Polly was so intrigued by the tale that she forgot her

first shattering surprise. "This is the best story I have ever heard, Van!" she laughed. "But I shall not call you Vanessa because I might do it by mistake at the wrong time."

"Y-you mean you will not disclose all?" Vanessa asked. She had been wondering if she should dress in her half brother's clothes now and make her escape before the viscount became alerted to her deception.

"Of course not!" Polly cried. "This is too thrilling an adventure." She straightened the jacket over Vanessa's shoulders. "We had better return to our duties," she said with an impish grin, then turned sober. "And remember, Van, if ever you get found out, I'll help you escape!"

The two shook hands, their pact made.

Vanessa was still trembling from residual shock when she entered the private dining room. The viscount glared at her with annoyance. The food was on the table before him, and he had started to eat.

"You are as bad as a woman," he said sourly. "A simple change of uniform should not have taken so long."

"I am sorry, my lord," she murmured as she hurried to pass a platter. "The dust was difficult to wash off."

"And you had to hunt for some herb," he said mockingly. "Which one did you use this time?"

He leaned towards her, and Vanessa looked at him in surprise. She hadn't known he was aware of what she rubbed on her skin.

His movement brought him close to her, and they stared at each other, inches apart. He looked into her dilated eyes, the green clear as a woodland pool. A man could drown in those eyes, he thought, and pulled back, confounded by the notion.

"There is still the scent of lavender in your hair," he said in a strained voice. "I take it you did not have time to snatch something else from the garden."

Vanessa's heart beat painfully against her ribs as she carefully moved a platter closer for his inspection. When she dared look at him again, he was scowling darkly at his dish, as if not liking what he saw.

Vanessa saw that a pallet had been placed at the foot of his bed for when they retired. She did not know if Roberts had placed it there automatically or if the viscount had ordered it. She was thankful only that she wasn't forced to sleep with the men doubling in the servants' quarters. That would have ended her disguise immediately.

Tomorrow night they would be at Sir Bartongale's home. She had an uneasy sensation that the adventure would then reach its climax and her days as page to the viscount would be over.

The thought sat heavily on her. In spite of the constant apprehension over being uncovered, she had enjoyed being with his lordship.

The viscount relaxed in the chair before the small fire lit to remove any lingering dampness. Vanessa folded down the bedclothes and tested the mattress for freshness.

"It has been well aired," she commented. "Do you wish me to place a warm brick at your feet?"

He looked up from the London paper the innkeeper had supplied. It was two days old, but the news was new to him.

"No, it is not necessary. The night is warm enough." He examined her over the paper. It would take a long time before a man would tire of watching such graceful movements, he thought.

His face hardened. Instead of woolgathering, it would behoove him to attempt to uncover what new trick she might be contemplating.

"Here's an article on sheep you will be interested in," he said. "Come and read the caption."

Vanessa came eagerly, happy to hear the renewed warmth in his voice. She had been sorely distressed by his cool attitude towards her.

He shifted in the chair, indicating that she should sit on the low armrest. Vanessa stilled her surprise and gingerly took the offered position.

The viscount placed his arm around her waist before holding the paper in both hands so that they could read it together. Vanessa stared glassy-eyed at the sheet, immobilized by the sensations running through her at his touch. Her shoulder was pressed against his chest, and his face was inches from hers. Her heart beat tumultuously from his proximity. She thought she would faint.

"The article is on the lower left," the viscount directed. "Do you find it?"

Vanessa's senses swirled as she tried to focus on the printed words. She was so overcome by the clinging aroma of the soap he used that she did not hear the derision behind his words.

"It doesn't offer much information," he continued, letting the paper drop to the floor. He heard her sigh of relief, but when she made to leave, he placed his hand deliberately on her waist, effectively blocking her escape.

"What do you think I will find at Sir Bartongale's?" he asked. He carefully deepened his voice, increasing its seductive timbre. "Will his daughter be a repeat of the Wesley brats, or will she be more up to mark?" He leaned closer to her and saw her tongue run nervously over her lips. His smile held a hint of cruelty as he let his lips brush her shoulder, as if accidentally.

"I-I wouldn't know," she gasped. "D-didn't your father give you a description?"

"No, he didn't," he murmured. "Perhaps it is just as well. I wonder if she will have silky black curls like yours."

He raised his free hand and twisted a strand around his finger, prolonging the contact.

"B-black hair isn't fashionable," Vanessa managed to offer.

Wayne was well aware of the tumult raging in the slender form he held captured against him. He had deliberately contrived the situation as a test. He was confident she would fall into his arms, turning her face to offer her lips. It was a golden opportunity for her to try to enmesh him in a seduction.

He released the curl and let his finger trail down her neck until his hand rested on her shoulder. He caught his breath over the clinging softness of the warm skin. Dammit, why didn't she turn to him so he could accuse her! Didn't she know he knew her for the doxie she was?

She remained a statue with her face averted. Anger rose in him. All he had to do was tighten his arms around her . . . What was she after? Was she waiting for him first to open his purse to her? The familiar tightening came to his chest, and he fought the desire to shake her until her teeth rattled. Something had gone wrong; his response was different from that which he had planned. What was she doing to him?

The desire for revenge had suddenly lost its appeal. His anger slipped away from him as he felt the trembling of her body. He was now aghast at what he had been attempting to do and released his hold, letting her move away.

A pained expression crossed his face when he saw her quivering lips and suspiciously bright eyes. He longed to gather her in his arms, gently to soothe away her agitation.

Instead, he remained stiffly in his chair as she quietly let herself out of the room, murmuring that she had forgotten to give Polly a message.

Wayne raged at himself. What a despicable cur he was to inflict such torture on a girl who had repeatedly proved herself innocent! He fervently hoped she would never know the extent of his base nature.

The viscount had an uncomfortable feeling that he needed to revise his first guess at the reason for her deception.

Sir Bartongale's estate was not as large as Baron Wesley's, nor the house as old, but then, it was not entailed. He had built it after retiring and being knighted for outstanding performances during his years in India.

Upon their arrival the butler led them to the drawing room. Sir Bartongale's posture was superbly erect from years of army life. In comparison Lady Bartongale appeared faded, showing the effects of the hot Indian climate on women.

Vanessa's attention centered upon the daughter, Ivy, and she drew her breath in sharply. This was no coy, bovine hopeful. Here was a woman of her own age but full-blown, ripe, and disturbingly attractive. The blond hair was set in the latest fashion; the red lips were alluring in a provocative pout. Vanessa saw the speculative challenge in the bold blue eyes before the lashes dropped demurely while she made a deep curtsy upon being introduced. She held her head so that there was a full view of the deep cleavage displayed by the low décolletage of her gown.

The viscount's mask of haughty boredom did not slip, but from her position by the door Vanessa saw the quick gleam of appreciation in his eyes. Vanessa hated the girl on sight.

"I should recognize you immediately, my dear Larimor!" Sir Bartongale exclaimed. "You are the image of your father when we were young together. You bring back many fine memories!"

"He speaks fondly of them also," the viscount answered with a faint smile. "In fact, I suspect they have increased with the telling."

"Yes." He laughed. "It is fortunate we remember the good and forget the worrisome adventures of youth."

They chatted for a few minutes while Vanessa watched quietly from her post by the door. Lady Bartongale, she saw immediately, was as faded as she appeared. She would not be the aggressor that the baroness Wesley had been.

Now the daughter was the one to watch. Vanessa had quickly noted how the bold eyes swept over her, examining with calculating evaluation before she dismissed the page as too young to bother with. There was bigger game in the form of the tall, handsome viscount with hair brighter than her bottles could produce.

Miss Ivy moved provocatively to the viscount, entering the conversation and calling attention to herself.

Vanessa assessed the situation quickly. The mother had given up the battle to control her vivacious daughter, while the father had retreated manlike, leaving no one to guide the young woman. He wished only that one of the ardent swains would soon ask for her hand. Perhaps the viscount would become enamored by her obvious attractions. The letter from the earl had stated only that his son was passing through, but something more might come of the meeting.

Being new, the house was built along spacious lines, and the viscount's bedroom was larger than the one he and his page had shared at Baron Wesley's. There was a large dressing room attached, and Vanessa carefully hung the viscount's clothes on hangers while Roberts took care of his bath and shaving before dressing him for the evening meal.

Her small trunk was there also, and her heart beat faster. A reprieve! Was it possible that she would not have to face sharing a bedroom with the servants?

"Will you be wanting me to stay with you still, my lord?" she questioned as Roberts flicked an imaginary piece of lint from his sleeve.

Wayne adjusted the fit of the jacket over his broad shoulders before answering. "It is evident that Sir Bartongale has no control over his charming daughter," he said astutely. "Perhaps between the two of us we will have continuous success with our partnership in preventing the decision of whom I chuse to marry taken from my hands."

Vanessa hid her pleasure. He had not been blinded by Miss Ivy's beauty! He saw her for what she was.

The evening became a torture for Vanessa. How could a woman who was no older than she know so much about luring a man! One minute the voluptuous girl was demurely coy, the next boldly inviting. Her tactics had a calculated effect, and Vanessa saw the viscount's gaze wander frequently to the tantalizing lips pouting at him, while enjoying a full view of the low-cut gown as she bent toward him in conversation.

The mother seemed unaware of the daughter's performance; the father ignored it. Vanessa writhed in her position by the door, a forgotten shadow watching the seduction.

Why should it cause her so much concern? His lordship had indicated he was alert to the daughter's schemes.

Then the reason behind her anxiety flashed through her like a lightning bolt. This pain searing her was jealousy. She was in love with the viscount!

The knowledge staggered her. It couldn't be! Yet her

heart told her the truth, and she closed her eyes in the agony of her discovery. This was the end; she must depart. But even as she admitted the necessity, she knew she could not leave him until he discovered her true identity. She was existing on borrowed time, but the need to be near him was too intense to permit her to terminate the association yet.

"Wainwright. What a charming name!" Miss Ivy murmured. The two had moved towards the french doors near Vanessa. "It becomes you, my lord, but it is such a mouthful. Surely you have a more intimate name?"

"I have many intimate names," he answered with a faint lift to one eyebrow, "but my friends call me Wayne."

"Then it will have to be Wayne for now, won't it?" She smiled provocatively. "Perhaps later I can test your other names!"

He gave a small bow. "That," he said mockingly, "will be entirely up to you."

That night the viscount was resplendent in a pale blue robe which made his blond handsomeness all the more striking. Only by concentrating hard on her task could Vanessa keep her hand steady as she poured his evening glass of wine.

She had a wild desire to run her hand through his thick blond hair, to lay her head on his broad chest. She had never experienced such wanton emotions before. Was this how the women he wooed and won had reacted to him? She could imagine the trail of weeping women left behind when he became bored.

"The fair Ivy let me know that her room is the first around the corner of the hall," he said musingly as he tasted the wine.

Vanessa looked at him in horror. Would he accept the

invitation? "Do you think it wise to investigate?" she questioned in a small, strangled voice.

He gazed at her mockingly. "Perhaps not, but it could prove interesting. She looks like a very giving woman."

He examined his page with appreciation. He had ordered Roberts to find a robe so that she could be more comfortable during these nightly sessions. It was a deep blue and accented the blue glints resting in the black hair now curling silkily across her forehead. That creamy skin would be the envy of any woman. He fought the inclination to trail his fingers along her neck, recalling its clinging softness.

Wayne shifted restlessly. These thoughts were flitting through his mind much too often, disconcerting him. His attempt to penetrate the reason for her deceit had foundered. Maybe he should take advantage of the thinly veiled invitation awaiting down the hall and hanged be to any consequences.

His fitfulness drove him from the chair, and he paused by the dresser. He glanced into the mirror and encountered the wistful expression of the girl gazing at him.

He turned abruptly and faced her. "Van," he said brusquely, "what are your feelings about women?"

She looked at him, startled, then lowered her lashes. There was a strange expression on his face.

"I'm afraid I don't understand," she murmured. "I have few women friends."

"But you find them attractive to you?" His voice was hard, demanding an answer.

She spread her hand in a gesture strangely appealing. "Attractive? I do not think I'm old enough to feel anything that strongly." Her voice sank into a whisper.

"What about men? Do they appeal to you more?" His

hand was on the silver hairbrush on the dresser, shifting its position.

She licked dry lips. How could she answer him—not men, only you, my lord?

"For some reason I find I have to be on guard where older men are concerned," she managed to whisper. That, at least, was the truth.

He pushed the brush roughly aside and jammed his hands into his pockets. He stared out the window as he took several deep breaths.

"You are a strange lad," he said finally. "I keep feeling that there is more to you than what you tell. You say you come from poor circumstances, but only a blind man could remain unaware that you were born for better things. You have an innate grace, a comeliness."

He stopped abruptly and turned to her with an angry gesture. "Sometimes I think you are really a witch and I should never have taken you on as my page!" His voice was harsh as it whipped out savagely.

She gazed at him stricken, having no idea what had caused the denouncement. Then her green eyes clouded in misery. He hated her!

Her pale face shimmered in the light from the single candle. There was a luminosity in those strangely compelling eyes, as if tears were hanging there. He was overcome with the desire to console her, and his arm went across her shoulders. She gave a little sigh, and her head rested on his shoulder. His lips were pressed to her forehead before he realized what he was about.

"Get to bed, Van," he said, his voice taut with suppressed emotion. "This crazy trip I am forced to go through is making me react foolishly. We are both tired and belong in bed."

Vanessa lay huddled in bed, alternately hot and cold

while she thought about the strange conversation. She shivered, recalling the raw anger directed at her, completely bewildered about the cause. Then her love surfaced to warm her as she was swept with the remembered tenderness of his kiss. 'Twas merely a brotherly kiss, she cautioned firmly. How long would she stay now, knowing of her hopeless love? Her heart said: until he uncovered her masquerade and threw her out in disgust.

CHAPTER ELEVEN

"What do you think of Roberts's hand?" Polly asked worriedly.

Vanessa looked at her in surprise. "I didn't know anything was wrong," she answered. "He sent me down with this shirt for you to remove a wrinkle. What's wrong?"

"He pierced his thumb with a pin the other day, and last night, when I was washing, he came down to see if there was a salve to ease the pain. I made him soak it in hot water and put on a poultice my mother used to make. He said it gave him some relief, but I'm worried. It looked very angry."

Vanessa glanced at her friend, noting her deep concern. Was it possible an affection was growing between the two? While Roberts gave unstinted devotion to his lordship, his life appeared singularly barren otherwise. What a wonderful solution for these two if his lordship would condone such a marriage.

"I'm sorry to say I did not notice," Vanessa admitted. "I'll ask when I take back the shirt."

"You took long enough!" Roberts snapped when she returned. Vanessa looked at him in surprise. It was not like him to be so abrupt. Then she saw the flushed face, the feverishly bright eyes, and could guess how ill he felt. He was cradling a bandaged hand to his chest.

"Hold the shirt for his lordship and button it for him," he ordered.

She was forced to face the viscount, and her breath drew

in with a muffled gasp. The fine cotton undershirt did not hide his wide expanse of chest, the muscular arms and broad shoulders. He wore his riding breeches, which snugged his narrow waist and hips.

She held the shirt for him, then stood before him to do the buttoning. She was overwhelmingly close. Surely he must hear the pounding of her heart! Her trembling fingers brushed against his skin, and her hand was immediately on fire.

The reaction was so intense that her glance flew up to meet his eyes. They were strangely brooding and held hers for a heart-stopping moment before he stepped back from her.

"I can do this," he said curtly. "See what has to be done for Roberts's hand. It looks as if it needs a doctor's attention."

"It is not necessary, my lord," Roberts protested. "Polly is taking care of it. I will have her put on another poultice."

"Nevertheless, I wish Van to unwrap it so that I may inspect it," the viscount ordered.

Wayne frowned when he saw the red skin tightly stretched over the swollen thumb. When the jacket was removed, an angry red line was seen extending up the arm.

"Notify Sir Bartongale immediately to contact his physician," he said firmly. He had seen these red lines before and knew they indicated infection.

He reached for his jacket, hiding his concern. He was inordinately fond of his valet. To lose his service now was unthinkable. The page certainly could not substitute!

He glanced at the slim girl and stared. She was cradling the painful limb in one hand while the other was rubbing lightly along the arm and down to the thumb, as if trying to draw the angry inflammation out of the original pinprick.

The face was a mask of infinite tenderness and concentration, yet Wayne had the uneasy sensation that the girl was not aware of what she was doing, was not even in the room. Her eyes were half-closed, glazed over with a faraway expression.

A look of pain crossed the sensitive face, and it became flushed as if with fever. A stab of apprehension ran through Wayne's breast. Was the infection perhaps catching?

He moved involuntarily towards the two, then stopped. Roberts's face, which had appeared burning with fever, was now its usual, slightly florid color. Wayne knew before he checked the hand that the swelling would be down.

The bandage was stained, as if a boil had been lanced. The poisonous substance was draining, and the viscount breathed a sigh of relief, knowing immediately that Roberts would now get better.

The man's eyes were wide as he flexed his hand, not believing the pain could possibly have disappeared so quickly. "Polly said you had healing hands," he said in awe. "I did not believe her story, but I see I am in your debt."

"Keep it soaked with hot water," Vanessa instructed. "I'll run down to get the herbs to make a poultice to keep it drawing."

"No," he protested. "With my lord's permission you will have to take over my duties until my hand improves. I do not want to stain his clothes. Polly will take care of the poultice. Hers were most soothing."

Vanessa smiled at his eagerness as he left. Polly would

be only too happy to take care of his needs, she was certain.

The fatigue which always descended after one of these sessions settled on her. The viscount was immediately aware of her weariness and stiffened. There it was again, the desire to lay a comforting arm around the slim shoulders and pull the head onto his own shoulder.

"Get my hat and whip," he ordered sharply. "I assume you wish to ride Grey Ghost this morning?"

Vanessa pulled away from her exhaustion and hurried to comply even while she was smarting from the taunt in his voice.

Miss Ivy was waiting for them in a smart light blue riding outfit which accented every curve. The blue gave color to her pale eyes and made her hair more golden, although the sunlight gave it a certain brassiness.

"I ordered my horse and learned you, too, were intent upon riding, so I'm inviting myself to join you." She smiled saucily at the tall man.

"The pleasure is mine," the viscount answered, and Vanessa fought a depression while watching his appreciation as his glance went casually over the curvaceous figure. "I must warn you, though. Diablo insists upon a brisk run first. Shall we meet somewhere when he is satisfied?"

She gave a quick laugh, her eyes bright with anticipation. "You haven't yet seen my horse. He, too, demands his run. Shall we see who wins the race?" There was a thinly veiled challenge in her words.

A young footman handed her her gloves and whip. Vanessa's gaze sharpened upon seeing the adoration barely shielded in his eyes.

The grooms brought the animals around. Miss Ivy's horse was indeed spectacular but not in Diablo's class.

Her lips pursed with annoyance when she saw the third

horse. "Surely you don't need your page with you even when you ride!" she exclaimed. "I heard it was the latest in London for gentlemen to have one dance attendance, but you must have had enough of him last night. I swear he is like a shadow!"

The viscount never looked more haughty. "I just bought the horse, and it needs the exercise."

"Then I will ride it. I'll send mine back."

"I'm afraid it is not broken to a lady's saddle, and I would not wish harm to come to you," he returned. Something in his voice warned her not to press.

She gave an irritated shrug and let the groom lift her up. He handed her the reins, and Vanessa saw with astonishment how his hand lingered over hers.

"You do not wish me to attend today?" he murmured, his eyes bold on her face.

She pulled away before turning to smile coquettishly at the viscount. "I have no need for you today, Henry. I have his lordship to protect me."

He stepped back politely, his head lowering, but not before Vanessa saw an unguarded glint of angry frustration in his eyes.

What goes here? Vanessa wondered. Was the boredom of country life driving the young girl to dally with the servants? Henry was a handsome young man in a heavy, earthy way, although now his face held a dashed expression.

Vanessa was accustomed to Diablo's racing off his first flush of energy. The viscount gave him his head and rode a distance before returning to meet them.

Miss Ivy soon gave up the unequal race and settled to a fast canter. The beauty of her face was marred by its grim set. She was an excellent rider and indeed looked handsome on the horse in her snug-fitting outfit and the tall hat with a wisp of veiling. She had hoped to catch the viscount's attention with her expertise, but so far he was concentrating only on his horse. She was not used to any man's ignoring her so.

Ivy had caught the viscount's quick glance of appreciation the night before. The gossip about his lordship's amours in London had alerted her to a possible way to capture his attention, and she had dressed accordingly.

Her mother had protested weakly, and her father had predictably closed his eyes. Ivy had been so certain of her seduction that her frustration still clung after she had waited fruitlessly for the viscount to come to her room.

The viscount topped a rise and pulled Diablo to a halt. Both were breathing hard from the exertion, but he felt better for the exercise. Last night green eyes had kept invading his sleep. He thought he had exorcised that particular devil, yet this morning, when the girl's hand had touched his skin when buttoning his shirt, it had been like a sting of fire. Hell's teeth, what devilish thing was happening to him?

He glanced down the hill at the two riders galloping towards him. His face hardened as he took in the ripe allure of the leading rider. Miss Ivy might ease this turmoil for an evening. The invitation had been clear enough.

He shrugged away the temptation. She was too like a spider, and her traps would be just as carefully laid as the ones the baroness had attempted. No. He might have considered dallying with her under other circumstances, but now for some reason the thought of sharing a bed with her was repugnant to him.

His gaze went to the other rider, and his chest again tightened in an unpleasant way.

Witch! Green-eyed sorcerer! he fumed inwardly.

Yet he couldn't help noticing the air of innocence, a

certain purity of the figure, doubly apparent by the contrast with the other.

His hands tightened on the reins, and his annoyance grew. Dammit, there was no reason for this odd uncertainty gnawing at him. Somehow he would extract his revenge and dismiss her when they left here. With that settled, Wayne awaited their coming.

Vanessa was immediately aware of the viscount's black mood when they reached him. Usually after this first run the two would canter beside each other, relaxed and talking about anything which came to mind. It was a golden time.

Now with the intrusion of Miss Ivy everything was different. Could the viscount be feeling the same regret over the loss of their privacy? The possibility was soothing.

"You are wicked, my lord," Miss Ivy said severely as she and Vanessa cantered up to him. "Is this how you ride with a lady—ignoring her so that your page must ride protection?" Her full red lips pursed seductively, softening her words. "If you don't think of your horse, think of me. I, for one, crave a rest."

Her hands fluttered helplessly. He dismounted obediently and lifted her from her horse.

It was smoothly contrived, no doubt from experience. She was in his arms, her body snug against his while smiling teasingly at him.

Really, Wayne stormed within himself, did she think these obvious overtures would beguile him? She had not done her homework well, or she would have known he had to be the hunter or there would be no interest.

He glanced over her head to meet green eyes. They held an unreadable expression which immediately placed him on the defensive. What right did a mere chit have to indicate disapproval! Perversely he found himself answering Miss Ivy's teasing smile with one of his own, and he drew her arm through his.

"Shall we take a little walk?" he asked. "A pause now will make the ride back more enjoyable. Van can watch the horses."

He tossed the last over his shoulder as he led the now-glowing girl down a narrow path to where a brook could be heard.

A pain twisted in Vanessa's chest. He sounded as if he actively disliked her!

What was happening? Sensitive as always to other people's emotions, Vanessa had felt ever since the conversation last night that something had changed between them. Whereas before, when they were alone, there had been a wonderful easy exchange, now a wall was being erected and the viscount was receding behind it, taking the precious easy rapport and the sensation of being protected with him.

Vanessa's shoulders drooped as she patted Diablo's arched neck. Again she was alone in the world, and her intense loneliness was doubly painful because she had been in the sun, felt the warmth of another's interest and the security of his shield.

She had fallen in love, helplessly and hopelessly. She had blinded herself with the hope that she could serve him with a silent devotion. Peagoose! she berated herself.

For some reason, she knew not why, he now appeared antagonistic towards her. It was time to leave before her duplicity was discovered, before his anger became overwhelming. His disgust would be more than she could bear.

A faint scream came from the path they had taken, and she heard the viscount's voice sharp with concern.

Without thinking, Vanessa hurried down the path and

stopped short in consternation. His lordship was lifting Miss Ivy in his arms and carrying her to a fallen log.

Her arms were around his neck, and she placed her head on his shoulder, but not before Vanessa saw the gleam of triumph in her eyes.

Vanessa began backing away, but the Viscount heard her. He placed his burden on the log and called to her.

"Come here," he said imperiously. "Miss Ivy has apparently twisted her ankle. Will you remove her boot so that we can see the extent of her injury?"

Vanessa winced under the curt command but hurried to comply.

"Couldn't you do it, dear Wayne?" the girl cried. "I'm in such pain, and a servant never has the right touch for a lady." She inched her skirt up as she extended her leg until she was exposed audaciously to the knee.

"You have nothing to fear with Van. He has healing hands and will be careful," the viscount answered coolly, standing to one side so that Vanessa could kneel before her.

Vanessa bent to her task, ignoring the prolonged gasps of agony as she carefully slid off the riding boot. She stepped back so that the viscount could assess the exposed ankle. There was no swelling or hint of a bruise. It was all a sham, a contrived act. Vanessa had been aware of the angry glances directed at her for destroying the effectiveness of the plot. In the past this act of helplessness and swooning had precipitated all sorts of interesting capitulations.

"We cannot have Miss Ivy in such evident pain, can we, Van?" the viscount said dispassionately. "This is an ideal opportunity for you to demonstrate your healing art."

Vanessa tensed upon hearing the scornful undertone in his voice. What had she done to cause this complete reversal of his feelings towards her? Why was he showing such contempt; why was he so obviously rejecting her?

Her instincts, which were always alerted to true suffering, assured her that this injury was all an act. Surely the viscount with his quick perception was aware of this also. Then why demand she enter this farce? The answer was clear. He was intent upon demeaning her. Anger rose sharply within her. She would not be a part of this pretense.

She stared at him, her eyes bright with resentment. "Do you intend for me to treat her as I did Diablo when his ankle was strained? The brook is cool and will bring down the swelling," she said caustically.

He stiffened at her allusion. He well remembered her standing in the river with the horse docile under her crooning voice. His eyes narrowed with reciprocal anger. How dare this girl defy him?

"I am referring to how you helped the abigail Polly," he said icily.

"I can help only when there is an injury I can see." Her answer was a challenge. Her chin firmed while her slender body tensed with defiance. Their gazes met in a stormy clash of wills.

"Take care of her ankle!" he seethed.

"Are you ordering me, my lord?" she asked. He realized with shock that her fury matched his own.

Somehow this confrontation had disintegrated into a contest between them, and Wayne raged, knowing he must establish mastery over this obstreperous page. He had been correct. This chit must be sent away, and he ignored the odd sense of desolation deep within him.

"I am amazed you tolerate such insolence from a servant," Miss Ivy exclaimed. She had been listening open-mouthed to the exchange. "He would not be allowed long in our household!" The two ignored her. They were still glaring at each other, locked in their private battle.

"Wayne!" Miss Ivy called sharply. It was intolerable that attention was being diverted from her. "I don't know what the argument is about, but I assure you I will not be touched by him. My ankle is not as bad as I feared. Please replace my boot and have the horses brought here. I wish to return home!"

"You have your orders!" the viscount said through clenched teeth. "Get the horses!"

Vanessa turned to comply, her head high.

Wayne glared after her. It must be his anger which imprinted the grace of the receding figure, erect with proud rebellion. Reluctant admiration stirred in him, but he firmed himself against it as he turned to help replace the boot on the foot which showed no evidence of injury.

CHAPTER TWELVE

They returned to the house, the viscount riding beside Miss Ivy, now glowing under his attention. His blond head was bent towards his companion as if he were intent on her every word.

Vanessa rode in the approved position several paces behind. It took all her willpower to keep her shoulders square as her anger drained away.

Somehow she had placed him upon a pedestal, a man above all others, almost godlike. She had been stirred by their exchange of ideas, their searching conversation. They had laughed over the same nonsense. What foolish dreams she had harbored! She had envisioned a future with such a continuous sharing, page and master eager for the evenings when the rest of the house had gone to sleep so that they could talk undisturbed. Foolish peagoose!

He was a man like all the others, quickly enamored of a pretty face however empty the head, intent on what was willingly offered.

Her disappointment was so intense that she had to hold herself firmly in check so as not to shame herself with tears. He ignored her completely when the flunkies hurried to take their horses, and he escorted Miss Ivy into the house as if she were a fragile flower. Vanessa's mouth trembled in her distress. He became more attentive to Ivy whenever he caught Vanessa's eye on him.

He did not bother to look at her as he curtly dismissed her after they had emerged from the dining room following a prolonged breakfast. Nevertheless, she sat outside the drawing room door, listening to the indistinct murmur of their voices—Miss Ivy's light and flirtatious, his deep and drawling. Although dismissed, she sat guard in case he had a change of heart.

The ambivalence of her position drained her of energy. Did he or did he not want her near as previously requested? She waited in the hall, hopeful of a mending of the strained relationship. That afternoon Sir Bartongale was taking him to inspect the stables. Would he request that she participate like the last time?

She recalled the thrill she had felt when he had chosen the superlative horse for her use. The special rapport which had flowed between them was now gone. A woman whose every gesture was a promise had reduced her dreams to silly nonsense—which, indeed, they always had been.

The family met in the hall. Vanessa stood erect, awaiting his order.

The mother fluttered a minute before confessing she thought it best to take a nap. "The weather is so unseasonally warm," she said vaguely. "I find I do best if I rest during the hot part of the day."

"A good idea," her daughter agreed. "I shall do likewise since Papa and his lordship will be spending the afternoon at the stables. I much prefer to be awake at night."

Her lashes fluttered as she gazed at the tall viscount. "We shall have the evening to continue our conversation," she murmured softly for his ears alone. "Mamma and Papa wished to have a party tomorrow so that the neighbors could meet you, but I persuaded them to wait another day. It will allow us more time to become better acquainted."

The viscount gazed down at her from hooded eyes, his

expression the habitual mask of faint boredom. He gave a slight bow of approval, then turned to follow Sir Bartongale. Vanessa moved to follow, but he stared coldly at her for a moment.

"I will not need you the rest of the day," he said curtly. "You could lend assistance to Roberts so that he can rest his hand."

Somehow she made her way to the kitchen, seeking Polly to help overcome the pain of his blunt words.

"What is wrong?" Polly asked, noting Vanessa's troubled face.

Vanessa pulled in a long breath. "It's nothing. I-I . . . oh, nothing!"

"Has his lordship discovered?" Polly whispered apprehensively.

"No. It is nothing like that." Now that there was a sympathetic ear, Vanessa was reluctant to discuss the matter.

"How is Roberts's hand?" she asked, searching for another topic.

"I can never thank you enough for making it better," Polly said softly. "He comes frequently to have the poultice changed."

"I was willing to do it, but he preferred your touch," Vanessa offered, and was rewarded by the happy glow on her friend's face.

"I find him very interesting," Polly said shyly. "We have so much to talk about while he's sitting soaking his hand."

The words stabbed at Vanessa. Yes, she knew how interesting a man could be!

Roberts entered, searching for Polly to apply another poultice. The two settled in a corner of the kitchen, unaware of the bustle around them as their heads bent to each other while they talked.

Vanessa left, driven by restlessness, and went upstairs to sit on her pallet in the dressing room. If only the viscount would look at her with that special tenderness Roberts's face held when he talked to Polly!

She thought of the voluptuous girl now occupying the viscount's attention. In contrast she would pale to insignificance, even if he had met her as a girl.

She stopped in front of the mirror. Was she so poor in appearance? She could never understand why the men in the village seemed interested in her. Her slim form held no allure, and certainly she never encouraged them.

Her hair was a rich blue-black but others had a similar color. True, her skin was milky white and finer-grained than that of most of the women. It must be her eyes, those awful green eyes. So many had commented about them until they had become a cross she felt forced to bear. If only she had been blessed with her mother's lovely blue eyes.

In spite of the hardship her mother had endured in her marriage, there was a refinement about her which had lifted her above the other women of the village.

Again Vanessa wondered about her mother's origins. She certainly must have been a gentlewoman by birth to have known how to read and write and been able to teach her daughter. What had precipitated so disastrous a marriage to the gardener? On her deathbed she had said it was to give Vanessa a name, but what a price she had paid! Why had her mother's family rejected her, and why had her lover allowed his parents to stop their elopement? For the first time Vanessa felt anger towards her unknown father for ruining her mother by his uncaring demands.

A picture rose before her of her mother's head with the

same raven hair as hers bent patiently over the fine needlework which seemed always to have been in her hands and which had given them a livelihood.

Vanessa suddenly felt the need to communicate with her parent, to feel once more her protective love. It drove her to the trunk, and she rummaged in its depth for the one possession made by her mother. She shook out the dress, recalling her mother's careful fitting, then the two of them admiring the result.

It was a lovely dress of fine pale green dimity with little bows in a rosy color nestling in the scalloping of the bodice and skirt. She had loved it dearly, and now, holding it against her, she yearned to wear it once again. The need overwhelmed her. To have it on would restore her femininity. She now realized how her soul revolted against the needed masquerade.

Without further thought she folded the dress into the shawl she carried it in and dashed out the door. She couldn't try it on here. The danger of being discovered was too great.

Vanessa hesitated by the smaller stable where the viscount's horses were stabled. The men stood some distance away, watching one of Sir Bartongale's horses perform.

Quickly she saddled Grey Ghost and led her at a fast trot to the nearest wood, where the pines acted as a barrier. When certain that she was undetected, she gave the horse her head and covered the path in a gallop. It was as if the beast felt her urgency and need for secrecy by finding the pine needles which muffled her speeding hooves. A small glen opened up before them, and Grey Ghost slowed to a stop before a stream.

Vanessa became immediately enamored of the pretty scene before her. The little sun-dappled clearing was protected by the encroaching forest. The horse nibbled the grass as she gazed about.

Her agitation receded, soothed by the quiet glen. No one would see her here, and she swiftly dismounted. She removed the page's outfit, which was becoming increasingly distasteful to her.

She was a girl with the first upsurge of a woman's emotion, and the necessary disguise had now become a bitter hindrance, effectively preventing her from acting as her heart desired.

The shallow little brook beckoned, and Vanessa knelt on the sandy bottom to splash contentedly in the cool water. Lady Bartongale was correct. It was unseasonably warm, and the bath was refreshing.

Then carefully, almost reverently, she slipped the dress over her head. She smoothed the wrinkles out as best she could and gave a sigh of satisfaction.

She felt whole again. The masquerade had been necessary for the protection it offered, and she would have to return to it. But for this brief moment she was herself once again. She went to the brook and bent over a small pool to catch her reflection. She stared at her image, bemused by how much softer her hair appeared when she wore a dress.

"Meridel!"

Vanessa froze upon hearing the deep voice.

"Meridel!" The call was repeated in a strangled agony.

She turned quickly, wondering whom the man was talking to. She had never heard of anyone with that name but her mother.

A tall, gaunt man stood at the edge of the glen, his horse's reins in his hands. The pine needles had evidently muffled the sound of his approach.

Vanessa glanced around, looking for the woman he must have been calling, but there was no one else.

"My God, are you a wood nymph sent to haunt me?" the man exploded. He was gazing from deep-set eyes, and Vanessa realized he was speaking to her.

"I-I'm sorry, sir," Vanessa stammered. "I am not the one you are seeking. My name is not Meridel." Her voice quivered over the name as it brought a vision of her mother to mind.

"No, I can see that now," he said, passing his hand over his eyes. "But the similarity is uncanny. What is your name?"

"Van . . . Vanessa." She was in a dress. She could speak her name proudly.

"Are you from around here?" he questioned. "I have not seen you before."

Vanessa glanced at him warily. If he were a friend of Sir Bartongale's, he might be invited to the party tomorrow and look for her.

"N-no, my lord. I am traveling through and came here only hoping to find a place to escape the heat." That, fortunately, was true enough.

He glanced around the glen and gave a slight smile that eased the grim lines on his face. "I had the same thought in mind. The brook comes from deep within the earth and brings a refreshing coolness to the air. I come here frequently when I wish to be alone."

"I shall leave then, my lord," she offered. There was no doubt in her mind that he was titled. While his clothes were dreadfully out of style, they had been made by an excellent tailor. Besides, his proud carriage would have labeled him as such to any discerning eye.

"No, do not move," he ordered. His sunken eyes again

fastened upon her. "You intrigue me. It is not often one finds a wood nymph on one's property."

Vanessa gave a slight gasp. "I didn't know I was trespassing! I thought this was still part of Sir Bartongale's estate," she said in apology.

He raised an eyebrow. "Then you are from my neighbor's house. Our property marches together for a distance. I was about to refuse the invitation for tomorrow night's party to meet some viscount visiting him, but now that I see who else is in the party, I shall have to accept. I am curious to see how a wood nymph acts when surrounded by lesser mortals." A smile softened the stern lines around his mouth.

His words came lightly, but Vanessa felt trapped. Then she rallied. He would not recognize her as a page. No one ever noticed servants. And perhaps the viscount would still be angry with her and not require her services.

"Why, don't you know, my lord, a wood nymph can be seen only by those bewitched? I fade into the woodwork and cannot be seen by man!" A dimple formed as she smiled teasingly at him.

He caught his breath in a sharp gasp, and his face paled. "I must know more about you," he said. His deep voice again held the hoarseness of his first call. "Your mother. What is her name?"

Vanessa was impaled by the intensity of his demand, and she answered, unable to deny him.

"Meridel," she murmured, and stopped, realizing that she had never heard the rest of her maiden name.

"My God," he whispered. His hand went to his horse as if he needed its support. "I knew it must be so when I first saw you."

"I-I am supposed to look as she did when young," she admitted. "You called me by her name. Did you perhaps know her?" Was this truly happening? Her heart was pounding so that it was difficult to breathe. Had she finally found someone who had known her mother? Had her instinct to travel north carried her to the area where she had been born?

She leaned forward eagerly. "Oh, tell me about her!" she cried, excited hope sending color to her cheeks. "I know nothing about her parents. She told me so little!"

A flash of pain crossed his face. "You talk as if she is . . . gone."

"Yes," Vanessa said soberly. "The winter was cruel last year, and she contracted a fever in her lungs. There was nothing we could do."

She closed her eyes against the remembered pain. She had been able to help so many with her gift but had been helpless to aid the one she loved most.

"I knew," he murmured as if to himself. "The loss was complete. I finally gave up all hope of ever finding her again."

Silence pulsed between them as they both looked searchingly at each other.

"Y-you haven't told me your name," she said hesitatingly, "or how you knew my mother."

"Forgive me," he said. "I am Lord Stuart Thornton, Earl of MacLowry, the owner of this estate." He came across the glen and bowed over her hand.

He raised his head to gaze intently at her, and she drew her breath in with a sharp gasp. He was close now, and she could examine the gaunt face and see into the shadowed, brooding eyes. Her gaze was incredulous, her face ashen with surprise.

His hand closed convulsively around hers, and he stared back at her, green eyes meeting green eyes.

"It . . . cannot . . . be!" he exclaimed after a long pause.

Vanessa remained speechless. Her mother's words were ringing in her ears. "Looking into your eyes, I can remember the great happiness once mine." Vanessa had assumed she was talking about her parents, but now she knew the answer. It was her lover she was speaking of! The shock of the revelation immobilized her.

"Vanessa!" Her name came in an agonized cry as realization also dawned on him. It then seemed perfectly natural to be enclosed by strong arms and to find her head resting against his chest.

She was home at last! The sensation was overpowering, and she gave a little cry as tears of happiness ran down her cheeks. She looked at him in wonder and saw a matching dampness on his face.

"Can it be true?" she whispered. "Are you my father?"

"We cannot deny the color of our eyes," he cried, his face alight with joy. "It is a strong trait in my family, but was not in Meridel's."

His gaze was hungry on her as if he could not believe what had transpired. "A daughter! I have a daughter, and such a lovely one!"

He threw back his head, giving a laugh of exultation. "I came here bedeviled by my loneliness, and now I am the proud possessor of a wood nymph, an angel, an incredibly beautiful, enchanting goddess!"

He drew her close in his arms again, their very tenderness a warm haven. "Oh, Meridel, Meridel, thank you," he whispered fervently against her hair.

He held her by the shoulders as he again examined her face, as if wishing to engrave it on his heart. "We have so much to talk about, to explain. I must learn everything about you. The years, long years lost! We must catch up with them. Come, we will go to my castle—no, *our* castle," he amended with a smile, "and find each other!"

Vanessa's heart plummeted as she drew away from him. The viscount! she thought with rising agitation. She had forgotten him completely.

"No, I cannot," she said, agonized. It had all come too quickly. She needed to get away, to hide until she could sort out what had happened. She felt as if she were standing at a fork in a road and must decide which path to take. Her future, her happiness depended upon it.

There was no doubt in her heart that this man was her father, but he had rejected her mother, forcing her into a disastrous marriage. How far could Vanessa trust him now? What was he going to do with a daughter no one knew about? After the first flush of recognition would he reject her? How could he present her to his family, his friends? The half-formed questions swirled through her mind, the problems seemingly insurmountable.

And there was the viscount. She accepted the fact that she would have to leave, and soon, but her heart cried out against making the parting now. Every day, every minute she was with him were doubly precious because they were numbered. Her love desired only one more evening, one more kind exchange to place in her memory for the black future when she would see him no more.

"I must leave," she said. "They will be expecting me."

The frown was black on his brow. "Do you think I will risk losing you now that I have found you?"

"Please, you do not understand," Vanessa persisted. "I have a commitment which I must bring to a close. Then, if you wish, I will meet you again."

"I do not understand," he said. There was a stern expression on his face very similar to one of the viscount's, and it wrenched her heart.

"I will go with you to Sir Bartongàle and tell him whatever story you wish, but I insist that you pack your trunks and come home with me," he said firmly as one used to having his orders obeyed.

He gave a start. "You are not spoken for or married, are you? I see no rings."

"No, my lord," she murmured. Her expression saddened, and a droop came to the sensitive mouth. He wondered for a moment about the cause.

"Please, I request your understanding," she begged, looking pleadingly at him. "I will try to meet you here tomorrow, but I must go unattended now. And please, tell no one about this meeting until we can speak again."

His frown deepened. He looked for a long time into her eyes before giving a sigh. "I could not resist your mother when she pleaded in the same manner. One would think in twenty years I would have learned better. All right, my Vanessa, I will do as you wish but only if you promise to come tomorrow."

"I will if I can," she assured him, "but my time is not my own."

His face hardened. "I will wait, and if you do not come, I will storm his house, demanding to see you."

"No, please!" she cried in alarm. She placed her hand on his arm, her face raised in entreaty. "You said you were invited to the reception tomorrow night. I-I cannot explain everything now, but I shall later. I might not be there. Even if you see me, you must not talk to me. Then I promise you I will meet you here the following day and go with you."

Her lashes fell to hide the pain in her eyes. All she wanted was one more day to be near her love, even if he still ignored her. Then she would go to this tall man who, incredibly, was her father and satisfy their mutual curiosity by exchanging stories before she moved on.

He stared at her for a long time, then said gently, as if

reasoning with himself, "I have no claim on you except through my heart. I must trust your promises, or I shall lose forever all faith in mankind.

"Please, Vanessa, do not fail me. I lost your mother because I bent to others and did not do as my heart desired. Do not let me lose you because I listened to you and again ignored what I know is right."

He was pleading. Vanessa knew it was a rare occurrence. Pride was deeply ingrained in him, but she had reached beyond it and, indeed, into his heart.

A small smile of relief trembled on her lips, and she leaned forward to place a light kiss on his cheek.

"I promise," she vowed. "If I cannot come tomorrow afternoon, I shall be here the following day. Then all our questions shall be answered. I, too, have many!"

He placed a tender kiss on her forehead, and it was as a benediction. She gazed at him for a moment, her eyes bright with unshed tears. Then, turning swiftly, she gathered her telltale page's clothes, fortunately hidden under the shawl. Before he could assist her, she was on Grey Ghost and spurring her on the trail.

CHAPTER THIRTEEN

Vanessa's return flight was swift. She paused only hurriedly to dress again in the page's outfit. She then crept into the dressing room where her cot was placed, still thinking incredulously of what had happened in the little woodland glen. Could it be true? Now in the safety of the room the event seemed a farfetched dream. She had longed to find her true father, yet it was now difficult to believe that what had actually occurred was not just another vivid dream woven from her longing.

Her father! There was no denying that the clear green color of their eyes matched, giving credence to their quick assumption. And he was an earl! It was too incredible, too like the fairy stories she had read.

That he was an earl somehow hadn't surprised her. A castle always seemed to be involved with her daydreams about him. What heaven it would be to visit, perhaps live in one!

Then her dreams toppled as reality reasserted itself. How could he think his family, his friends would accept her, his illegitimate offspring? That the king had admitted as much about his own offspring born of his mistresses did not take away the stigma or ease acceptance by one's family. In his eagerness and surprise of discovery he had not fully realized the implications. He must now be having second thoughts.

She would not subject him to that embarrassment. She would keep her promise to meet him once more and learn answers to her questions about her mother, then make her escape.

"What are you doing here? I told you to take care of Roberts!"

Vanessa jumped to attention. The viscount was standing in the doorway, glaring at her. She had been lost in her thoughts and had not heard him enter.

"Polly is giving him poultices," she replied. "He did not need my care."

"Is that why you sneaked off this afternoon?"

Her head jerked up and she looked at him with alarm. Had he seen her ride off? Had he followed and seen her in a dress? Her face turned white with apprehension.

"Don't look so surprised," he lashed out. "I saw you take Grey Ghost and go into the woods. Whom were you meeting?"

"I-I wasn't meeting anyone," she protested. "I was seeking a cool place."

His eyes narrowed, as if he were wondering if he should believe her. "It would be wise if you remembered that you are my page. As such, I expect you to be available in case I have need for you."

She bowed her head and caught her lower lip between her teeth to stop its quivering. He *had* announced that he had no further need for her that afternoon.

Wayne turned abruptly to the window to banish the sight of the girl. Damn her! he raged. He took a deep breath to gain control over himself. If it weren't ludicrous, he would have accused himself of lashing out at her from jealousy. When she was out of sight, he wondered what she was doing. Yet when he was with the twit he felt about to explode from annoyance. Now he found himself bending his ire on the defenseless girl.

Wayne's friends would not have believed his behavior.

He prided himself on having complete control. He never behaved this irrationally.

"Have water brought for my bath," he ordered with more constraint.

"I've spent the afternoon with the horses and don't want to take the stable odors to dinner."

He turned back to the girl and gave a bitter smile. "You had better change also. I wish your attendance. The fair Ivy is becoming too amorous for my taste. Nothing annoys me more than when I have to put up a defense. Women can be so senseless. I obtain no enjoyment if there is no chase."

The room was filled with sudden sunshine. It was as if a heavy stone had been lifted from her chest. He wasn't enamored after all!

"You wish me to stay with you as before?" she asked hopefully.

"It makes it easier," he admitted wryly. "You may as well earn your keep."

Her heart leaped. She would be near him, and that was all that mattered now. She would have tonight and tomorrow.

She hurried to tell a flunky about the hot water and then to alert Roberts. Polly was with him, and Vanessa loathed interrupting them. Roberts was talking as if attempting to convince Polly of something, while she stood with her head bent, listening. Something about the droop of her shoulders warned Vanessa that all was not proceeding smoothly. Whatever the problem, they would have to unravel it later. His lordship could not be left waiting.

Vanessa looked questioningly at Polly when Roberts left. There were two bright spots of color on her cheeks, and she looked hard pressed to keep back the tears.

A lovers' quarrel, Vanessa guessed. Polly could at least work out her problem. Her own love had no chance.

"Is there something I can do?" Vanessa asked softly.

Polly gave a bitter smile. "No," she said grimly. "I had some dreams, but I have cast them aside. I should have known that a penniless maid cannot expect much from life."

"It can be difficult," Vanessa said understandingly.

Polly nodded. "I have discovered that already. That is why I can understand your masquerade. If I didn't have so evident a woman's figure, I, too, would try to pass as a lad. You were smart as well as brave to do it."

Vanessa wondered exactly how smart the scheme had been. It had given her a breathing spell but had solved nothing except the problem of hunger. That it had crushed her heart was her own fault.

"It hasn't been easy," she murmured. "I will have to leave soon."

Polly looked at her with surprise. "But when his lordship was talking to Roberts before, he was asking questions about you. He left us both with the impression that he was happy with you as his page."

"W-what type of questions?" she asked apprehensively, pressing her hand over her breast to still the rapid beat of her heart.

"He requested information about where you came from. We could not help him. You have never told us anything." She looked questioningly at the still girl. "Do you think he suspects anything?"

"I think it wise to leave," she whispered. "Luck has ridden too long on my shoulder. I cannot tempt fate any longer."

"Then I will go with you," Polly said quickly. "There is no reason for me to stay once you go. Since I cannot disguise myself in the same way as you, I can travel with you as your sister and use your masquerade as a shield."

Vanessa looked at her, aghast at such a scheme.

"Do not say no!" Polly pressed. "One of us should be able to find work so that we both don't go hungry. And with me along to give credence to your being a boy, all will appear more believable. There must be some people who wonder why you don't shave." She grinned mischievously. "I can say it is a family trait. Please, Van," she said, once more serious. "I do not want to stay any longer. If you won't take me along, I will have to go on by myself, unprotected. You know what will happen to me then."

"You can't think of me as giving much protection," Vanessa said weakly.

"Being with one who seems to be a man is safeguard enough," Polly said firmly.

Vanessa saw the reasonableness of her arguments. She remembered her lonely wanderings before she had reached the inn. They would give each other needed companionship.

"All right," she said, capitulating. "Tomorrow is the ball. I plan to leave the next afternoon. I-I have a commitment I must attend to first."

They clasped hands solemnly. Vanessa hurried upstairs with the strange sensation that they had bound themselves together for life.

A heavy melancholy now weighed upon her shoulders. All would soon be over. The viscount would travel on, going out of her life and quickly forgetting her.

Vanessa took her solitary meal while the family was being served. Roberts brought down the viscount's clothes for Polly's washing and spot cleaning. He usually lingered to talk with her, but this time he was gone when Vanessa checked on the girl.

Polly was leaning over the tub, and when she looked up in response to Vanessa's greeting, her eyes appeared red-rimmed. The lovers' quarrel evidently had not been patched.

Vanessa's slender figure was a picture of despondency as she waited in the hall for their supper to be finished. In spite of the marvel of finding her father, her future had never looked so black. Soon she would be leaving behind the two most important men in her life.

From what his lordship had said, Vanessa concluded that Miss Ivy had lost position as a possible bride. She was fiercely happy. She could not bear to think of Ivy's becoming his countess. She would not know how to make him happy. But what of the next woman he was to inspect? It was better that she was leaving. This way there could be no torture, envisioning who would eventually wear his ring, share his bed . . .

A game of whist was started in the cardroom with Vanessa sitting quietly in a corner. In spite of her afternoon nap, Lady Bartongale moved early to retire. Seeing the hesitant glance she sent to her daughter, Vanessa had no doubt who had instigated that decision.

After talking about some breeding stock he had heard of, the baron left also, apologizing for some paper work he had to finish before the morning's post. He gave a slight cough and tried to hide his embarrassment. "If you will excuse me for leaving, my dear Wayne," he said, his gaze darting about without settling on anyone. Would the page stay as a surrogate chaperon? he wondered.

Sir Bartongale flushed and harumphed again. Damn his daughter, placing him in such an unconscionable position! Still, if it helped her catch a lord, he could ask for nothing better. He could transfer his worries onto other shoulders.

He mopped his brow and managed to exit without seeing the mocking lift to the viscount's eyebrows.

Wayne went to stand by the handsome mantel, then turned to gaze down at the girl reclining against the soft pillows of the sofa.

Vanessa had to admit that in the soft candlelight Miss Ivy appeared very alluring in a silvery blue dress sprigged with pink rosebuds, a cluster of which nestled in the blond hair curled high on her head.

"Must you stand so far away?" Ivy smiled enticingly. "You appear too tall and remote. Come, sit by me," she invited with a pat to the pillow beside her.

"But then I could not enjoy the full effect you make, my dear Ivy," he replied, not moving.

"You can enjoy more if you are closer," she murmured seductively.

Wayne's eyes became hooded as he noticeably retreated farther behind his haughty mask. "I am sure," he agreed smoothly. "But prudence dictates otherwise. Since your parents have left, perhaps you wish your maid in attendance?"

A faint flush of annoyance stained her cheeks. "Surely, my lord, you are not intimating that I have cause for anxiety from you," she said with some sarcasm. "I would not be concerned even if you sent your page away." The hint was entirely unladylike, but Ivy did not care. He was proving to be more of a challenge than she had expected.

"Your faith warms my heart," he returned mockingly. "But you may rest assured, my dear child, that I shall observe all proprieties."

"Your humor appeals to me," she said, bristling. "I have not considered myself a child for many years."

His glance went coldly, insolently, over her fully ripe

body. "I apologize," he murmured. "I was referring only to your birthdays, of course."

She rose from the cushions to hide her agitation. Her plan had been to lure him to her boudoir, where she could show him how adept she could be. Surely, with his reputation as a rake, that is what he would desire from a wife.

"I believe you are being the tease," she protested while moving to him so that he could get the full benefit of her perfume, heavy with the odor of tuberoses and jasmine. She had been told once by one of her admirers that it drove him to distraction. Tonight she had need of all her armament.

"Tease you? Never, my dear Ivy," he parried. "I am too cognizant of the honor your parents have presented. I would never misuse their daughter in so cavalier a fashion. I shall be rested soon and continue my travels. I plan to check my estate farther north."

She hesitated, not knowing what to make of this. She knew the precarious position she was in. Rakes preferred married women bored with dull marriages to unattached ones. Irate parents were likely to descend, demanding marriage as a redress.

"My parents feel the honor is theirs and wish only to make your sojourn comfortable and memorable." Her lips pouted provocatively as she gazed up at him. "I, too, concur with their wishes."

"You have succeeded admirably. My father recommended that I stop here instead of staying at an inn. School ties are still strong, and he thought I could carry some messages."

"You must concede that there are more comforts available here than in any inn!" She was leaning forward so that he had a full view of her daringly low-cut bodice.

"I agree," he replied. "Your father's stables are excellent for my horses, and the countryside makes for interesting runs."

She blinked, not expecting this response. "Horses cannot be all you think about!" she snapped, forgetting in her frustration her role of the siren.

He drew himself tall and gazed down haughtily. "A gentleman worthy of the name thinks of his horseflesh before himself. Their comfort was my prime concern when I made my decision to pause here."

She tossed her head as she moved from him, and her eyes lit on Vanessa standing patiently by the wall.

"I fain you are enough to try a woman's soul!" she exclaimed petulantly. "I believe even your page would have more concern for my feelings and would not waste time bandying words so unnecessarily."

She came over to the silent page and smiled provocatively at the new object of her attention. Vanessa stared at the floor, fighting the flush that rose in her cheeks.

"You see, he is not immune to the fact that I am a woman," Ivy said triumphantly. "I had not realized how handsome he is." Her bold eyes roved speculatively over Vanessa. "He is slender and not without grace. You chose well, my dear Wayne."

She turned back to the tall man. Her teasing smile froze on her lips upon encountering the thunder on his face. She had hoped to rile him out of his indifference, but she backed away instinctively under the force of his expression. What had caused this reaction?

"I see you are not above teasing," he said, his voice deceptively silken. "But servants, of course, are beneath your consideration."

Miss Ivy gazed at him sharply, and Vanessa wondered if he had, after all, seen the exchange between her and the footman and groom. She had discovered long ago that his slumbering eyes missed little.

"You are being insultingly rude," Miss Ivy said angrily, her red cheeks not needing the added artifice of coloring. "I refuse to listen further to your insults. I hope that on the morrow you see fit to apologize."

With that she swept out the door, her back stiff with indignation.

Wayne's gaze was sardonic as he watched her departure. "And you, my dear Van. Did you consider me insulting?"

Vanessa gave him a fleeting smile, seeing the laughter in his eyes. "Very definitely, my lord, but not without cause."

"And should I apologize?"

"It would be the gentlemanly thing to do."

"Then you consider me a gentleman?"

Vanessa searched his face. "Very much so," she answered in a low voice. "A wonderful, kind gentleman who took two waifs into his protection when they were homeless."

An odd expression crossed his face. It disappeared immediately, and she was not certain what she had seen.

"Alert Roberts that I shall be up shortly. Then prepare me a cup of hot mulled wine," he ordered brusquely. "I need to sleep soundly tonight."

She hurried to do his bidding. He sipped the wine when prepared for bed. There was little conversation that night, and Vanessa hugged herself against the pain of loss. She had so hoped that there would be a few more warm memories to store for the bleak future.

The viscount remained uncommunicative, and when finished with the mulled wine, he went to bed. Vanessa snuffed out all the candles except those by his bedside and the one necessary to light her way to her cot in the dressing room.

He watched idly as she reached up to open the drapes. It was another warm night, and he preferred the windows open wide to admit any vagrant breezes.

Wayne's eyes narrowed as he watched the flowing movements of her slender body. The candlelight flickered softly over her skin, offering golden highlights to its perfection.

Vanessa paused by the bed and gave him a tremulous smile as she bade him good night and went softly to her cot.

How could he have thought that a lad could have such grace! Only a girl of gentle birth could move so sweetly. A recognizable tremor came to his limbs, and he tossed angrily in his bed.

A vision rose in his mind of her dressed in the height of fashion and under his protection. He could place her in the house he kept in London, an easy walking distance from his own. Her beauty would cause considerable comment when he promenaded with her or had her perched on his high-stepped phaeton.

Was that what she wished for? It would be the quickest way to stop her constant invasion of his thoughts. Experience had taught him how possession caused women to lose their allure for him.

Wayne considered the prospect, then gave pause. He was not one to play with servants. The idea had always been abhorrent to him. But this girl was different, and ah! what better way to extract payment from the chit for daring to trick him so! Her deceit was its own provocation.

He recalled the sensation of the slender body in his arms the night he had held her entrapped on his chair, and he in an instant was out of the bed.

Wayne paused by the door to his dressing room and gazed down at the form outlined by the sheet. There was enough moonlight coming through the window for him to see the dark hair on the pillow, the easy rise and fall of the chest in sleep.

The vision of green eyes was before him again, wide with interest while he recounted a story, bright with excitement when on a good run on the horses, crinkling with humor when laughing . . . and always, always, the underlying innocence that shone within them.

Wayne was appalled by his intent. How could he have envisioned bedding the child? He drew in a slow, ragged breath, reached for the door, and drew it closed.

Vanessa lay on her cot, fighting the tears. Already she was washed by a sense of intolerable loneliness. She fought against her longing and tried to turn her thoughts towards the wonder of finding her father.

A slight sound from the other room alerted her to a movement, and she wondered if she should investigate. Then she realized that the viscount was walking about. The wine evidently had not produced the desired sleep.

He paused by her door. The moonlight in the room behind outlined him as he gazed down at her.

Vanessa did not move as she watched him from under lowered lashes. She forced her breath to remain even as if in sleep, despite a suffocating tumult growing in her.

Finally, when she thought she could no longer stand the pressure building within her, he reached out and closed the door.

Vanessa stared unbelievingly at the closed partition. He had never done that before. Why had he acted so?

Her heart plunged. It was symbolic of the growing rejection she had been conscious of, a silent anger which rose unaccountably at times and was directed against her.

Now the tears did come. Her desolation was complete. She berated herself for her idiotic behavior, but her heart accepted no reasoning. She had been willing to worship from afar, knowing that there would never be a response from him.

Still, her female's heart bemoaned the fact that he would never know her as a woman, never see her in a dress, never remember her as anything but a boy. The men in the village had found her attractive. She had secretly hoped that somehow, someway, he would come to regard her as a desirable woman, that she would see a gleam of appreciation in his eyes.

For one desolate moment she considered fleeing the next day, then reprimanded herself. She was part of the elegant picture he projected. No one living in the country had a page in his household. It was an affectation the *beau monde* played with. She would stay through the entertainment being given in his honor. From the bustling of the servants, it was apparent it had grown into a large affair. If the viscount wished her in attendance, she would remain for this last festivity.

Sleep, when it came, was fitful and full of vague dreams, which caused her to rise the next morning with shadows darkening her eyes.

CHAPTER FOURTEEN

Polly sat dejectedly beside Vanessa while they ate breakfast. Both pushed the food around their plates, unable to take more than a light sampling.

"I asked Roberts if I might have an advance on my pay," Polly said at last. "I told him I needed to buy some clothes, which is true enough, but I thought it best to request it so we have some money when we start off tomorrow."

Vanessa came out of her troubled reverie to agree. "It behooves me to do the same. Do you think he will think it odd if I make the same request?"

"Why, no!" she said with a touch of belligerency. "He knows we both were hired with nothing but what was on our backs. It is only wages due us!"

Polly's tears were perilously near the surface, and Vanessa looked at her with sympathy.

"You love him, don't you." It was a statement. Suffering with the same affliction, she recognized the symptoms.

Polly brushed angrily at her eyes. "It was crazy for me to let it happen. I thought he felt the same, and I lived with impossible dreams for a few short days."

"Surely he is free to marry," Vanessa said.

"Marriage is not what he suggested," Polly answered, her voice quivering with anguish. "I so wanted to agree, but I could not face the consequences."

Vanessa nodded. No matter how secret their meetings, the other servants would have found out. Then, when

Roberts had tired of Polly, her position would have become intolerable. She would have been ostracized and would have had to leave, with luck without child. Meanwhile, Roberts would be secure in his position, but Polly would be a woman marked. The cruelest would be the other women servants, while the men would think Polly fair game when she was no longer under Roberts's protection.

"It is time we both left," Vanessa said bitterly. "I don't know what the future will bring, but at least we have learned not to give our hearts so freely again."

Polly looked at her questioningly, and Vanessa paled. Her unguarded mouth had uttered her painful thoughts.

"You are in love with the viscount!" Polly cried. "Surely you . . . I mean . . . he . . ."

"Don't be a fool!" Vanessa snapped. "I am only a boy, someone he was kind enough to use as his page. I am merely a servant as far as he is concerned."

"But you love him," Polly persisted.

Their eyes met, and they saw the same pain lying in the depths.

"We are both fools." Polly sighed.

"But we have learned our lesson," Vanessa replied stoutly. "Tomorrow afternoon, when Roberts is occupied dressing the viscount for dinner, we will depart."

By that time she would have met with her father and there would be nothing more to hold her. Vanessa had found that Sir Bartongale's plan for the afternoon was to take the viscount to visit a breeder's stable to inspect new stock, and she would be free for that last meeting.

The house was in a turmoil in preparation for the evening's festivities. Extra help had been hired from the village. Vanessa heard that there would be thirty guests, and her apprehension diminished somewhat.

Her father, if he came, would not be likely to recognize her in such a crowd. She would be a servant and, as such, would blend inconspicuously into the background. Besides, he would be seeking a young girl and would never think of looking for someone dressed in male clothing.

Vanessa's only giveaway would be her eyes. She would have to remember to lower them if he should come near.

She and the viscount had taken their usual ride before breakfast, but it had been as unsatisfying as the evening before. The viscount rode Diablo long and hard, and Grey Ghost barely managed to keep up with him. At first Vanessa wondered what demons he was trying to outrun, then realized sadly that the returned black mood was no doubt a result of the conflict Miss Ivy must have stirred in him the evening before. Upon reflection was he now wishing he had accepted what had been offered?

She had then given up the torturing thoughts. She was on a magnificent beast, racing in the still-crisp morning air next to the man she loved, and for the moment that had been sufficient.

That afternoon any hope of completing the tentative meeting with the earl had to be abandoned. Roberts unexpectedly demanded assistance to assure the perfection of the viscount's clothes for the evening. Vanessa suffered silently under his surliness. He seemed to take pleasure in harassing her over small details.

The valet's deportment surprised her. He had been the most amiable of taskmasters up to now; she contributed his caustic words to the pressure upon him to present his lordship in top form.

"You are a good friend of Polly's," Roberts said, minutely examining a pair of white silk stockings for a possible pull.

"I find her an entertaining person," Vanessa admitted.

She continued, realizing that this was an opportunity to praise the girl and make Roberts realize how shabbily he was treating her. "I have nothing but admiration for her," Vanessa continued. "It is evident her mother taught her well, even if they did not have a full purse in the family. In spite of the deplorable situation the last mistress left her in, she has not lost her sense of humor. I always thought humor was an important part of a person's makeup. If I ever marry, I will make certain my spouse has a full measure of it."

"What is a chit of a lad like you talking about marriage!" he cried, and Vanessa backed away from his thunderous expression. "The viscount would never permit his page to have a wife. How could you conceive supporting her without a salary? Or do you expect her to take care of you?" His voice was heavy with scorn.

Vanessa was unable to suppress a laugh. He had twisted her words, giving them a ludicrous interpretation.

"Now who is being ridiculous?" she said. "I was only speaking rhetorically. Polly is too old for me, besides being too smart ever to consider me as a possible marriage partner. She is more your age."

Roberts's face paled as he busied himself sorting through the fine linen handkerchiefs. He said no more, but his hostility abated.

Vanessa took her own uniform to Polly for pressing. It was the fanciest one in the trunk, of pale yellow satin with heavy gold braiding down the front.

Polly frowned while examining Vanessa's offering. "Why didn't you bring it to me earlier?" she grumbled. "Roberts has piled me with more than enough work. He had me redo two outfits despite there being no apparent need."

"I'm sorry, I'll do it myself," Vanessa said agreeably.

"No, you won't!" she returned sharply. "I know my job. I've been properly put in my place."

"There is no need to grouse at me," Vanessa said soothingly. "I have had enough from your Roberts. All afternoon he's been acting as if a thorn rode under his skin. He's the most unreasonable person in existence."

Unaccountably Polly's face crumpled, and she burst into tears. "You do not know him!" she stormed. "He can be fine, and gentle, a-and wonderfully kind!"

Understanding dawned. The poor girl was torn apart by her love and the approaching separation. Was she having second thoughts about rejecting his offer, even though the marriage ring had not been included?

Vanessa placed her arms around the sobbing girl and patted her back in sympathy. Tears were perilously close in her eyes. Both of them had committed the unpardonable sin of falling in love with unattainable men.

"So this is where you have disappeared!"

They looked up, startled, to see Roberts standing in the doorway, glowering angrily. They moved apart guiltily, wondering what had happened now.

"You were hired to assist me," he stormed at Vanessa. "You can make your amorous advances on your own time! You are needed upstairs."

Both girls paled. At any other time Vanessa would have hurried to do his bidding, but a new recklessness arose in her because of the unjustness of his accusation. After all, tomorrow they would be far away from his domination.

"If you took time to see the evidence before your eyes," she seethed, "you would notice that I was only giving condolence to someone in distress. You, of course, would have no cause to recognize the reason behind it!"

Her look of haughty disdain would have done credit to

the viscount. She swept past him, her chin high, her back rigid with barely controlled resentment.

Polly gave Roberts a searing look and turned to the laundry tubs. He was left staring helplessly at her bent back, all anger drained from him.

The guests started arriving on time. They were not members of the *ton*, with whom it was fashionable to arrive late.

Naturally the viscount was part of the receiving line. His elegance bedazzled everyone. The champagne-colored velvet jacket was cut to perfection, accenting the broad shoulders and narrow waist and hips. The long tails backed the satin breeches in a pale peach. No man could show a stronger turn to his legs smartly encased in silk stockings. The points of his collar were just the right height, and the neckcloth, tied in an intricate manner, did Roberts's expert fingers proud. The fobs on his gold chain glittered with precious gems.

Such resplendency would be hard to match, and the Bartongale family stood proudly beside their guest.

Their daughter was not to be outdone. Her gown was the exact shade as the viscount's personal colors, and Vanessa was certain that it had been chosen with care. The décolletage was daring in the extreme, considering the voluptuous bosom which needed to be kept under control. The silver shot material was thin and clinging, and there was evidence of the underslip's being wetted.

Ivy was indeed the object of envy by every woman who passed, not only for her daringly attractive dress but for the handsome lord which rumor said was here to ask for her hand. Most expected the engagement to be announced this evening, and many eyes searched her hand for a tell-tale ring.

Not until Vanessa saw the families arriving did she wonder about her father, the earl. Would he bring a wife, and perhaps children? A queer sensation went through her. She might have half sisters, although she could never publicly claim that connection.

The earl arrived late, when those on the receiving line were thinking of disbanding.

"My lord!" Sir Bartongale cried happily upon hearing his neighbor announced. "You do me a great honor by attending this function, sir. I know it is not your habit to give time to frivolities, but the supper, I guarantee, will make your attendance well worth your time."

Vanessa's heart beat a rapid tattoo against her rib cage upon seeing the tall, gaunt man. Again she was struck by his erect carriage, the arrogant angle to the head so poignantly similar to the viscount's.

Again, his dress was of an older vintage, but impeccably tailored. His was the elegance of a bygone era, and she gazed at him proudly. He was her father, the man her mother had loved even to death. Whatever condemnation Vanessa might feel about his abandonment of her mother, she could not deny a lifting of her senses, a respect tinged by love.

Vanessa's eyes shone with pride when the earl was introduced to the viscount. She gave a silent blessing filled with love, wishing that they would have reason to talk and learn to admire each other.

The viscount searched out the earl, and they retired to a corner, much to Miss Ivy's chagrin.

Even as they conversed, Vanessa saw the earl's gaze move searchingly around the room, and she knew he was looking for her.

When their drinks became low, it was her duty to refill

the glasses. The footmen were accustomed to having her dance attendance and would not approach the viscount.

She had not envisioned this problem's arising and now shook with apprehension. True, the earl and the viscount held the highest titles in the party, but she had not thought that she would have to approach them together.

Praying fervently for anonymity, she took the decanter of fine Madeira which the viscount preferred and approached them, careful to keep her eyes lowered. Dear God, she prayed, let them remain too interested in their conversation to be aware of me!

Only by total concentration could she keep her hands from trembling. She performed her duty, her head bent in a servile position, so that she did not see the thoughtful expression crossing both men's faces as they discontinued their conversation until after she had left. She was nearly overcome when replacing the decanter. She had been so careful to hide her eyes that she had forgotten about the just as exceptional color of her raven hair. Had the earl recognized it? Her general appearance was what had alerted him in the woodland glen. She had always been the picture of her mother except for her eyes.

Only with a stern grasp on her quivering nerves was Vanessa able to concentrate again on the scene before her.

The two men were now separated. Sir Bartongale had the earl in tow, and several men were conversing earnestly with him. His face was stern, as if he had difficulty controlling an anger. Miss Ivy was standing triumphantly next to the viscount, engaged in an animated discussion with the small group surrounding them.

Feeling safe now, Vanessa permitted herself the pleasure of gazing lovingly at the viscount, to drink in the handsome picture he made.

These were country people, so supper was announced

early. The earl, holding the highest title, offered his arm to Lady Bartongale, while her husband led an ancient dowager to her seat. That partnered the viscount with the daughter of the house, and Ivy placed her hand possessively on his arm as they followed the procession to the dining room.

Extra footmen had been hired to do the serving, and Vanessa was free for several hours. Twelve courses had been planned. The menu included wren's soup, glazed mutton, pigeon pie, and baked, freshly caught trout, ending with an exciting raspberry sorbet packed in ice.

It was an ambitious dinner which Lady Bartongale had supervised with efficiency. Apparently her vagueness descended only when she was in contact with her husband and daughter.

Vanessa wandered into the laundry room. Polly was pressing the cleaned clothes, her face set in lines of angry determination.

"Has Roberts been annoying you again?" Vanessa asked.

"I don't wish to hear his name again!" Polly cried. "All I hear is—'this stain still shows; there is a wrinkle still apparent; the viscount expects perfection, and I intend he has it!'" She mimicked Roberts's voice to perfection. "Tomorrow he can struggle with this antiquated iron himself and see how well he can do it," she said grimly. "The only thing preventing me from throwing the clothes at him is the satisfaction of imagining his vexation over the extra work when he discovers I'm not available for his browbeating tomorrow. You haven't changed your plans, have you?"

"No," Vanessa said firmly, recalling the danger of near discovery when she filled the two wineglasses. "Tomorrow in the midafternoon we shall leave. I-I have something to do after luncheon and will take my clothes with me. There is a bridle path north of the stables which leads to the woods behind it. Do you think you can get there unnoticed by three? I will meet you there, and we will begin our journey together." She gave Polly a strained smile. "We are healthy and should have no trouble finding work."

"Roberts gave me my wage, which should help," Polly answered bravely. Her face was pale. Once again she would be without the security of a position. The thought was unsettling.

Vanessa nodded. "I have mine also." It had been given reluctantly, but she had been surprised at the generous amount. "We will have to be careful in its use. If we are lucky, there will be clean barns to sleep in until we find work."

Polly suppressed a shudder. She had not thought beyond the initial escape. Still, if her companion could consider such a thing, she would not show her distaste.

The trays lined with crystal bowls filled with the pink ice were leaving the kitchen, and Vanessa left hurriedly. The final sweet was being served. The ladies would then repair to the drawing room, leaving the men to their port. When they were finished, Vanessa would again have to stand on duty.

The men did not tarry long. They soon joined the ladies in the main salon. Two musicians were produced. One sat at the piano, and the other lifted his violin. The modest orchestra played dance music for the younger guests while the older ones retired to the smaller salon for a game of whist and gossip.

Vanessa stood mutely by the wall, watching the viscount politely partner each girl. His effect upon them was apparent. They were not used to the attentions of so titled a man. Some were mutely panicky, others frenetically gay, while still others seemed reduced to nervous giggles at everything he said. The viscount bore their reactions equally, his face showing its habitual haughty boredom, but Vanessa was vividly aware of the disgust roused in him by such vapid creatures. No wonder he preferred more experienced married women.

Vanessa closed her eyes, picturing the delight of being in his partner's place, and a tremor shook her. This dancing looked so easy, so enchanting! Yearning rose in her breast for what could never be.

There had been so few opportunities in her life to enjoy this lighthearted pastime. There were occasional village dances, but how different they had been from this!

Miss Ivy was again in the viscount's arms. Even though watching them was agony, Vanessa could not take her eyes from the two. They admittedly made a handsome couple. Both had blond hair and blue eyes. While he was tall and arrogantly devastating, she was voluptuously feminine. Miss Ivy was short, barely coming to his shoulder, and Vanessa was never more conscious of her own height.

If she were in his arms, she would have only to lift her head to meet his lips. She winced at the pain of the thought. To be in his arms, to feel his lips . . .

A movement by the door caught her attention. The earl stood there, evidently not playing this hand. He glanced over the dancers before his gaze went to her.

Quickly she averted her head but not before sensing his anger. Had he recognized her? She dared not look back, and her heart thudded with a suffocating beat as he moved closer. He paused near her, and they both watched the dancers for a moment.

"I want to see you on the veranda," he said in a tight, controlled voice. "I shall be waiting for you."

He stood stiffly by her side, his eyes resolutely on the dancers. Still not glancing at her, he passed out through the tall french windows open to the warm evening breezes.

He had recognized her after all! Panic ran through her. Her first inclination was to escape upstairs. Then reason returned, and she followed him nervously.

He had not unmasked her. He was giving her the courtesy of first seeking her explanation. If she refused, she was certain he would approach the viscount, and she shivered, imagining his flaming denunciation when he learned the truth.

She would explain as best she could. When the earl left, revolted by her story, she would have no reason to remain. She was certain he would go immediately to the viscount. Somehow she would have to alert Polly. They could just as easily leave this night.

The earl was standing by the stone railing at the edge of the slated veranda. His gaunt face was in shadow, but his erect carriage bode no good for the outcome of their talk. She moved timorously towards him and stood with her head bowed, her hands clutched together to hide their trembling.

"Well?" he said coldly. "I could not believe it true when I first saw you. What is your excuse?"

Vanessa licked dry lips. "It is an involved story," she began.

"That I can believe. But in the prudence of time I assume you can give me a shortened version."

She flicked a nervous glance at him, searching for some sign of his previous affection, but his face seemed carved from stone. She took a deep breath and plunged into her tale.

"It started when I had to leave my home." She explained her position after she had discovered that her tiny home was padlocked against her and that her half brother had taken off to sea. She quickly described her fright upon seeing the approaching carriage belonging to the squire, her face reddening at the telling, and of how her brother's clothes then offered a solution to how she could travel alone.

A look of incredulity flashed across his face, and he made a move towards her, but her head was bent, too intent on her story to notice.

She told of her starved condition and how grateful she had been when the viscount offered her a position as page.

"How fortuitous for the viscount," he said icily. "It isn't always one can travel with a woman incognito. I thought better of him!"

Vanessa's face flamed. "You are wrong!" she declared, horrified at having placed the man she loved in the wrong. "He thinks of me as a mere boy of sixteen. Look at me in these clothes. If you did not know otherwise, would you think me anything else than what I portray? He does not know I am a woman of almost twenty." There was a hint of bitterness in her words which the earl wondered about.

"But certainly you must attend him in his room," he persisted. He wasn't certain of a page's duty.

"He has Roberts, a very well-versed valet who jealously guards his position," she answered. "I am sent to fetch things, and I make certain to be out of the room while he dresses."

He gazed at her for a long moment, digesting her incredible story while trying to hide his abhorrence at her disguise. "You know I cannot allow my daughter to remain in such a position," he said. "You are returning with me immediately to my home, where I can take care of you. We must get you out of these outlandish clothes, and forget this deplorable episode."

"I-I planned to leave tomorrow after our meeting," she admitted. "I realize this masquerade cannot continue."

"You are right," he said with some vehemence. "But I will not permit you to stay even one additional night."

Vanessa paled. She had been clinging to the hope that there would be one more evening together. She desperately craved one last precious exchange of laughter, of teasing each other's minds in exhilarating exchange. It was all she asked before she left the viscount's side forever.

"I promised I would meet you tomorrow, and I shall," she protested. "I am pledged to stay here until then."

He frowned, ready to argue, but she hurried on. "If you press, I shall leave and you will never see me again," she threatened. It was her only means of stopping him.

He took in the obstinate thrust to her chin, the determination of her stance. "You must promise not to interfere," she insisted.

"I promise," he muttered reluctantly even while giving grudging admiration to this lovely creature who was part of him. "I do not know why, but I give you my word not to demand your immediate removal. But I shall have a promise in return. Tomorrow you will come with me."

"Agreed," she answered readily. "I cannot see why you should want me," she said reflectively. "I am not someone you can hide in a room. Whatever story you manufacture, people will recognize that we have the same eyes and will wonder what the true tale is."

"I realize that," he answered. "I admit that I care not a whit, but I must protect your reputation. Ever since I found you, I have been searching for a plausible story. I had a cousin who took to the Continent to escape pressing creditors. We have not heard from him since. My story is that you are his daughter. I heard of his death, and you have been asked to return to be under my protection. That will account for our eyes being alike."

He would give this lie for her! Her eyes misted with affection.

He drew his breath in sharply upon seeing the tenderness in her face. His throat tightened. This exquisite creature, a reincarnation of his lost Meridel, had been sent to him to ease the lonely years left to him. He could not lose her now.

Still, he knew he must tread lightly. Life had made her independent, and he had to prove himself worthy of her love. He had sensed her resistance when he had arrogantly ordered her to accompany him home.

"I have never married," he said slowly, feeling for the correct words. "I therefore have no known heirs. What I have will be yours, Vanessa."

She gazed at him wide-eyed, overcome by his offer.

"I do not deserve it," she whispered. "I have no need for more than small comforts. In spite of your assurance about the prepared story, I cannot put you in the position to live a lie. You must see that it is best I do not stay."

He was surprised that his offer was being rejected. Time was what he needed, time to accustom her to the comforts he could offer.

"It need only be a short visit," he said persuasively. "Allow an old man a little pleasure. I promise that when you wish to leave, I will not stop you."

"You are not an old man," she protested.

"Indeed, he is not if he entertains any notion you are to visit him!" the viscount said icily from the doorway.

They both turned, startled, to meet his blazing eyes. Vanessa blanched. How much of the conversation had he heard?

"I realize, sir, the attraction my page has for older

men," he said, leveling his fury on the man before him. "I am surprised, though, at your audacity while a guest in this house. I was aware of your interest when he poured the wine and have kept an eye on you since."

The earl showed reciprocal wrath. "You insolent pup!" he raged. "How dare you make such an accusation? It is enough to draw you out!"

The viscount's lip curled. "I do not match swords or pistols with men old enough to be my father, though, by God, if I see you annoying him again, I shall!"

Vanessa looked frantically at the two as they glared at each other. The air was electric with their animosity. If she didn't intervene, there could be blows.

"Please, please!" she cried, running between them. "You have misinterpreted our conversation, my lord." She moved to the viscount, and her hands rested on his chest as she implored him. He glared down at her to meet her beseeching gaze. An odd expression crossed his face, and his hands went of their own volition to cover hers where they rested against him, holding them in place.

They stared at each other, and Vanessa had the earth-shaking sensation that they were standing isolated on a hilltop while the world fell away from them.

She had no idea how long they stood so transfixed, but suddenly she was alone. He had stepped back, stopping abruptly by the open window.

"I am forced to take your words as true," he told her stiffly. "Perhaps now you will see fit to do your duty and not disappear without permission." He turned and went inside.

"The arrogant fool!" the earl raged. "I should take a whip to him! Under no circumstance will I permit you to remain in this house for another minute!"

Shaking violently, Vanessa moved to placate her father. "You gave your solemn promise," she said resolutely.

"That was before I saw him for what he is! It isn't often that I misjudge a man so erroneously. I shudder to think how he will berate you later."

"He shall ignore me," she said sadly, and her heart sank, knowing it to be true.

"It makes no difference. I cannot envision sleeping tonight while worrying about you." His face was taut as he gazed at her. "I would approach Sir Bartongale immediately, but I realize it would not do for them to associate you with their guest's page. However, I shall order my carriage, and you will leave with me."

"Please," she whispered, her hands lying beseechingly on his arm. "Give me these last few hours." Her voice broke as she fought to control her tears. Although the viscount might berate her or ignore her, she could not forgo this last bit of time with him.

The earl saw the threatening tears, and pain tore through him. Twenty years ago another maiden had looked at him in the same way when he had been forced to leave her.

"You love him!" he said accusingly.

Vanessa swayed as she closed her eyes. Her secret was out! Her expression had been unguarded under her duress.

His arms were around her, and she leaned against the tall, wiry man, her head pressed against his shoulder. "Vanessa, Vanessa," he murmured with a catch in his voice. "You foolish, foolish girl. You have stirred yourself a proper kettle of fish."

"I know," she whispered. "But it is my—our secret. I could not prevent it from happening. He is completely unaware of it, and that is my salvation."

He looked at her with bewilderment. Had ever a man

inherited a daughter under such a set of conditions? Of one thing he was certain. Now that he had found her, he would fight for her, do everything in his power to give her the happiness he suspected was seldom hers. He brushed the silky hair from her cheek with a tender gesture. He had reached his decision.

"I have walked into your life. It is only proper that I let you bring this to a close. However, you must promise in return that from tomorrow on I become your protector, my daughter."

She looked up from the comfort of his arms, her face soft with relief. "Yes, Father," she whispered.

She raised on her toes and placed a soft kiss on his cheek before hurrying to follow the viscount into the room. He would be watching for her return, she knew.

She did not see her father stare after her, deep in thought, his fingers over the spot where her lips had touched. He finally drew in a deep breath and went to give his respects to his host and hostess. He would hurry home. Rooms must be prepared; servants, alerted. His mind was a mass of plans, and not until he was in his carriage did he realize that he hadn't felt such happiness in years.

He could now review dispassionately that young rascal's accusation. The viscount had heard the last of their conversation and naturally had arrived at such a conclusion, although the inference exasperated him sorely.

Surprising how heated the young lord had been, he mused. He could understand overseeing the morals of a young lad in his employ, but surely he had been overly intense. He had observed that moment when Vanessa had come between them and they had looked at each other. With any others he would have considered them lovers. Was the viscount perhaps aware of the masquerade? The earl almost turned the carriage around at the thought but paused. He had to prepare the way at home.

Those many years ago, when he had returned after having been forced by his parents to take the European tour, he had entered a period of wild debauchery to drive away his despair at failing to find his love. The earl was not too old to recognize the special look of innocence which clung to his daughter. She was untouched. Her story must be true. The viscount had no idea of his page's true identity.

The earl's first reaction upon arriving at the party had been bitter disappointment at not seeing his green-eyed daughter. His shock when he recognized the page pouring wine had held him speechless. Only his promise not to pay her attention had kept him from demanding an immediate explanation.

The earl had held himself in tight rein until he was driven after supper to seek her out. His heart had lurched upon seeing her slender form standing quietly by the wall. Despite her outlandish uniform, for an instant she was his Meridel, exactly as he remembered her, untouched by time.

He recognized the soft, yearning innocence of her face, filled with love, and he discovered with a start that she was gazing at the viscount. As she thought herself safe from observation, her eyes had given her away.

The earl foresaw the problems the two of them would face should Vanessa's love be returned. Even if the viscount responded and reconciled himself to her duplicity, a man of his high position in society would encounter insurmountable obstacles to his marrying someone in Vanessa's circumstances. A man of nobility simply did not marry beneath his station. Vanessa's heritage was as good as the viscount's, but there was no marriage license to offer as proof. Bitter lines carved the earl's face. Years ago he never would have guessed that his overwhelming love would someday end this way.

The earl frowned deeply. From experience he knew that no problem was impossible to solve. Of one thing he was certain: If it were in his power, this child would be granted the happiness long denied him. It was up to him to assure her acceptance in society. Wisely he realized that this precious girl could not remain his for long. He thought long and hard on the way home.

CHAPTER FIFTEEN

With the earl's departure the other older guests felt free to leave, much to the pouting chagrin of the younger guests. Few dances were given in the country, and they had had an enjoyable time.

The dancers had been lightly chaperoned, most of the elders eager for the card game and their own gossip. Therefore, experimental walks had been taken in the garden with just as experimental pauses in the protective shade of various bushes.

Miss Ivy's face revealed her frustration. She had tried to raise the viscount's interest by flirting with an assortment of amorous swains, but her efforts seemed to have had no effect at all. At the end of one dance she had noticed that he was missing and had relaxed only when he returned alone. He had apparently gone out for a breath of fresh air. If only she had been alert and followed him! She was not having the desired effect on him, and she gnashed her teeth in bafflement. Tomorrow, after a good night's sleep, she would plan a different campaign. She had never lost a battle and was determined to win this most important one.

Vanessa waited impatiently for the frolics to end. She had spent a harrowing time convincing the earl she could stay, especially after the viscount's violent accusation. He had agreed, but she knew he would have overridden all her excuses if he had known she slept in the viscount's bedroom. She shivered at the thought of what her father's reaction would have been.

The viscount waited politely with his host until the last guest left, then informed Vanessa to alert Roberts. He wanted a bath. Vanessa knew it would fall to her to carry up the heavy buckets of hot water. Most of the servants were in bed this late in the evening. Did he make this demand in retaliation? His glance had been cool and indifferent, as if he were barely aware of her.

She struggled up with one bucket. She had been unable to prevent it from hitting her legs, and she was wet from the knees down.

The viscount looked at her with a curl of disdain and turned to Roberts. "That should be enough," he said. "I want only a sponge bath. It was a warm night to do so much dancing. I must think of the others living here. If Van were to bring more buckets, there would be a waterfall down the stairs."

Vanessa's face flamed at his caustic words. How foolish of her to have hoped for one last night to cherish. She should have left with her father.

Her mouth curved dejectedly as she gathered the viscount's discarded clothes, then hurried out as he approached the tin tub, untying his robe.

The kitchen was empty, the debris associated with the aftermath of a large party only partially cleared away. The exhausted servants had retired, planning to complete the clearing in the morning.

Vanessa placed the clothes in the washroom. Would Polly have time to do them before they left? Her fingers caressed the fine linen of his shirt, and suddenly her face was buried in it. She inhaled deeply of the perfume he used, the man scent, and her senses swirled. Tears started, and she cried as if her heart would break.

This was the end. She had never harbored false hopes for a return of her love, but she would have willingly settled for his friendship. For the past few days even that had been denied her.

She bathed her eyes in cool water, hoping his lordship would not notice their redness. She would claim a headache and the need for bed and realized with surprise that she did indeed feel a throbbing pain at her temples.

She dragged herself up the stairs, wondering what final denouncment he would heap upon her. Her mouth twisted bitterly. She had become his whipping boy, a role she would have been too proud to tolerate in any other circumstances.

Is this what love did to people, strip them of all respect, feed on the desperate need to be near the object of their loves? How demeaning! But she was helpless in its grip. Thank goodness she and Polly had made their plans to disappear.

Polly! So much had happened that she had forgotten about their pact. She had promised her father to go with him but could not desert the girl now. Would he perhaps find room for her in his household?

When Vanessa entered the bedchamber, she found the viscount already in bed, propped up with pillows and reading a book. She gave a little sigh of relief. She could slip into bed unchallenged.

She moved quietly around the large four-poster bed to the wardroom which held her cot, her eyes heavy with sleep.

"I want a word with you, Van."

Vanessa halted, standing dejectedly with her head bowed, waiting for his castigating words to fall.

His silence made her finally raise her head and look at

him. The intimate picture of him in bed precipitated a quivering along her nerves.

Vanessa was not surprised to see that the mask of boredom the viscount presented to others was gone now. At one time she had reveled in the pleasure of seeing his expression change with each shift of topic. Now she saw a firmness which boded no good, and she quickly lowered her lashes.

Wayne had been sorely provoked when he had come upon her with the earl. There had been something intimate about the picture they presented which had sent a sharp thrust of pain shooting through him. If he hadn't known better, he would have considered it akin to jealousy.

He was rapidly becoming tired of addressing her as a lad, but it would not do to unmask her now and face the embarrassing questions his host would raise. Once they were gone from this place, he would have the pleasure of taking her to task for her deceit.

"You need a few facts explained to you," Wayne began in a remote voice. "You are too handsome for your own good. For some unaccountable reason you still retain an innocent air about you. I daresay you have learned to cope with women lured by it, but there are others who examine you also."

Vanessa's face crimsoned, knowing what was coming, but not how to stem the tirade. She knew how men looked at her. She had experienced that discomfort since reaching maturity. It was an odd twist of fate which made immune the one person whom she wished to attract.

"You were incorrect about your assertions to the earl," she said stubbornly.

"Perhaps I am thick-witted," he said bitingly. "I have gone over the conversation I overheard, and I cannot give the words any other meaning. Perhaps you can explain them more clearly to me." He had, in fact, been apprehensive that the earl had uncovered her subterfuge.

Vanessa's lower lip extended in a mulish expression. She was trapped. There was no possible explanation she could give.

He examined her angrily. This chit, whom he thought pliable, was proving to have a deplorable stubborn streak. He had tolerated as much as he could. He had expected to play the cat, taunting a mouse, but the game had suddenly become unpalatable.

"It is late, and I have no desire to argue," he said, dismissing her. "We will go into this further in the morning."

Wayne watched her hurry to her room. He stared at his book in disgust, then tossed it aside angrily. He had not digested one word since opening it. He blew out the candles and settled into bed.

A grimace flitted across his face. Resentment burned in him over the awkward position in which he was now placed. Dammit! No creature should have the ability to stir him this way. He bitterly cursed the day he had ever come upon her. The whole trip had been ill-fated from the beginning, although it had begun auspiciously enough with the letter from the willing baroness Audrey.

As he thought about Vanessa's silken body, his restlessness grew. He tossed in bed, wondering if he should avail himself of the offer from down the hall.

A muffled sound came from the next room, and he was instantly alert. It was not repeated, but he was certain it was a sob. Wayne lay rigid in bed, horrified by his overpowering desire to go to the chit and soothe her. He had been a brute, accusing her of such an evil transgression with the earl, but he had been driven as if by the devil himself.

Recalling his heated words, he now felt embarrassed. It would have been sheer folly if the earl had called him out. Aside from her deceit, the girl's attitude towards him had been above reproach. It was one aspect of the charade which puzzled him. Could it be she had no ulterior motive?

His hand went to his chest, and he frowned into the darkness. He had tried to avoid remembering, but now in the black solitude he again felt the slender hands quivering under his as they lay on the broad expanse of his chest. Again he was looking into her beseeching eyes, conscious of the odd sensation of their being as one. His breath came rapidly, and he found his heart pounding at an alarming rate.

Wayne hit the pillow in his frustration. Damn those eyes, those green witch's eyes! Tomorrow he must send her away.

CHAPTER SIXTEEN

Vanessa awoke from a deep sleep. From the set of the sun she realized it was late. Had the viscount gone riding without awakening her?

She rose sluggishly, remnants of an unhappy dream clinging to her. She remembered crying bitterly over something, and the dream's depression still lay heavily upon her.

She dressed hurriedly and stopped at the doorway to stare fascinated at the bed. The long body of the viscount lay sprawled across its length. The sheet wound about him indicated that he, too, had suffered a restless night.

The viscount's face was slightly flushed, his blond hair rumpled. He looked heartrenderingly vulnerable, like a young boy, and it took all her willpower not to smooth his hair from his forehead.

Vanessa's face was filled with longing tenderness, and the intensity of her gaze must have caused him to open his eyes. They stared at each other for a breathless second. In that moment of sleepy awakening there was no pretense, and she quivered at what she saw in his eyes.

The awareness was gone instantly, and his lordship became fully awake. He gave a muffled oath, and she was left wondering at the heavy beating of her heart.

"Why are you standing there?" he said sharply. "Get Roberts. You can't even attend to the simple duty of waking me in time for my morning ride!"

Vanessa retreated in confusion. Not until she gave Roberts his order did her heart stop its mad beating. She was filled with a fierce happiness. She had been given her going-away present after all. In that one sleepy moment he had been poignantly hers. She did not try to decipher what had happened when he had first awakened. It was breathlessly similar to what had occurred the night before when his hand had covered hers.

The morning seemed to drag interminably. Several times the viscount seemed at the point of telling her something. Then he would turn away, his mouth set in a firm line.

At least his manner was coolly agreeable, and she was thankful for that. If he had been caustic, she was afraid she would have dissolved into tears. She was filled with a dull ache, knowing that this was her last bittersweet time with him.

She managed a moment of whispered conversation with Polly. "Are you still prepared to go?" she asked. "If you wish to remain, I will understand. There is a slight change of plans. Can you leave a half hour after I do?"

The pale girl was visibly shaken, but she stiffened her shoulders resolutely. "I will be there." She gave a hysterical giggle which indicated the tension she was under. Her eyes then widened as she stared at the door.

Roberts had come in to give them a baleful glare. The fool! Vanessa fumed. Instead of glowering at them in jealousy, he should make Polly an honest offer. He would have to go far to find a better helpmate.

At last the late breakfast was over, and the men prepared to ride to examine the touted bloodlines of a neighbor's stable. As soon as she heard their horses pound down the drive, Vanessa ran upstairs to retrieve her small bundle of clothes. She would have to keep on the outfit she now wore but would change into her dress as soon as she reached the safety of the trees.

Vanessa managed to leave the house undetected, her bundle clutched in her hand. She longed to say a last good-bye to Grey Ghost, the lovely mare the viscount had bought for her use. Her lips quivered, remembering the joy of their morning rides together. Those memories she would hug to her heart.

She traveled a circuitous route which shielded her from view from the house. As she slipped into her dress, she made a silent pledge. The events of the past two weeks must not be allowed to cause her further anguish. She was meeting a wonderful man who was her father. He had shown amazing compassion and understanding, and for as long as he desired her to stay, she would devote herself to making him happy. She would not let her heartache encroach upon this new adventure.

Her only problem was Polly, and she was certain the earl would give her a position. If not, her obligation was to the girl, who was giving up steady employment to go into the unknown upon her instigation. Vanessa walked down the path, beset by mixed emotions, until she reached the quiet glen.

The earl was staring thoughtfully into the little running brook, and she took in the quiet elegance of his tall figure. This was her father! The knowledge caused a lump to rise in her throat.

He turned upon hearing her, and the light which sprang into his deeply set eyes caused her to give a little cry. She ran the remaining distance into his open arms. He held her gently, tenderly, as if afraid she might disappear.

"Ah, Vanessa," he murmured. "I was being tagged by the very devil with fear you might not come, that the whole incredible discovery was a figment of my imagination."

Vanessa smiled at him, suddenly shy. Her precipitous catapult into his arms had come naturally, but she knew it was not maidenly. He must think her conduct hoydenish!

The thought was farthest from his mind. He was like an excited youngster, anxious to take her home.

"Come," he urged. "My carriage is waiting down this path. Once you are settled, we can have our promised talk. There is so much I want to hear about your . . . mother."

"First I have a favor to ask of you, sir." She hesitated and gazed anxiously at him. Would his kindness extend this far? "I have a friend, Polly, who was in the viscount's service also. We planned to leave together, and now I cannot desert her. She has no place to go. She is an abigail. Would you know of anyone needing such services? She has been most kind to me."

"By all means, she must come with us!" he quickly agreed. "She will be the answer to a problem I have handed over to my housekeeper. I had no need for a lady's maid in my bachelor existence but realized you would require one."

Vanessa blinked, overcome with the idea of having her own handmaiden. Was this the life he offered? Then she thought happily of Polly. She would be more like a friend, someone to confide in when she was heartsore, when she remembered whom she had left behind.

She flew over the path to find Polly waiting nervously for her arrival. As she pulled her along, Vanessa explained in hurried sentences what had transpired. The poor girl gaped in amazement, and even when sitting behind them in the phaeton, she could hardly grasp the unbelievable story. Polly could only hang on as the formidable earl, who was supposed to be her friend's father, urged the horses to a fast trot. Somehow the tale would be straighten out later, but for now her head fairly spun. For the moment, at least, the bleakness in her soul at leaving behind Roberts, the man she loved, was driven out.

The earl did indeed own a castle. It was small but boasted a crenellated roof and towers. There was even a moat, now a mere puddle of water with ducks in it, and a drawbridge which was permanently in the lowered position.

The horses' hooves echoed hollowly as they rode across the bridge. A lackey ran out to hold the animals when the earl pulled to a stop before a large brass-studded oak door.

He turned to his daughter with a smile. "Welcome home, Vanessa," he said simply, and her smile hung tremulous with excitement.

She looked wonderingly at the stone edifice before her. Was this to be her home? It was built of local grey stone. The narrow windows indicated its advanced age, but all seemed in good repair.

The earl offered his arm, and Vanessa placed her hand on it as they walked up three broad steps. The heavy door was thrown open as if on cue, and they moved into a baronial hall.

Vanessa's first impression was hazy. There was too much to assimilate: tapestries, which later she learned were priceless, hung on the wall; a suit of armor stood beside a fireplace large enough to walk into. Above it was an impressive coat of arms, and this more than anything made her realize the remarkable change in her position in life.

A line of servants stood by the broad staircase, waiting to be introduced.

203

"Minton, the butler, my dear," the earl started. "Minton, meet your mistress. My daughter, Lady Vanessa."

Vanessa looked at him, startled. That was not the story concocted last night! She collected herself quickly as she smiled charmingly at the grey-haired man bending over her hand. It would not do to protest before the servants.

"Welcome to Moorhaven, my lady," he intoned, and Vanessa wondered at his look of satisfaction.

Many were old servants, their lives one with the castle. They had been thrown into a tizzy last night, when his lordship had arrived from the party. The earl had called his butler and housekeeper to the library. They had hurried to the call, wondering about the unheard-of order.

His story had been well prepared. He had just received a message, he had informed them, that his daughter, whom he had thought lost to him, was coming home. He need not tell them the full story now. Surely they must remember that as a young man he had been sent on his tour of Europe. While visiting Italy, he had become enamored of a beautiful contessa. They had been married, but when it came time for him to return, she refused to leave the comforts of her home in sunny Italy for an England she had heard was always dismally cold and inhospitable. Only then did he realize how her parents had indulged her every whim. When he insisted upon her coming, they had backed her in refusing to make the change.

He had returned alone, hoping she would come to her senses during his absence, but the months had dragged on until he realized there was faint hope for a reconciliation. Now they knew why he had never married to produce an heir. Divorce, of course, was out of the question.

Not until years later did he learn that there was a daughter. He made an effort to visit her but was refused, and he finally decided that a girl's place was naturally with her mother.

Imagine his surprise upon receiving a missive two days ago stating that his daughter was now in England. In fact, she had spent the last few years being educated here. The grandparents and mother were now dead, and she naturally wanted to meet her remaining relative. The earl paused again, satisfied with the rapt attention being given to his tale. Of course, his joy had at first been tempered by doubt. Before bringing her home, he must inspect her to make sure she was not an impostor. Therefore, he had not said anything to them before now.

Upon his seeing her, all doubt had vanished, and now the house must be made ready. The state bedroom suite next to his must be prepared. He would bring her home the next afternoon.

The earl cast glances at his servants as he glibly continued his story. If they took it as whole cloth, the gossip which leaked out would do much to clear the way for Vanessa's future. They were old retainers, had been part of his inheritance. He had kept the story close to what they knew. After all, he *had* spent the year in Europe, so the marriage could have taken place then. They had also weathered his few years of wild living when he returned. He had been desperately trying to bury his pain upon being unable to locate his only love. They would now attribute that period to heartache over a fractious wife.

He watched them assimilate the story, fitting the segments into what they knew about him. If they still had doubts, he was certain that seeing Vanessa would dispel them.

The earl had lain awake far into the night, searching for ways to perfect his story. Upon sunrise he had risen to call his valet. Clausen not only was a faithful servant, but had proved to have a solid head on his shoulder as well. Above all, he was very discreet.

The earl told the true story to Clausen, after first swearing him unnecessarily to absolute secrecy. He then sent him posthaste to Edinburgh. The earl's own carriage would carry him there quickly. In Clausen's hands rested his daughter's ultimate happiness.

Now, as he introduced Vanessa to each servant, from the butler to the lowest scullery maid, he saw them capitulate to the slender girl's graceful charm. He saw with satisfaction that each of them noticed her remarkable green eyes, so like his own, the talisman he had depended upon to make his story completely believable.

The pictures in the gallery clearly showed the same color eyes handed down through successive generations.

"Is her ladyship's luggage to follow later?" Minton asked the earl when the last maid bobbed a shy curtsy and left the hall.

Vanessa paled. How did one explain their absence?

"It should arrive tomorrow," the earl replied. "I ordered her to come posthaste and let the cases follow. I sent Clausen to supervise their shipment. I think tea is in order; then a rest might be desirable. Please show Polly, her abigail, to the rooms."

With a decorous "Very good, sir," Minton bowed himself out. He was bursting to see Mrs. Blake, the housekeeper, and compare their reaction to the incredible occurrence. No one could deny those eyes! His lordship's story must be true. This explained the periods of moodiness from which no one had been able to rouse him.

Vanessa barely controlled her questions until Minton deposited the heavy ornate silver service before her. Mrs. Blake followed, carrying the tray with thin sandwiches and delicate cakes.

"You shouldn't have told them I was your daughter," she cried accusingly when the door was closed. "We agreed I would be a sort of niece."

He gazed at her somberly. "You made that story impossible to carry out when you called me Father. I was not going to deny myself the pleasure of hearing it from your lips again." The air pulsed with emotion, and he changed the subject. "I take two sugars and a spot of milk in my tea," he said, smiling.

Vanessa poured carefully, thankful that she had on several occasions observed Mistress Martin perform the ritual at the squire's house.

The earl watched the natural grace of her movements, and a wonder that his love could have produced so lovely a creature filled him.

She nibbled tentatively on a sandwich, every glance a question until he capitulated to her silent pressuring.

"It is best I tell you the story I told the servants," her father said, replacing his empty cup. "Last night we both realized the need for fabrication of some sort of background for you. The one I decided upon fitted in with my own life."

Quickly he ran over the story first related the night before.

"Have you ever been to Italy?" he asked. "It would be good to use a town you know as your place of birth."

"There were times we had nothing but bread and weak tea," she answered, giving a smile to tender her gentle rebuke.

He lowered his head to hide the flash of pain. What an unthinking dolt he was! Her story had indicated the difficult times they had suffered. "It is of no consequence," he said.

"No one locally has been there. I will, however, give

you some books I have on the country, and you will have to take lessons in the language. As soon as I can get my estates in order here, I intend to take you to Italy so that any future questions can be answered realistically. Would you like a trip through the Continent?"

Vanessa's face glowed. The books she had read had made her dream of such a trip. Could it actually come true?

His stern features softened. He had thought he would never make the tour again after the bitter memories of that first enforced exile. Now he was anxious to unveil the sights to this lovely creature.

"We'll do it," he said with boyish enthusiasm. "But for now I will satisfy your curiosity about your home. Come, we will start with the state rooms. Tomorrow Mrs. Blake can show you the rest."

The main room was as impressive as the entrance hall. The furniture was handsome and undeniably old. Large Dutch and Flemish paintings hung on the walls. The banquet hall could seat thirty guests with ease. Each room had a huge fireplace, and Vanessa guessed that in the winter fireplaces were a necessity to make the rooms livable. It had been a hot June, but the rooms were still chilly. The sun's warmth could not penetrate the thick stone walls or flow through the narrow windows.

The grandeur was overwhelming but slightly depressing, the gloom accented by the occasional slit of light which managed to find its way inside. While clean, the rooms had an unused air about them, and the earl informed her they were seldom occupied.

"I open them only when I entertain," he admitted. "And I have had little cause to do that. Now it will be different," he said with satisfaction. "The news of a daughter's sudden appearance will soon be known in every household. I will be expected to give a reception to introduce you formally to the neighborhood."

Vanessa looked apprehensive, but he smiled reassuringly. "Do not fret, my dear. I shall remain by your side and see that it does not become an ordeal." The rooms he now led her through were more to her taste, smaller and less intimidating. Evidently this was where the earl did his living. There was a library lined with books she was eager to start investigating, a study he said he used as his office, and a small drawing room with comfortable, though faded, furniture.

"I never realized the need for redoing," he said with some surprise, seeing his apartments with new eyes. "I will leave the task in your capable hands."

The delicious aroma of roasting meats came from one corridor, and the earl pulled out his pocket watch in surprise.

"How thoughtless of me, my dear," he apologized. "I have been intent upon showing you everything instead of allowing you time to rest. I will take you to your rooms immediately."

Vanessa had never beheld so lovely a bedroom. The walls had been paneled and painted a pale blue. Flowered carpets were thick and soft underfoot. A chaise was upholstered in a gold and blue silk which matched the bedspread on the huge four-poster bed. The pale blue canopy was covered with sprigs of tiny pink rosebuds, while chubby pink cherubim decorated the ceiling. The dresser, the chair, and the desk were white, the carvings rubbed with gold. It was a room fit for a bride. Vanessa glanced up at the tall man beside her. His eyes were brooding upon her; his sadness was apparent.

"Yes," he said softly. "I had it prepared for your mother while I was searching for her. Now her daughter—our daughter—will finally use it."

She quivered at the pain in his voice. "Then you did not intentionally desert Mamma?"

He stiffened in indignation. "Desert her!" he exclaimed. "How dare you even suggest such a thing!"

Seeing her step back from his anger, he immediately apologized. "I forget, my dear, that you do not know my story. We will speak further after dinner. I am as impatient as you to unravel what happened twenty years ago."

Polly came hurrying from an adjourning room when the earl left, her eyes wide with excitement. "I am overwhelmed, Lady Vanessa!" she cried rapturously. "Come and see the rest of the fabulous rooms."

She opened a door to show a tremendous wardrobe. "Can't you see all these hooks and shelves filled with your clothes? And look here, a separate room for your bath with a fireplace to take off the chill. And come here," she urged, pulling Vanessa to another room. "It is small but ideal for my use. See, I have a private entrance to the hall so I need not disturb you. In most homes the abigail sleeps upstairs, which makes it difficult always to be in attendance."

Her happiness was contagious, and the two girls hugged each other, giggling from sheer excitement. They examined the rooms once more.

"I could learn to be content here," Vanessa said wistfully. "It shouldn't take long to forget . . . what might have been." Her eyes misted, but she wiped angrily at them and smiled.

"Do you think the earl can be approached about new clothes for you?" Polly asked. "Men don't think about such things, but you can't continue wearing only one dress."

"I don't know," Vanessa admitted. "Perhaps he will let us go to town tomorrow so that we can buy some material to make some. We don't have to hoard our money now for food and lodging."

"Well, for tonight we will have to do with what we have, my lady. Let me help you off with your dress so that I can at least press it. It is so rumpled you look as if you slept in it. I was so ashamed before all the servants when you were introduced. They must think me a terrible lady's maid. I can only hope they think that the ride here was long and difficult. Why are you looking at me so?"

Vanessa was standing before her. "You cannot call me Lady Vanessa," she protested.

"That's who you are." Polly bristled. "The earl introduced you so before the servants. It would never do to let them hear me call you anything else. Especially Van," she ended impishly.

Vanessa gave an uncertain smile, tinged with pain. The name immediately brought the viscount to mind. Polly recognized the desolation in Vanessa's eyes, and her lips firmed. They both had been forced to turn their backs on hopeless loves.

Briskly Polly unbuttoned Vanessa's dress and hurried out with it to search for the ironing room, leaving Vanessa to soak reflectively in the tin tub painted with bright garden flowers.

The ironed dress was a vast improvement, and Polly arranged Vanessa's hair to curl artfully around her face before weaving in ribands she had found in a drawer.

The earl, looking every inch the lord of the house, was waiting for Vanessa at the foot of the stairs as she descended. For an instant she saw the handsome, dashing man who had captured her mother's heart.

His eyes were broodingly on the slender girl as she

descended, and he felt a pang of regret that he could not make time stand still. Anyone as lovely as she would not be with him long. She would set the countryside on its ear after being introduced next week at the reception ball he planned, and the young cubs would soon be lining up to ask for her hand.

They did not eat in the echoing banquet hall. He led her instead to a room bright from the setting sun, where six could eat comfortably.

"I thought you would prefer eating here rather than being formal," he said, sitting her opposite him. "You will note that I had the windows enlarged in these rooms to let in more light. It was an arduous task chipping at two-foot-thick walls, but worth the effort."

While the footmen changed the courses, he described to her the countryside, the neighbors and their families, and the extent of his holdings.

"I try to balance the land's use," he explained. "The tenants grow an assortment of produce. I have left much in woodland for game and logging. In the hills farther north I also run sheep."

Vanessa immediately recalled her conversations with the viscount on that subject, and the earl was amazed at her knowledge as she intelligently discussed the details of his project.

She was no vacuous female. Her quick mind had caused her to rise above her environment, and pride warmed him. He did not believe that women were only ornaments. If his daughter were to inherit his lands, he would want her to know how to handle them, at least how to check on them through the bailiff. Normally it would be a husband's job, but he had seen too many valuable estates mishandled when inherited by untutored men.

The meal ended all too soon. The earl could not remember when he had enjoyed himself so much. It was a rare situation—a learned teacher and an avid pupil.

They retired to the salon, and when Minton exited after placing the coffee service before her, Vanessa gazed at her father expectantly, waiting for him to begin his story.

He placed his cup reluctantly on the table, mentally steeling himself against the pain which always tore at him when the subject was brought up. Still, if he wanted to know what had happened, he had to tell his part of it.

"I met your mother when I was a youth still in Oxford," he began. "There I found my interest lay in mathematics and science. There was a Professor Smithson whose brilliance attracted me, and I sought him out whenever possible. It wasn't long before the other students teased us about being like father and son.

"It was true. I came late in life to my parents, after they had given up hope for a child. My father was a difficult man, always demanding perfection. Since that was impossible where I was concerned, he preferred to ignore me. My mother devoted her time to her horses. The hunts and races were her whole life."

He paused, frowning, a faraway look in his eyes. "When Professor Smithson invited me to his home one evening for dinner to discuss further an abstract formula he was devising, I was only too happy to accept. He was not in the habit of doing so, although other professors did so frequently.

"I soon discovered why. His wife had been highborn but had been ostracized by her parents when she chose to marry beneath her station. She had soon found that the salary of a don could not support her as she demanded, and she had become an embittered woman. I now understood why he spent so much time at the university.

"I soon forgot my observation when a vision of loveliness came to sit at the table with us. I imagine I was formally introduced to their daughter. All I remember was that her name was Meridel, and I thought I had never heard a more perfect name for so beautiful a maiden."

Again the earl paused. The memory was strong and produced such an exultant expression on his face that Vanessa's throat constricted.

"For six months I lived, breathed, and dreamed with Meridel ever on my mind, all intensified by the knowledge that this heavenly creature reciprocated my feelings. We managed several secret meetings as lovers the world over do. And as lovers our dream was to be married as soon as possible.

"There we ran into problems. Her mother would not consider it. I might be a prospective earl, but at present my pockets were hard let." The earl's face reflected remembered bitterness.

"When the end of term came, I vowed that I would enveigle my father to permit the marriage. I was only twenty to your mother's seventeen, and we required parental permission. But I was sure when my father saw the loveliness of the flower I had captured, he would give his blessing.

"As soon as I introduced Meridel, I realized our hopes were doomed. I was informed that he had other marriage plans for me. My father would not consider any plea.

"In the manner of lovers we were beside ourselves, vowing that we would not wait until we came of age. We made plans to run off to Gretna Green, a day's fast run from here. We hoped that our parents would then give their blessings.

"We accomplished our escape, but Lady Luck soon laughed at us. We were only halfway there when night fell. Then a wheel buckled after hitting a pothole, and we could go no farther. We had deliberately searched out the back roads and were in a deserted area. There was nothing we could do but wait until daybreak and assistance.

"It became chilly, and I placed the rugs under the tilted carriage to ward off the dampness. We made our bed there."

The earl's face was pale, and he rose to pour a glass of brandy. He now stood before the small fire as if seeking its warmth, and he finished the story, his back towards the quiet girl.

"Yes, we were discovered the next day. We were dragged home like escaping convicts. I was ordered to take a year's tour, as had already been planned. I raged like a bull but could not move my father, and Meridel was quickly bundled off.

"We were allowed only ten minutes to say our good-byes, with the family in attendance. I vowed that I would return for her as soon as the year ended and I was no longer under their jurisdiction. She was ushered out, and I was left heartsick. I could not even touch her, have one final kiss.

"That was the last I ever saw her."

The sentence was spoken in a whisper of agony. Tears coursed unheeded down Vanessa's cheeks. She longed to go to him, to offer sympathy and understanding, but she sensed his need to be alone to conquer his grief.

"Once I told her I wished I had her pretty blue eyes instead of my coloring," Vanessa said softly. "She assured me that seeing my green eyes reminded her of the happiness she had once possessed. I thought at the time that she meant someone in her family because she spoke with love. I now know she meant you."

He turned to her, his face lit with joy. "Thank you, Vanessa," he said humbly. "Those words are a gift beyond compare. In deep despondency, I thought she had married because she had learned to hate me, that I was alone in my steadfast devotion. But why did she not wait?" he cried painfully. "I could not find the answer to that."

"Perhaps because she found herself with child and did not know which way to turn," Vanessa murmured. "You said her mother was much like your father. What could she do with you away for a year? I know there was a breaking away from her parents. She spoke gently of her father but never of her mother. I never met them. I didn't even know their names or where they lived."

The earl sank into a chair and buried his ashen face in his hands. "I drove her to it!" he groaned hoarsely. "I wrote to her at least once a week, but when I received no answer, I realized her mother must be intercepting the messages."

He took a deep breath before continuing. "When I returned, I discovered that the professor had died and the house was occupied by others. I hired runners to search for Meridel's mother. When I found her in a small apartment, she heaped scathing remarks upon me, telling me that Meridel had married another man. I was stunned but determined to find her. She would never tell me where Meridel was and never mentioned there was a child.

"Whom did she marry? I had no name, so I could not go any further."

"I can only guess at what occurred from what little I've been told," Vanessa said in a low voice. "Evidently, when she learned she was with child and perhaps had been thrown out by her mother, she went to see your parents, seeking help.

"On her deathbed she gave me the barest outline of what had happened. Your parents must have denied her petition to contact you but offered her money. Evidently one of your gardeners was outside the window and heard everything. Anxious for the money, he offered to marry her. I can understand how desperate she must have been. What was to become of her with a child and no husband for protection? It was the only avenue she could take.

"I remember that he was handsome when I was young. It was only later when drinking became an obsession . . ."

The earl jumped from the chair, his expression like a wild man's. "The gardener!" he shouted. "Oh, my God, forgive me, Meridel!" With that cry of torture he stumbled blindly from the room.

It was a long time before Vanessa had the energy to follow. She sank into bed, grateful for sleep to still her whirling thoughts. Her questions had been answered, but she felt that she had lived a lifetime since that morning.

CHAPTER SEVENTEEN

"Pardon me, my lord," Roberts said, entering the bedroom where the viscount had repaired to dress for dinner.

Wayne glanced at his valet, noting the worried crease between his brow. "What is it, Roberts?" he asked indulgently. Roberts appeared exceptionally perturbed, and he wondered if the problem was a stain that wouldn't erase from a garment or an improperly starched neckpiece. It was time Roberts married, he thought, before he became a fretful old maid.

"It is Polly and, I believe, Van, your page," he answered.

Wayne became immediately alert. He raised an inquiring eyebrow at his valet. "What have the two done now?" he asked.

"I-I do not know," Roberts replied. He rubbed his hands together in agitation. "They are nowhere about. I went to speak to Polly and could not find her. When the maids said she had gone out early in the afternoon, I became worried. A stableboy said he had seen her go to the woods behind the house and," he continued, his voice tightening in anger, "he had also seen Van enter the woods a short while before."

"Why your anxiety? There are no rogues about to accost them." The viscount turned so that Roberts could remove his jacket. He didn't want Roberts to see the concern the news gave him. Why this cold dread spreading in his chest?

"I believe they have left," Roberts cried in anguish. "I should have been aware of the possibility when they both asked for their wages."

"What!" the viscount exclaimed. "Why should they wish to do that? Were you harsh with them?"

Roberts's face reddened. "I did remonstrate with Van for showing too much attention to Polly. I did not realize their affection ran so deep. They must have taken off in retaliation."

The viscount examined the troubled expression on his man's face. Could it be he was enamored of the abigail and was suffering from jealousy? He would have laughed over the situation except for the apprehension spreading within himself.

Poor Roberts! He still did not realize that Van was a girl and his jealousy misplaced. But where had the two gone? This was indeed an odd way for Van to end her masquerade.

"Perhaps they have only gone to town and misjudged the distance," the viscount said in a dismissing voice. He would not permit Roberts's announcement to perturb him. "If they are not back by supper, you are to discharge them. I will not have servants who wander off without permission."

The viscount swallowed hard against the rage rising in his chest. How dare the ungrateful creature take off like this! Hadn't he housed and fed her when she was destitute? He breathed deeply to smother his anger. Roberts's assumption that they had absconded must be incorrect. There must be a simple cause for their delay in returning.

Neighbors had included him in an invitation to dinner with the Bartongales. Afterwards he would deal severely with the truant chit.

When he returned later that night, he did not need to

ask Roberts if the two had returned. Unhappiness clouded the valet's face. Only by strong forbearance did the viscount restrain himself from further questioning. He was well rid of the troublesome twit, he assured himself grimly. Her departure assured him of a night untroubled by her irritating presence.

Unfortunately it was not so. The bedchamber proved hauntingly empty. He found himself listening for the slightly husky voice rising in question. The sound of her musical chuckle kept echoing in his mind, and the flickering candlelight caused dancing shadows, reminding him of her graceful walk. He tried to read but finally threw the book down in disgust. Green eyes were gazing at him from each page.

Anger welled up in him. No woman had ever bedeviled him like this. He was well rid of her. He had requested Roberts to bring him a brandy. For some reason he could not partake of wine, as was his custom. There was no dark head bending near him to replenish his goblet. He refilled his glass and knew he was well on his way to being foxed, but the visions kept dancing before him. Damn the girl! Did he have to hunt her down so that he could properly denounce her and rid his mind of her?

Wayne fell into bed and scowled into the darkness. The drinking had loosened his pretensions, and he now looked into his heart, groaning aloud over what he saw there. He was possessed by a green-eyed witch, and he recognized his agony as love.

He pounded his pillow in self-derision but faced the truth of his discovery. The question now was what was he going to do about it. His mind whirled in a fever of excitement. Marriage, he knew, was impossible under the circumstances. He would find her and set her in his *maison d'amour.* He burned with the need to hold her close, to possess her soft lips.

Tomorrow he would start a search for the two of them. His morning ride would now have a purpose. They shouldn't prove difficult to find. They could not have traveled far on foot.

The earl was at breakfast when Vanessa came down in the morning. Sometime during the night he had come to terms with his private devil, but the toll taken showed in the deepened lines on his face.

"There is no need for you to rise this early, my dear," the earl said, ringing for a fresh pot of coffee.

"But I consider this the best time of the day," Vanessa assured him. "I have no riding outfit, or I would have asked to go with you to see the properties you described so well last night. Which brings me to a problem."

She paused, looking at him anxiously. "I have only this dress and must make more. Is there some way we can go to town to buy some material? Polly and I can then start sewing a presentable wardrobe."

"I have considered the problem," he said with a smile. "I have sent for some dresses for you, and if we are lucky, they should be here tomorrow. I do not think it wise for you to go to town at present."

A shadow crossed her face. "I-I do not think I would be recognized, but you are right. Someone from Sir Bartongale's might see Polly."

"The viscount has never seen you in a dress?" he asked quietly.

Vanessa shook her head sadly. "No, to him I was only a boy."

His gaze took in the soft droop to her lips, the obvious

dejection, and he gave a small sigh. How twisted were the strands of one's life, and how difficult to unravel them!

"Since you are not properly outfitted as yet," he said, "I will have my phaeton brought up and will take you around in it this morning. There is much I can show from the carriage."

It was another warm day, but with the raised top protecting them from the sun, Vanessa found the ride enjoyable. They made several stops at tenant houses. At each she saw the respect shown to the tall man beside her, and her pride in him grew.

His feelings were evident, too, as he introduced her. "My daughter, Lady Vanessa," he said proudly. After the initial start of surprise, the tenant's pleasure was apparent.

"Aye, 'twas no doubt she was bred of him," they gossiped as the carriage drove on. "Those green eyes have come through again." They could hardly wait until the house servants arrived with the full story!

It was almost bedtime the next day when Minton announced the arrival of the carriage with Vanessa's new clothes.

The earl rose quickly. "Does he have many packages?" he asked. At the butler's nod he ordered them to be taken to Vanessa's room.

"My valet has returned from Edinburgh with some success," he said to her. "I won't hold you back because I know you want to see what he managed to find."

He smiled indulgently as she ran eagerly up the stairs. He then went to his study to wait with some impatience.

"Well?" he asked when Clausen came in. "Were you successful?"

The man handed him a leather packet. "I had to spend all the money you gave me, sir," he said apologetically.

"Since you wanted it as soon as possible, I deemed it best not to waste time haggling over a price."

The earl nodded absentmindedly, as if impatient to be alone. "It was a long trip. You must have had a hectic time with little sleep. Get something to eat and go to bed," he ordered.

"And, Clausen," he continued as the man reached the door, "I want to add my personal thank-you."

The valet bowed, a faint smile on his lips. He was exhausted, but it had been exhilarating doing something so outlandish. What he had done was also illegal, but for the master he would have done far more.

The earl sat down at his desk when the door closed and slowly undid the ties around the packet. He slid the papers from the compartment and scanned them closely, finally holding them against the light to examine them further.

He smiled grimly. A remarkable job. Money might not be able to buy happiness, but it accomplished much.

He replaced the slightly discolored parchment with the faded ink into the leather envelope. Taking a silver key attached to the chain holding his watch fob, he opened a drawer in his desk and placed the parchment under some legal documents, then locked the drawer carefully.

He returned to the drawing room and poured a large glass of whiskey. In this case, he would not rely on chance alone to unravel the snarled threads and weave the strands into whole cloth.

Vanessa and Polly were beside themselves with excitement. There were six large boxes, each containing a dress lovelier than the next. There were also round hat boxes with delicious concoctions in them, as well as satin slippers with matching gloves.

"I cannot envision Clausen's handpicking these." Polly

giggled as she opened the last box to reveal a collection of dainty laced and beribanded undergarments.

Vanessa joined in her laughter as she sank onto her bed. Was all this hers? Her wildest dream had come true.

"Quick," she said, "help me into this green dress. I must go to the earl and thank him properly."

Polly dressed her quickly, and they eyed the enchanting result. "Methinks," Polly said drily, "his lordship led an active bachelor's existence if he could order clothes to such a close fit!"

Vanessa made a moue as she slipped on the matching slippers. "He is very much a man, isn't he? You do not think the viscount or even your Roberts is any different?"

The girls stared at each other in dismay, their joy immediately disappearing.

"I-I didn't mean that," Vanessa faltered, her throat tightening with distress. She fled the room to escape Polly's accusing eyes. How could she have been so unguarded? For a moment they had been so gay, forgetting the heartache riding so close to the surface.

Vanessa found the earl at his desk in his study. "Look, am I not pretty?" she questioned, pirouetting inside the doorway.

The earl stared at her for a bemused moment. "Ravishingly beautiful is a better description," he said approvingly. "I made a rough estimate at your size and gave your coloring to Clausen to take to the dressmaker. I hope what was on hand is acceptable? There is an order for more, and they will be sent when finished. I have decided not to rent out my house in London this season, and when we go there, you will personally be able to chuse what you wish."

She clasped her hands together, her eyes round with wonder. "I can never thank you enough," she said huskily.

"I do not ask for thanks," he returned, his voice deeper than usual. "I want only your happiness."

She flew to his side and raised on tiptoe to place a kiss on his cheek. "Thank you, Father," she whispered.

Once again, as he watched her leave, his fingers moved lightly over the place on his cheek still quivering from the soft kiss. He had been amply repaid.

The days passed quickly. The earl bought her a dappled grey horse heartbreakingly similar to Grey Ghost. He had seen her affection for the beast at their first meeting in the glen. He had bought the hack as a replacement but cursed himself for reviving memories when he saw her first stricken look.

They rode together every day, keeping to the north of his property. To the south was the joint boundary with Sir Bartongale, and the earl prudently avoided that area.

On Saturday more boxes arrived from Edinburgh, and both girls cried with special delight over one breathtaking creation in white gossamer silk shot with silver threads. The bodice had sprays of flowers embroidered with pearls and sparkling diamanté. It was a fairy costume Vanessa happily envisioned wearing at the reception the earl planned for the following Saturday.

In spite of the wonder of her complete change of fortune, the love so plainly given by her father, and the reciprocating response in her, Vanessa fell into a black mood of despair on Sunday.

On this day the viscount had said he planned to leave Sir Bartongale and continue to his next assignment. She had not expected ever to see him again, but as long as he was in the neighborhood, she had entertained wild dreams.

They would meet accidentally, she fancied, and he

would become enchanted enough to pursue the earl's daughter. They could build on a new beginning, he never knowing of their previous contact. It was all unsubstantial. The farfetched possibility disappeared now that he was leaving. The earl came upon her in the library. He paused in the doorway, examining her pensive face, a book lying unheeded on her lap.

"What is it, Vanessa?" he asked gently, coming to her.

She gazed at him, her eyes bright with unshed tears. "I am an ungrateful wretch," she said, fighting for control. "Pray, pay no attention to me."

He sat down on the sofa beside her and took her hand. "I can see you are in distress. Let there be nothing between us, my dear. Together we can fight the dragon."

His sympathy broke down her reserve, and she was in his arms, sobbing uncontrollably.

"There's no d-dragon left to fight," she wailed, burying her face against his shoulder. "He leaves today, and I'll never see him again!"

He did not need to ask whom she was referring to. He held her against him, gently smoothing her hair. When her crying slowed, he handed her his handkerchief, and she shamefacedly wiped her eyes and blew her nose.

"What do you want me to do?" he asked when she was again in control.

"There is nothing anyone can do. That part of my life is over, and I will soon forget it," she answered, but her woeful expression denied her brave words. "I'm not the first woman who foolishly gave her heart to someone who did not reciprocate. I shall survive like all the others." She tried a quivering smile which tore at his heart.

"Your love is one-sided only because he has not seen you as a woman," the earl said, and could have immediately bitten his tongue upon seeing the flash of hope spring to her face.

It quickly faded, and she rose resolutely to replace the book she had attempted to read. "I don't want you to think me ungrateful, Father. You have given me everything a girl could wish for. I promise you won't see me moping about like a silly schoolgirl. Now, if you will forgive me, I shall go to freshen up after this childish exhibition."

She forced a bright smile, and he watched her leave, a thoughtful expression lingering on his face.

Wayne had spent a restless night, wrestling with the problems brought on by his admission that he had at last fallen in love. While he could not envision his father's blessing such a union, he found that marriage was what he desired with the enchanting girl. Anything less would not suffice.

But first he must find her. He informed Roberts he planned to institute a guarded search. He did not wish to alert the neighborhood, especially the Bartongales, to the intensity of his concern over the departure of his page. He hid his surprise when Roberts requested permission to ride with him. Two could cover the area more quickly, he admitted, and bring the hunt to a rapid conclusion.

Wayne thought first of the nearby river, remembering Van's description of following the waterway when she had left her home.

Each traveled in opposite directions to cover the area. They rode until common sense told them that two persons could not have traveled so far on foot. When backtracking, they stopped at each farmhouse to ask if two wayfarers had passed by.

Upon obtaining no results, they took to the back roads

before searching along the main one connecting the towns. Each day they went forth with single-mindedness, returning in the afternoon to plot the next move.

Wayne said nothing of their search to Sir Bartongale, although that astute gentleman could not help noting the long, unexplained rides taken each day. When asked if he would like to extend his stay, the viscount had accepted the offer with relief. Surely the next day would bring the quest to an end!

Roberts's strong attachment to the girl Polly was described in a halting explanation. He had become enamored of the lively abigail with her quick humor and had thought she was of the same mind. Yet, when he had offered for her, she had turned him down in anger. Van had come upon them then, and Roberts had retreated, hurt and confused. Further advances had received the same rebuff. It was only on the afternoon after they had disappeared, and upon reviewing where he had gone wrong, that he realized the interpretation she must had placed on his words.

"I was so involved with the asking," Roberts confessed, red-faced, "that I assumed she knew I was intent on marriage. However, in retrospect, I can see that my fumbling words could have been construed in another way. No wonder she had nothing but scorn for me. There was never a bigger fool than me! I must find her, my lord, even if it is only to tell her the truth of my intentions."

Roberts's expression was so woebegone that the viscount placed an arm across his shoulder in condolence. "We shall find them," he said with an assurance he was far from feeling.

The days passed swiftly for Vanessa. The castle was overrun with extra help scrubbing and polishing the rooms. Indescribable aromas found their way from the kitchen, and Mr. Bloomsbury, the chef, informed her of the growing lists of delectables he was preparing. The long table in the state dining room would be opened to the fullest, to be laden with food for the midnight meal.

The floor in the main hall was waxed for dancing, and the minstrels' gallery cleaned and made ready. Aided by two footmen, Minton supervised the daily polishing of the silver which he brought from the safe. Mrs. Blake wore a harried expression and was intent on instructing her own army of cleaners. Even Polly was uncommunicative, her fingers busy making minute adjustments to the dresses which now came almost daily with the post from Edinburgh.

Vanessa rode mornings with the earl on his daily inspections. In the afternoons he had short sessions with her over the various ledgers he kept on his estate.

"You have inherited your grandfather's love of figures," he observed, noticing her rapid grasp of the complexities of estate management.

"My father's also," she added quickly, and they exchanged a companionable smile.

On Tuesday morning the earl urged her to ride with a groom in attendance instead of with him, as was their custom.

"I must inspect a problem with Sir Bartongale's property," he explained. "He will meet me there to see what has to be done about a crumbling fence we maintain jointly."

Vanessa watched him ride off, a wistful expression on her face. Her father was protecting her again, careful to prevent recognition by the Bartongales.

He could not do so forever. Would they recognize her at the reception when she was dressed in her lovely gown? She hoped she had escaped close examination because she had been a servant. Vanessa clasped her hands to still their trembling as a shiver of apprehension ran through her. What would be the outcome of their meeting on Saturday?

The viscount rode Diablo in an easy canter. It was a lovely, clear morning, but he stared ahead, unseeing, a heavy frown settling on his brow. They had been on their quest for a week, and soon he must abandon the fruitless search. Indeed, he was making a fool of himself over his persistence. Still, while his head agreed, his heart rebelled, driven by the witchery of one maiden.

A group of riders were ahead of him, and he recognized Sir Bartongale examining a crumpled line of stone fencing. His daughter sat restlessly on her horse. This was a good time to tender his regrets and give his intention to move on to follow his father's list of prospects. Only a fool would continue the way he was.

As he approached, Wayne recognized the Earl of MacLowry and realized the men had met to discuss the stone fencing. He tensed, remembering the crass words spoken hotly at their last meeting, and made to go. Sir Bartongale saw him and called to him, desiring him to offer his suggestions on the problem.

An agreement was soon reached on the matter of the boundary fence, and Miss Ivy introduced the subject of the reception being given that Saturday, intent on extracting information about the long-lost daughter being introduced.

The earl turned to the viscount to extend an invitation to attend. Wayne was about to refuse, stating he would be long on his way, when for the first time he looked full into the earl's face.

The earl had been in shadow that night when they had exchanged words over Van. Now the sun was full on him.

He had a good look at the austere face and saw the flash of green in the deep-set eyes. Wayne found himself thanking the earl for the invitation.

The viscount joined the Bartongales on their ride back to the house. Ivy was full of the latest gossip about the sudden appearance of the earl's supposed daughter. Before, when the subject had been raised, Wayne had been hard pressed to remain in attention, bemused as he was with his own problem. Now he listened intently.

"There has been much speculation over the poor girl," he said drily. "The earl does not appear to be easily taken in by a fortune hunter."

"I hear she is uncommonly attractive," Ivy said petulantly, and Wayne understood why she was belaboring the subject. She would not enjoy competition. "It is well known how a pretty face can make a man act brainless, though one would scarcely think a man of the earl's caliber to be so taken in. Still, a man is a man, no matter what his age," she added shrewdly.

"Saturday night should offer some answers," he said, and wondered over the intensity of his anticipation. He recalled the earl's green eyes, so similar to another pair which haunted him.

Surely there were few people with such distinctively colored eyes. Could the reason Van had taken on her disguise been to reach her father? He shook his head over the questions swirling in his mind. He would have the answer to the most important one at the end of this week. He was certain the rest would then fall in line. He urged his horse on, conscious of the acceleration of his heart.

When the earl returned from his meeting, he was strangely quiet. Not until after dinner did he relieve Vanessa's curiosity. The telling left her badly shaken.

"Sir Bartongale's guest rode up as we discussed the fence," the earl said, watching her reaction from the corner of his eye. "It seems the viscount has not left after all."

Vanessa was thankful she was sitting. The blood drained from her face so quickly that she felt faint. "H-he is staying with them still?" she asked weakly, licking dry lips. Then Miss Ivy had won her battle! "W-was his daughter with them?" she cried in agitation.

"Yes, they all were riding," he answered. Her pain tore at him, but he held himself in check. "When the subject of your reception came up, I was placed in the position of having to invite him to attend."

Her face showed her agony as she waited for the viscount's answer.

"He said he would be honored to attend. I also heard a strange story," the earl added slowly, a twinkle in his eyes. "It seems his page left with a maid he had hired, and the viscount is spending many hours searching diligently for them, asking whomever he meets if the runaways have been seen."

"He has no right to do that!" Vanessa cried in indignation. "True, we left precipitously, but one would think from the anger he was showing me that he would have been happy to see the last of me!"

Her dismay brought color back to her cheeks, and her father was relieved that she placed that interpretation on the news. He had had to alert her that the viscount would be coming. The shock of seeing him unexpectedly might otherwise have proved too severe.

During the rest of the week Vanessa was torn in diverse directions. One minute she was riding on a wave of high anticipation over the prospect of seeing the viscount once more; then the next she was plunged into despair as fear tore through her. She could imagine his disgust once he recognized her as his ex-page.

Polly became fiercely protective when told of Vanessa's tortured premonitions. He would not dare treat her unkindly! she declared crossly. She was Lady Vanessa, and his equal! Both their fathers were earls. Polly did not know how the matter would be smoothed over about being born on the wrong side of the blanket, but she was certain the earl would manage that worry. Hadn't he resolved every other one? Her faith in him was already unshakable.

Vanessa was more cognizant of the problems, but she could not control the return of her hopeful daydreams or the resultant dashes into gloom.

The arrival of the fateful day came as a welcome relief. That night the viscount's reaction to her would decide if later her pillow would know her tears of despair.

Polly insisted Vanessa take a nap, but it became a torture for her to lie still. Instead, the girls chatted quietly, still in wonder over the change in their fortunes.

Finally, the time arrived for Vanessa to start dressing, and Polly struggled to hide her elation over the exquisite creature emerging under her careful attention.

"If you had a veil, you would look like a bride," Polly breathed in awe as she adjusted a dark curl to lie beguilingly against Vanessa's cheek.

"The dress is a dream!" Vanessa cried, enchanted by the stranger in the long looking glass.

Free from the bindings she had needed in the page's uniform, her figure now proclaimed its sweet maturity. She frowned slightly at the low-scooped neckline, which gave an unbroken view from the soft swelling of her breasts upward through the long curve of her slender neck.

"Perhaps we should have a riband around my neck?"

she asked hesitatingly. "There seems to be so much exposed flesh!"

Polly examined her critically. "It would be nice if you had a string of pearls or diamonds, but since you haven't, it is better not to do anything. You have such lovely skin it has a beauty of its own."

A knock came on the door, and Polly opened it to reveal Clausen.

"His lordship requests the privilege of coming to see her Ladyship when she is presentable," the valet said.

"Whenever he is ready," Vanessa replied, and Polly straightened the room with quick dispatch while they wondered at the message.

The earl arrived soon after, and they gazed in admiration at each other. Some of the boxes from Edinburgh must have been for him. He was exceedingly handsome in a pale green velvet cutaway jacket and matching silk pantaloons, accented by a gold striped waistcoat. The pointed collar and snowy cravat, tied in a manner Brummell would have approved, gave credence to stories that the earl had once been a tulip of fashion.

His examination of Vanessa was equally thorough. He was struck with her loveliness and once more wondered at the marvel of having found her.

"I meant to give these to you before, my dear," he said, indicating leather boxes in his hand. "I had them cleaned, and they have just arrived." The earl unsnapped a lid, and the two girls gasped at the fire leaping from the exposed jewelry.

Vanessa stared mesmerized at the narrow strand of diamonds accented by an emerald pendant. There were matching earrings and a bracelet in addition to an emerald ring surrounded by diamonds. The other box held a small diamond tiara, and he lifted it out to hand it to Polly.

"You will have to place this correctly, Polly," he said, bemused by their rapt expressions. "It should be perfect against Vanessa's dark hair."

"I-I cannot wear all of those!" Vanessa cried, overcome with their beauty.

"I agree," he admitted. "You have no need for so much adornment, but I wanted you to see the complete set. There are others in the vault, although I think these are the handsomest of the lot."

Polly fastened the tiara with trembling hands, happy for her mistress. The earl then placed the diamond necklace with the emerald pendant around Vanessa's neck.

Vanessa gazed, entranced, at her reflection in her mirror, then turned to the earl, her shining eyes vying with the glitter of the emeralds.

"You have made me into a fairy princess!" she cried, and kissed him in thanks. "I shall be proud to stand beside you tonight, King of the Fairies!"

"Then may I have the extreme honor of escorting my princess down to her court? Her subjects will be arriving shortly." He offered his wrist, and she placed her hand upon it. They went down the stairs, laughing happily.

Vanessa could not believe the sight that met her eyes. The dreary rooms had been transformed into a veritable fairyland. The many candelabra were ablaze with lights. Huge bowls of hothouse flowers had been placed before potted plants, and their masses filled the corners, adding to the enchantment.

The earl drew her before such a bower to receive their guests when Minton announced the first of the arrivals.

Vanessa braced herself for the ordeal, knowing that she would be under critical examination. She hoped she would pass as successfully as she had done with the servants and tenants.

The guests were too well-bred to stare when they arrived, even though they were racked with curiosity. Most were intrigued by the strange story circulating about the newly found heiress and would have come from a sickbed rather than forgo this initial scrutiny. Had the earl reached his dotage and been taken in by a fortune hunter?

They were immediately captivated by the gracefully charming creature, and their doubts faded.

"And, my dear, did you see those eyes?" they murmured behind their fans. "How lucky his lordship has his daughter by his side at last. What heartbreak he must have endured all these years until the good Lord gave her back to him! Did you see? He already has given her the MacLowry emerald. It does give one an odd sensation, though, doesn't it? Almost as if three green eyes were looking at one!"

The earl's demeanor was also noted. He stood proudly beside the slender girl, his gaze upon her with obvious affection. When giving her name in introduction, his voice held a lilt never before heard.

Vanessa was unaware of the effect she was having on the flow of arrivals. With each announcement from the butler, her nerves were stretched a little tighter. Soon the one name she was waiting for would be announced, and she was reaching a feverish peak which caused her eyes to shine brighter, her translucent skin to glow with a faint flush. Soon, heart-stoppingly soon, she would see him.

When Wayne reached his room after receiving the invitation from the Earl of MacLowry, he informed Roberts they would cease further search for the missing couple. He saw the despair on Roberts's face but had not the heart to tell him what he suspected in case he was wrong.

Wayne waited impatiently for the days to pass, consumed with the need to see if his supposition was correct. During the lonely hours while riding in his search, Wayne had occupied himself with thoughts on how to resolve the seemingly insurmountable problems so that his father would give his blessing to the marriage. He held his father in deep affection. It would hurt sorely if he rejected his choice for a wife. Yet even then Wayne knew he could not give Van up.

He cared not if the *ton* should look askance at such a merger. He was weary of the artificial world they represented. He would retire to the country. He had several estates in different areas. What better way to rear their children?

Was ever a hopeful groom beset by such problems? Wayne recalled her stating that she was an orphan. What then was her relationship to the Earl of MacLowry? Yes, there were many answers necessary. But first he had to ascertain whether he had indeed found his bride.

Roberts was aware of his master's suppressed excitement as he dressed him for the reception. The viscount had told him how Van had disguised herself as the page, and he was properly abashed that he had been so involved with the abigail that he had not been alert to so infamous a deceit. Still, his lordship had not shown the expected anger, but rather the same intensity of purpose he experienced while they searched. Wisely he kept his conclusions to himself.

The viscount was soon resplendent in a dove grey cutaway jacket and gold embroidered waistcoat. White pantaloons hugged his muscular thighs. Roberts opened the box containing his collection of fobs, and he selected one with an impressive emerald. He was reminded of green eyes. Would it perhaps be a good-luck talisman?

CHAPTER EIGHTEEN

The yard was already filling with carriages when the Bartongales drew up before the entrance to Moorhaven. Wayne gave the castle only a cursory inspection. He was too intent upon what he hoped to discover inside.

They waited at the door to the baronial room as the butler announced their names in rolling tones. Wayne's glance went from the tall host to the girl beside him being introduced to the previous arrivals.

His breath escaped in a long sigh, and he realized he had been holding it in apprehension.

She stood beside the earl, elegant in an exquisite gown. His gaze devoured the creamy skin, the delicate curve of the swanlike neck, the raven hair arranged in fetching curls around her lovely face.

A soaring shaft of relief sped through him, sending his heart pounding at an alarming rate. His supposition had been correct. The suspicion which had risen upon seeing the earl's green eyes was based on fact. Here was his love. No wonder he could not find her after she had disappeared!

Wayne moved with the Bartongales to stand before his host. The earl introduced them to the slender girl by his side.

"Our neighbors to the south, Vanessa," the earl said, placing a reassuring hand on her waist. "Sir Bartongale and his lovely lady, and their daughter, Miss Ivy. My daughter, Lady Vanessa. Also their guest, Viscount Kingsley, Lord Wainwright Larimor."

Vanessa! Wayne thought. Of course! How strange not to have known her correct name until now!

Wayne's pulse gave an added leap now he was close to her. She was more beautiful than he had envisioned. Her eyes were kept demurely lowered as she curtsied to his bow. He fought a foolish desire to gather her in his arms and run off with her, to protect her from the speculating glances of the guests. She was too lovely to be exposed to the circulating gossip.

Wayne was too bemused by the violent reaction roiling within him to say more than the basic amenities before moving on to make room for the next arrivals.

"She's pretty enough," Ivy conceded begrudgingly as they moved away. "But I doubt she is his daughter. There is no resemblance. I daresay she is able to foster her deception because she has green eyes, and the MacLowry clan tends towards them," she ended waspishly.

"I feel I have met Lady Vanessa before," Lady Bartongale murmured vaguely. "Perhaps it was when we passed through Italy on the way to India."

Wayne diverted their attention by having a passing footman fetch them a cooling drink. He found his hands clenched in apprehension. How long before they connected the similarity between the earl's daughter and his page? When one saw her now, it would seem impossible. He only hoped the careless attention given to a servant might have left a poor impression.

A footman offered a glass of champagne, and while sipping it, Wayne further examined the entrancing creature still greeting the guests.

Pictures flashed before him of the evenings they had spent together. He had jokingly told her that his enjoyment of conversation with her was part of what he searched for in his wife. What truth he had spoken in jest!

Wayne waited impatiently for the dancing to begin. He had an overpowering need to hold this exquisite girl in his arms. Her father, the earl, would naturally have the first dance. He, as the next highest in title, would have the second.

The Bartongales moved with him around the floor, introducing him to friends. He answered abstractedly with the proper social responses. His gaze kept returning to the pair by the door, especially to the slender girl curtsying gracefully to the late arrivals. At times he saw her search the crowd. Was she looking for him? He was not certain when her gaze moved quickly away from his.

Finally, everyone had arrived. With a signal from the earl the musicians changed their soft background music to the opening dance.

Lady Vanessa placed her hand lightly on her father's arm, and they moved to the dance floor. When they had made their first round, others joined them, and the floor was soon bright with swirling couples.

The viscount stood up to Ivy, performing his duty. The dance ended when the earl and his daughter were before him. He callously abandoned Ivy as he stepped forward to claim the next set.

"I shall be happy to place my daughter in your care, my lord," the earl said. "I find myself woefully out of practice."

The earl placed Vanessa's hand in the viscount's in a surprising gesture and signaled the musicians to start again. There was a scurrying for partners with the intermission being cut so short.

"Are you always so quiet, my lady?" Wayne asked after they had circled once around the floor. She had faltered on the first steps, but now she moved with him, light as a feather. Was she embarrassed by the first stumbling? He wished she would not keep her eyes lowered. Still, the fanning of those dark lashes were enticing against such creamy cheeks.

"No, my lord," she said in a husky whisper. "I was waiting for you to begin a subject so that I would know on what topic you wished to converse."

Wayne drew his breath in sharply. He had forgotten how he enjoyed listening to the husky inflection of her voice. Already he was imagining their spending evenings beside a fireplace.

"What do you think of this countryside in comparison to Italy?" Wayne asked. He had heard the story given out by the earl, and his curiosity was piqued over how it would be embellished.

The slender figure stiffened under his hand. "I have been in school in England for a number of years, so I am accustomed to your strange weather."

His eyes glinted with amusement over her fabrication. "I noticed your perfect English," he continued after leading her through an intricate dance pattern. "They taught you well, or should I say you are an apt pupil. You are without an accent."

"After meeting my father, can you doubt where I inherited my ability?" A demure smile curled her lips, and he had the outlandish desire to stop in the middle of the floor and kiss their softness.

Wayne glanced around the large room. He had an urgent need to have her alone. So many questions needed answering! Most of the houses had half-lit antechambers where one could discreetly disappear. It would be difficult doing so here, though, with nearly every eye upon her.

The dance ended, and immediately three odious bucks

were crowding in attendance. The successful claimant moved her triumphantly to the floor.

Wayne reached for a glass of champagne from a passing footman before he turned to watch them make the opening steps. He met her gaze full upon him.

He caught his breath over the impact the green eyes made upon him. Suddenly the enormousness of the problem facing him descended on him. He had been thinking in terms of marriage, but he well knew that her situation with the earl was false. How could he possibly hope for his own father's approval to such a match? Her background made no difference to him. He loved and desired this girl for his wife. His jaw clamped tight in frustration.

Would he have to give up all hope for their marriage? No! he thought fiercely. He'd give up everything and take her to Europe to live if all else failed. He paused in thought. He had seen similar exiles wandering through Europe. Could their marriage survive if they joined their ranks?

His weeks of worry and frustration exploded in anger. How dare this chit perpetrate this hoax upon him! He must be addlebrained to call this infatuation love! His interest was piqued, nothing more. He would quit this area and forget about the touch of magnolia skin, the silkiness of raven hair, the enchantment of a witch's green eyes.

"Would you prefer some brandy?" The earl stood beside him, his eyes hooded as he took in the heavy scowl on the viscount's brow. "You appear perturbed."

"Perturbed! I should call it far worse!" he cried, giving vent to his anger.

"I would suggest you take hold of yourself," the earl murmured with some sympathy. "There are ears bending to hear what is being said. Perhaps we could go into it further tomorrow at, say, ten in the morning?"

Wayne managed to pull himself together with considerable effort. "I shall be here," he answered stiffly, "and demand a proper explanation to this outrage perpetrated upon me!"

"If that is your attitude, perhaps we had better cancel the meeting," the earl replied coldly. "I will not have Vanessa exposed to any unpleasantness, least of all from you. She has suffered enough."

The green eyes surveying him were like ice chips. Their effect was like a dash of cold water, adequately ending his childish rebellion. Once before he had antagonized the earl. He dare not repeat it. No doubt her father would prevent any possibility of his seeing Vanessa again. He was quick to see a similarity in both their desires to protect the girl. Questions crowded for answers, but he was conscious most of all of a driving fear of losing her once again.

"I shall arrive promptly at ten," he said as soon as he could speak calmly.

"We shall be waiting." With that promise the earl moved off to speak to the rest of his guests.

The wineglass was emptied in one long draught. Wayne then retired to a corner to gather his scattered wits. His gaze seldom left the winsome figure as she swung from one partner to another. It was easy to see she had captured the approval of everyone. There would be a line forming at the front door after tonight. Someone so lovely, the heiress to the earl's rich lands, would be an admirable catch.

At midnight the company was led into the dining room for supper. Wayne did not follow. Tomorrow would be time enough to be near her. After hearing her story, he would have to decide how to proceed. That momentary rejection he had experienced was only a reaction to his frustration. The enchanting girl with the infectious laugh would somehow become his wife. Of that he was certain.

* * *

Polly's eyes were bright with excitement when she assisted an exhausted Vanessa out of her dress.

"I watched from the musicians' gallery," she bubbled. "No one could match you! I was so proud. You stood up for every dance. There will be many cards left here tomorrow."

"I daresay," Vanessa said disinterestedly. Her shoulders sagged, and Polly's gaze became thoughtful.

"He danced only one set with you," she said understandingly.

Vanessa could only nod her head. She had kept a bright smile on her face all evening, and now her throat had a familiar ache as she fought the threatening tears.

She had been so vibrantly alive in his arms! After the first fear of discovery she had literally floated with her happiness over finally finding herself where she had dreamed of being.

It had been a crushing blow when she realized that he intended standing up for only one dance with her. He had not become enamored of her after all, had not felt the attraction she had foolishly been hoping for.

"He didn't dance with anyone else, much to every woman's chagrin," Polly offered as consolation.

Vanessa had noticed, but that had been a small sop when every nerve had cried out to be in his arms again. The evening had been a hollow triumph, and she would gladly have exchanged the reams of compliments given so ardently for one from his lips.

She had hoped he would join the Bartongales, who had sat with them when they had partaken of supper, but he had been nowhere in sight. Miss Ivy had barely controlled her ire. Vanessa had hoped that no one noticed how she barely tasted her food. If people had, they had attributed it to the evening's excitement.

Now she could crawl into bed and let despair sweep over her. She had been careful when dancing with him to keep her lashes lowered. It had all been for nothing, she now realized. Her foolish dreams had proved to be a hoax, and now her pillow felt the hot tears of her heartbreak.

CHAPTER NINETEEN

Vanessa woke resentfully from her sleep. Polly stood over her, shaking her to wakefulness. Vanessa pushed her hand away, craving the oblivion which was slipping away.

"I'm sorry to awaken you, my lady," she said apologetically. "His lordship requested that I do so. He wishes you to be with him in his study by ten."

Vanessa sat up, blinking away the last vestiges of clinging sleep, which had finally come near dawn. The smudges under her eyes gave proof of its lack beforehand.

"What can he want?" she asked in surprise. "It is Sunday, and he does not ride as usual."

Polly gave a happy laugh. "Let me help you dress so he can tell you the reason."

Vanessa gazed at her in surprise. The girl seemed to be bursting with news.

"What has happened to make you so happy?" Vanessa asked.

"It's Roberts, my lady," Polly cried joyfully. "He came early this morning. His lordship told him about finding you last night. Roberts was here at daybreak, asking to see me."

Polly's face was rosy with excitement. It had been most audacious of Roberts to come at such an unseemly hour. He had bribed a kitchen maid to come up to awaken her.

"It was all a misunderstanding," Polly breathed ecstatically. "He intended we should be married."

Vanessa sat up in bed, torn by conflicting emotions.

246

"I'm so happy for you, my dear Polly," she cried, "even though I shall miss you sorely when you leave me."

Polly giggled mischievously. "We shan't worry about that at present. Here, drink your tea while it is hot, and then we must get you dressed. We mustn't keep the earl waiting."

Vanessa drank the tea quickly. It was just ten when Polly deemed her presentable and sent her down to the study.

Her father was sitting at his desk, and she paused questioningly upon seeing a tall man outlined against the window.

The viscount turned at her entrance, and both men saw the leap of joy on her face. It was immediately replaced with such an ashen look that both men thought she might swoon.

The earl moved to go to her aid, but she in an instant had herself sternly in hand. She was not one for vapors. The viscount had discovered her duplicity and come to heap his wrath upon her. Neither knew the effort it took to place a welcoming smile on her lips.

"Good morning, Father," she murmured. "Polly said you wished to see me." She gave a small curtsy to the viscount. "Good morning, my lord. You are out early after last night's dancing."

The viscount's control was remarkable. Upon seeing the flash of joy in her face, his heart had leaped up in response. At that moment he cared not one whit for explanations. He was happily content to feast his eyes hungrily on her loveliness.

"Please be seated, both of you," the earl ordered, breathing a sigh of relief upon seeing the bemused expressions on their faces. Perhaps guiding these two to a happy reconciliation would not be as difficult as he had feared.

"As you must have guessed, my dear," he began, gazing tenderly at the bent head of the girl, "Viscount Kingsley has come for an accounting of the folly you have pursued. It has caused him to question my ethics in allowing you to contrive so deplorable a masquerade."

"But you knew nothing of it!" she exclaimed, startled that the viscount should even hint that her father might be involved.

"You and I know that, but the viscount has not been informed of the whole story," he said reasonably. "I think you owe him an explanation. Don't you agree?"

Vanessa nodded even while cringing at the prospect. The time had come to explain her behavior. If he could not forgive her, he might in time understand the original necessity and how it had evolved into the deception practiced upon him.

"His lordship knows part of the story," she began in so strained a whisper that they both had to lean forward to catch her words.

"What I told you in our evening sessions was the truth," she said, giving a quick glance in the viscount's direction. His face was an immobile mask, and her heart sank.

She quickly skimmed over the uncomfortable relationship which had existed with her half brother and how she had been forced to rely upon his presence as a poor protection from men who annoyed her. When he had left without notice, and she had found that the squire had padlocked her house and was indeed coming down the lane for her, she had been forced to flee. Vanessa held her hands tightly on her lap as she relived that frightful moment when she realized the extent of her vulnerability.

Both men's fists were also clenched, but with anger. They held their tongues as she continued.

"When I found John's last wash on the bushes, I realized that the only way I could hope to survive would be to dress in his clothes and take on the masquerade of being a young man. I traveled several days until I was driven by hunger to find work. That is when you came upon me." She chanced another glance at the viscount but could not make out the changed expression on his face.

"You took me for a lad without a question. I-I only intended to stay that night—to see if there was anything further I could do for Diablo in payment for the food you gave me. That is how the masquerade started. You know the rest. I apologize, my lord. I never meant to cause you displeasure. Later, when you became angry, I realized you were sorry you had offered me asylum so I left. I did not wish to embarrass you further." Her gaze was beseeching, begging him for forgiveness.

The viscount rose abruptly and moved to the mantel, feeling acutely embarrassed. How could he explain his unwanted thoughts about the boy in his custody? Now he knew his tortured senses were telling him what his mind had not been astute enough to recognize.

"I cannot conceive that I was so befogged by my annoyance over my father's edict that I was so thoroughly taken in. You did make a comely lad," he admitted with a wry smile. "I had mixed feelings about having you in my household, knowing you would stir up the servants."

He glanced at the earl and caught his understanding look. A faint flush touched the viscount's cheeks, and he moved to the window.

The earl took up the story, telling how he and Vanessa had met and offering an explanation for the conversation the viscount had partially heard and misconstrued.

"My apologies," the younger man said. "But you can understand the position those words placed me in. I heard a man give what sounded like a proposition to my page."

"And you were jealous."

The viscount flared at the astute observation. He stared angrily at the earl, and their eyes met in a private clash. The viscount was forced to give way to the truth of the words.

"Yes," he admitted stiffly. "I can say it now that I am in possession of the full story."

"Only part of it," the earl said, and gave his own quick version. The viscount listened, not moving a muscle, while Vanessa sat dejectedly in her chair, silent and uncomfortable. Surely now he would leave in disgust. Why had the earl told the truth? If he had related the tale given to others, the viscount might have left without wounding her pride.

The question rose in the viscount's mind also. "This is not the tale making the rounds," he said when the older man finished. "Wouldn't it have been more prudent to be consistent, although you can trust me, of course, not to breathe a word."

"If there had been any doubt in my mind, I would not have told you," the earl replied coldly. "I strongly believe a person should know the full tale if he is to offer the necessary protection."

The long gaze the two exchanged seemed strange to Vanessa, but she was too heartsick to decipher it. She had come to accept her illegitimacy, but she could well imagine how someone highborn would react to it. For the first time she understood why her father had erected so elaborate a fabrication to explain her presence in his house. He wished to make her not only acceptable to society but also eligible for a proper marriage.

"And wishing to add to the credibility to the story given to others," the earl said, as if continuing a private conversation the two were engaged in, "I plan to take Vanessa to Italy so that she can study the country in depth. She would then become completely versed in the countryside as well as the language and answer correctly any probe put to her. She has an exceptional mind, as you must have discovered."

"It would also be an ideal place for a honeymoon," the viscount said, his gaze unwavering on the earl.

A faint smile softened the taut lines of the earl's face, and he relaxed visibly. "I agree. In that case I have something to show you."

He removed a silver key from his chain and opened the desk drawer. He selected the leather packet placed there recently and withdrew the faded papers, spreading them on the desk. Upon the earl's invitation, the viscount came forward to inspect them, then looked at him questioningly.

"This," the earl said with a small smile, thinking of the work of the efficient Clausen, "this is a document proving my marriage in Italy. And this tells of the birth of a daughter nine months later. Do they pass your inspection?"

The viscount held them up for closer examination. "You plan well," he said with new respect in his voice. "Were you so certain of me?" Relief flooded him. This was physical evidence which would smooth the path for their marriage.

"No," the earl admitted ruefully. "But I am usually a good judge of men, and my wager was on the assumption that Vanessa would not give her love freely to someone not up to mark. Still, if you failed the test, there were bound to be others who would need these documents. I am not too old to realize that I could not keep so lovely a flower under cover for my private enjoyment, no matter how much I longed to do so. Love might make two people blind but it was prudent to ensure that others were satisfied, with proper documentation should questions be raised." The earl's lips tightened. While a man in love might be willing to enter into a socially unsuitable marriage, he knew how cruel society could be.

To him there was no doubt. It was as if he truly had been wed. That night under the tilted carriage they had spoken words which had married them in the eyes of the Lord.

Vanessa came to stand by them at the desk, completely bewildered by the conversation she could not follow. The viscount had said something about a honeymoon, and that was seared in her mind, burying all else. Had he declared himself to Miss Ivy after all? Her face was ashen, but she went to him bravely to give her felicitations. Then she would be free to flee to her room.

"I would make certain that such an occasion never arose," the viscount said fervently, acutely aware of the slender girl standing near him. "My protection would be absolute. Still, I can appreciate the reasoning behind your planning. Have I, then, your permission?" he asked, keeping his gaze on the earl.

The older man smiled in response. "Perhaps it would be best to ask her first?"

The earl then left his place behind the desk and stopped before his daughter. Resting his hands on Vanessa's shoulders, he placed a tender kiss on her forehead. "Thank you for the happiness you have given me," he said huskily before leaving, closing the door carefully behind him.

Vanessa gazed after him, perplexed. Then a rising apprehension took precedence. She turned to the tall man beside her, her eyes wide with worry. "He sounded as if he were saying good-bye," she whispered. "What have I done wrong?"

Wayne smiled at her. "I doubt he will ever say good-bye to you, my dear," he said soothingly. "He stated a simple fact. You have made him very happy. A man can ask no more from a woman."

"It is the least I can hope to do," she replied slowly, not satisfied with his explanation.

"It is in your power to make others happy also," he said carefully. "Some of my most pleasant memories are of the evenings we spent together. I missed you when you ran off."

A shy smile curved her lips. "I found our talks pleasant also. That is, until you changed and became short with me."

He regarded her for a long moment. "And you do not know why I acted differently towards you?"

She shook her head slowly, wondering why her breathing was becoming labored.

"I was fighting an uncomfortable problem. I was bewitched by silky black hair I longed to touch, by a pair of green eyes that haunted me in my dreams. When I see you now, it is difficult to understand why it took me so long to see through your deception. My heart was telling me the truth."

Vanessa caught her breath as he moved a step closer and laid one finger along her cheek. "I wanted to feel the softness of your skin, so smooth and warm." The finger ran along the curve of her cheek until his hand was buried in her hair. He drew in a quick breath.

"It is just as I envisioned," he murmured, his voice deepening. Then with a rush of emotion, he cried, "Vanessa, how could you have tortured me so?"

She was in his arms, his lips warm on her forehead, her cheeks, her slender neck. Then, eagerly, hungrily, their lips met, and Vanessa was swept into a rapture beyond imagination.

"You vixen!" he murmured huskily when they paused to catch their breath. "You entrapped me from the beginning with those witch's eyes. I was lost in your spell from the first moment I met you. I knew I couldn't let you go. God, the torture you put me through, you and your infernal masquerade! I couldn't imagine what had happened to me. It was beyond all comprehension!"

He laid light kisses on the soft, pulsating mouth, then held her away. A worried expression came to her face. "Can you forgive the fraud I perpetrated on you, my lord?" she asked timidly. "Was it much of a shock last night to discover that I was not the youth you thought me to be?"

"Do you think I was blind all this time?" Wayne laughed. "My dove, I discovered your disguise the night Lady Wesley sent her daughter into my room."

Vanessa looked at him in amazement. "Then you knew the truth those times you placed your arm around me in affection?"

Wayne nodded, a mocking smile on his lips.

"And you were also teasing when you scolded me over Miss Ivy's ankle?"

His smile deepened, and Vanessa's cheeks grew warm. "Why did you not cast me out?" she cried in wonder.

"I wished to uncover the reason behind your trickery," Wayne replied. "I admit I was sorely vexed over the chit who dared try to perpetrate such a hoax upon me. My first intent was to teach you a needed lesson!"

Vanessa's eyes flashed green fire as she drew away from him. "Then that night in the inn, when you held me close, your intentions were dishonorable!" She recalled her bewilderment over his actions.

He grinned while clasping his hands around her waist, effectively preventing her escape. "I admit that was on my mind. But consider. If that was my full intent, would I have let you escape? Even then, dear heart, I knew I wanted more from you."

Vanessa's cheeks flushed a deeper hue, remembering how vulnerable she had been each night in his room. "Yet you remained honorable," she whispered.

The smile left his face. "I admit to having been sorely tempted," he replied honestly. "As soon as we left the Bartongales, I had planned to place you under my protection."

Vanessa paled. She attempted to pull away from him but was prevented by his firm grasp.

"I soon realized that was not what I desired for the woman I loved. You know, you have no recourse but to marry me," he said sternly, pulling her back into his arms. "I must make an honest woman of you, my enchantress. After all, you have been compromised. You have slept in my bedroom not once, but many times."

Vanessa looked at him in alarm. Was that his only reason for marrying her? "But, my lord . . ." she protested.

"My name is Wayne," he interrupted, and she saw the teasing smile on his lips.

"I understand there are other, more intimate names you are called," she said archly, recalling Miss Ivy's flirtation.

"And shall I teach them to you?" he asked huskily, a fire building in his eyes.

"Yes, oh, yes!" she whispered breathlessly. Her eyes were green pools reflecting pure joy. Dreams did come true!

"Witch!" he groaned, crushing her to him. "My green-eyed witch!"

The door opened after a light tap, and the earl gazed at

the entwined couple lost in each other's arms. His expression held a mixture of pain and happiness as he reclosed the door softly. He had missed the rearing of his daughter. God willing, he would soon experience the joy of dangling his grandchildren on his knees.